Murder
in
First Position

Murder
in
First Position

An On Pointe Mystery

by

Lori Robbins

LEVEL
BEST BOOKS

First published by Level Best Books 2020

This novel is entirely a work of fiction. The names, characters and incidents portrayed in it are the work of the author's imagination. Any resemblance to actual persons, living or dead, events or localities is entirely coincidental.

Author Photo Credit: Alice Kivlon

First edition

ISBN: 978-1-947915-74-9

Cover art by Level Best Designs

This book was professionally typeset on Reedsy.
Find out more at reedsy.com

To Glenn

Praise for MURDER IN FIRST POSITION

"Everything is beautiful at the ballet—until it's not in this exciting and unputdownable mystery where dance is the backdrop for lies, jealousy and murder."—Cathi Stoler, author of *Last Call: A Murder On The Rocks Mystery.*

"*Murder in First Position* is definitely *en pointe*! It's not often you find a novel, let alone a mystery, set in the world of dance, but from page one, it's evident the author knows both the ballet subculture and New York City from an insider's perspective. Filled with dead bodies, unexpected suitors, red herrings and the humor for which this Silver Falchion-winning writer Is known, *Murder in the First Position* will keep you guessing until the final curtain call."— D.M. Barr, author of *Saving Grace: A Psychological Thriller.*

"Magnificent Mystery. Robbins pens a wonderful mystery story in *Murder in First Position.* I have read works from this author before, and I really enjoyed it, and this was no different. The mystery surrounds ballerina Leah, whose rival was killed, and of course, everyone has eyes on her. I am vaguely knowledgeable about the strictness of discipline of professional dancers, but in this story, I think that lends to helping Leah try to clear her name while the police are right there, behind her. If you love a great suspenseful and mysterious story, this book should be next on your list. A very well-written story, and I enjoyed it. Robbins is a magnificent storyteller and adds that layer of suspense and mystery, as well as other sub plotlines. It's a perfect stage for murder, and this book has it. Magnificent story, kept this reader turning the pages. A definite attention grabber. The thrills and intrigue is written clearly and the characterizations are engrossing. Love this story. The author's technique of intense characters and great plotlines is a gift. I look forward to reading many more stories by this author.—This book is a definite recommendation by Amy's Bookshelf Reviews. [5 stars]"

Chapter One

I don't want dancers who want to dance. I want dancers who have to dance.
— George Balanchine

I was the girl all the other kids wanted to kill. Skinny, pretty, and confident, I was the target of much envy and very little affection. I realized later that people resented my extreme disinterest in their lives. But it was never personal, because all I ever cared about was ballet.

These days, I wasn't quite so dismissive, even though the gap between us had gotten wider than ever. Because while my former classmates were still young, I was old. Not too old to get pregnant, and not too old to make partner in a law firm, but definitely old for a ballerina trying to make a comeback. And for me, nothing else counted.

I wasn't bitter. One minute you were the newest baby ballerina and the darling of every critic. The next thing you knew, you were having knee surgery and *The New York Times'* dance czar was faintly praising you for your "mature artistry," which was ballet-speak for "time to retire." But I wasn't ready to hang up my pointe shoes. And Bryan Leister was my ticket to the future.

Bryan was only a few years my junior. As a performer, he was in his prime, but as a choreographer, he was a whiz kid. I helped him get started and get noticed, and now that ballet companies and Broadway were begging him to jeté with them, it was time to cash in every asset I'd amassed in that bank account.

I didn't have much time. American Ballet Company had commissioned a

1

new ballet from Bryan, and I wanted the lead role. If my performing career were to end soon, and persistent pain from my recently reconstructed knee indicated just that, then I wanted to go out with a bang. On my terms, not anyone else's.

I called Bryan the night before we were due to return from our summer break. I wanted to grab him before anyone else called in her chips.

"Bryan! It's me. How are you? How was Montauk?"

This seemed like a good opening. People loved talking about their vacations. At least over the phone you didn't have to look at any pictures. You could pretend you salivated over them on Facebook or Instagram.

Bryan's enthusiasm didn't match mine. "Uh, Leah. The summer was great. Yeah, it was great. Seriously, I've been meaning to call you, but I was, you know, about to leave for a really important appointment. Talk to you tomorrow?"

As *Call Ended* floated across the screen, I pondered his lack of interest. When we first met, he answered my calls as excitedly as a freshman girl who'd been asked to the prom by the captain of the soccer team. But Bryan sounded more like a college kid whose mother has phoned during his fraternity's beer pong competition.

I worried all night about whether or not I'd be cast in Bryan's ballet. Or any ballet. The next morning, I got up early and anxiously checked my email. If Grayson Averin, the *Times* chief dance critic, had finally written his long-promised feature article about my collaboration with Bryan, I'd automatically become a hot commodity. Powerful men would be calling me, instead of the other way around. I scrolled through my inbox, but no one of interest was interested in me.

As I waited for the downtown A train to take me to work, I scanned the day's news. I was looking for recent updates on two unsolved murders that occurred in Paris, during American Ballet Company's joint season with the Rive Gauche Ballet. The dance world didn't often make the front page, but the simultaneous murders of a Parisian ballet master and a Russian ballet dancer combined enough glamour, intrigue, and violence to keep the story in the headlines, even though the investigation was several months old.

I'd never had the pleasure of dancing with Valentin Shevchenko, who was missed most by those he'd seduced with his talent, as well as his resemblance, when naked, to a finely chiseled Greek statue. Not that I knew this from personal experience. The only time I saw him, he was fully clothed. If I had desired the pleasure of his company—which I hadn't—I would have had to stand in line. I was more shaken by the murder of the dark and intense Charles Colbert, who was stabbed in the same theater I'd danced in a few hours earlier. The thought of that horrific event still gave me nightmares.

As I entered the lobby of the ballet studio, a different kind of nightmare emerged when a barrage of texts pinged in rapid-fire succession. By the time I disengaged the phone from the depths of my dance bag, the alerts had grown to epic proportions, more suited to a state of emergency than the ordinary resumption of the dance season. I figured family and friends were messaging their support upon my return to ballet.

No hearts greeted me. No smiley faces either. And no bursts of confetti-filled congratulations. Instead, a horrifying series of condolences filled the screen. **Sorry! Hope ur ok!** Angry emojis filled the rest of the text. The second message, **Say what???,** included three green faces followed by a line of exclamation points. Facebook and Instagram erupted like firecrackers on the Fourth of July.

The links to each message were the same. *Ballet's Newest Power Couple: Bryan Leister and Arianna Bonneville Remake the Future of American Ballet Company.* When I clicked on the title, a dramatic photograph filled the screen. Bryan, looking feverish and passionate, had his hands wrapped around a young dancer's waist. She was bent backward, in an understandably ecstatic pose. The shock of seeing another dancer in my place was so disorienting, I forgot to push the elevator button. I stared at the picture, unable to look away.

A voice from behind jolted me out of my funk. "Totally amazing, huh?" Bryan, his arm draped over the shoulders of the girl in the photograph, had an annoying grin on his face.

I swallowed my gloom and congratulated him. "Hitting the big time, I see."

"Yeah, the article was pretty great. Have you, uh...well, you probably already know Arianna? Arianna Bonneville?"

I bared my teeth—the closest I could get to a smile—and greeted her politely.

Taller than me by a good five inches, she looked down her flawless little nose. "Of course I know you. I used to watch you dance when I was still a little girl." She flipped her long blonde ponytail over her shoulder and softly laughed.

Bryan wasn't stupid. He probably knew what I was thinking, and he sounded sincere. "Leah, you know I appreciate all you've done for me." He patted me on the back. "I'll make sure Friedrich keeps you on the rehearsal schedule. If you're up to it, of course."

I unlocked my jaw. "Thanks, Bryan. But I'm fine now. Better than ever. And I can't wait to get back into the rehearsal studio. I'm sure your ballet is going to be great."

The elevator door opened, and Arianna gracefully waved her hand, allowing me to enter first. I threw several sidelong glances in her direction, but she ignored me and communicated only with her cell phone as we rode upstairs.

Bryan avoided further eye contact by addressing his next words to the scuffed door. "I think you'll like our new ballet master. Friedrich Holstein is brilliant, and he has a lot of exciting plans."

I'd met Friedrich briefly, during our Paris season. In the two weeks we worked together, the only talent he showed was his genius for biting criticism. Of course, I didn't say what I was thinking. I already distrusted and disliked Arianna, and in the incestuous and competitive world of professional ballet, dancers could be quite ruthless in their quest for stardom.

When we got to the fifth floor, Bryan rushed into the men's dressing room. I called after him, "Hey! Before you go, I wanted to ask you—"

He held up his index finger, indicating I should wait. Seven long minutes later, I realized he wasn't coming back.

Dejected. Depressed. Disheartened. All those D-words, which followed up the all-purpose F-word. I still didn't say it easily, thanks to my mother's relentless training, but I was thinking it.

By the end of that painful day, I was bruised physically and emotionally. I headed for my favorite cafe, where I drowned my sorrows in a large latte, the calories of which I had unquestionably already burned off. Halfway through the drink, I remembered my appointment with Bobbie York, the costume mistress. It was late, but Bobbie worked ten- and twelve-hour days during the season, and there was a good chance she would still be at her sewing machine. I hoped she wouldn't have to let out my tutus. That would be embarrassing for me and would mean a considerable amount of work for her talented team of seamstresses.

I rushed back to American Ballet Company and took the elevator to the costume room, which occupied the entire top floor of the building. I entered the small anteroom, where double doors opened onto a large workspace, made bright by slanting rays of sunshine. The windows were open, and a late afternoon breeze blew the sound of honking cars and the scent of hot pretzels through the room.

On the bulletin board, someone had tacked up the photograph of Arianna and Bryan. Sick of seeing my humiliation trumpeted everywhere I went, I ripped it off the board, tore it into pieces, and threw the pieces into the trash.

The room was silent, except for the slight rustle of fabric. I figured Bobbie was in the bathroom, or taking one of her many cigarette breaks on the roof, which she had fitted out with a chair, an umbrella, and a large urn. The open doors told me she hadn't left for the day.

I sat on one of the wooden benches that lined the perimeter of the room and stretched my aching legs and feet. Ugly red and purple welts sprouted around the straps of my sandals, but I didn't take off my shoes. Once a dancer's feet were released from prison, they expanded to inhuman dimensions. I did loosen the straps across my instep. I was worried the shoes would cut off circulation to my feet and give me a fatal case of gangrene.

I lay down on the bench and used my lumpy dance bag to elevate my legs. It wasn't as uncomfortable as it sounded. Using my hands as a pillow, I leaned back and closed my eyes. The musty smell of the costume room, mixed with the scent of pretzels, perfume, and the faint odor of tobacco soothed me. I didn't go to sleep but fell into a half-conscious, dreamlike state.

The sound of a female voice roused me. I opened my eyes but saw no one. I'd never been brave, and the ghostly tone made me nervous, even though spooking me was probably Bobbie's idea of a humorous prank. Maybe she was getting back at me for being so late.

"Bobbie? Is that you?"

No answer.

Screw her, or whoever it was who mocked me with that disembodied voice. I marched back to the elevator, and as I waited for the door to open, I reached down to tighten the straps on my shoes. From this awkward vantage point, I saw, at the far end of the long narrow room, a large quantity of candy pink tulle, which sat on the floor in an untidy heap. I stood up and looked again. Not all of the fabric was pink. Some of it was red.

The breeze subsided and the air was still, but the pile of pink and red tulle moved. I was afraid it was a rodent. I didn't distinguish between mice and rats. Either possibility was terrifying, and a lifetime in New York City hadn't inured me to occasional sightings. No way was I waiting for the elevator. I grabbed my bag and threw open the stairway door. But the ghostly voice called me back.

The physical intelligence of a dancer's body was quicker than conscious thought. Before I crossed the room, before I approached the fairy-colored fabric, my knees trembled and my shoulder muscles twitched. My heartbeat climbed into my throat, and I breathed in shallow gasps that burned like screams.

The handles of a shiny pair of dressmaker scissors formed a shallow tent in the center of the pile of pink and red. And under the tent, the long blades of those scissors pierced Arianna Bonneville's back. Her eyes were closed, and her cheek rested on the floor. Blood soaked the thin fabric of her leotard.

The sight of her broken body brought me to my knees. I knew not to move her or touch anything. But I didn't know if Arianna was dead. I threw off the layers of tulle and brushed aside her hair. She didn't respond. I dug

6

in my dance bag for my cell phone, all the while exhorting her to hold on.

"Arianna! Arianna!" I whispered around a tight throat. She didn't answer. I punched nine-one-one with one hand and put the other on Arianna's back. She was still breathing. Her head was angled toward me. Her eyelashes fluttered and the lids opened a fraction of an inch. Her eyes turned upwards.

The scissors were locked in her back at a painful angle. One sharp point was buried deep inside her. The weight of the handles leaned to that side so the opposing blade was buried more shallowly. Most of the blood dripped from this wound.

What to do? Removing the scissors might cause more bleeding, which meant keeping the blades in place could save Arianna's life. But what about the blade that hung halfway out of her back? Should I press it back in? Apply pressure? Shuddering, I grasped the scissors and held them steady.

Over a burning lump in my throat I told the operator, "Ambulance—emergency—she was stabbed. She's—she's dying. I'm at ABC—American Ballet Company—sixth floor. Hurry!"

The operator, who sounded bored when she answered the call, sharpened her tone. She told me not to touch the weapon and not to hang up. I wanted to follow her instructions, but when I let go of the scissors, they slipped even farther and the bleeding intensified.

I dropped the phone and grabbed a piece of tulle. I wiped my hands and the scissors and concentrated on keeping the weapon steady. Tremors shook my body, but I stayed strong. Arianna's life depended on me.

Passing clouds darkened the room. A cool puff of wind, a harbinger of fall, blew across us. I patted her and kept talking, babbling that help was on the way.

Her fingers were cold. I reached up to the table above us and dragged a bolt of velvet fabric to the floor. One-handed, I wrapped a section of it around her, careful not to disturb the gaping wound in her back.

Bobbie York walked in, bearing two cups of coffee and her usual sour expression. When she saw the body on the floor, she dropped the cups and started screaming. I yelled at her to shut up and turned back to Arianna.

I felt again for her breath. "Help is on the way! Hold on, Arianna!"

She didn't move.

From behind me, Bobbie wailed, "Who did this to you?"

Arianna's eyes twitched open. With bloody fingers, I brushed her gleaming blonde hair away from her face, which left a red mark across her cheek.

Without moving, she looked at me through half-closed eyes and said, "Leah."

A trickle of blood snaked from the corner of her mouth. I grasped her hand—the one that had elegantly and dismissively waved at me a few hours earlier. But it was as lifeless as the rest of her.

Chapter Two

Dance is the hidden language of the soul.
— Martha Graham

Footsteps broke the silence. Medics surrounded Arianna, and a tidal wave of cops crashed through the costume room, trampling the fragile and beautiful fabric. The younger of two detectives, Jonah Sobol, took me to one corner, out of sight of the blood. The other, Detective Farrow, escorted Bobbie York to a different room.

Detective Sobol asked me again and again what happened. His voice was low and without much expression, and his brown eyes were so dark I had trouble reading what he was thinking. He looked young, but his deliberate manner belied his youthful appearance.

"Tell me again what you were doing here, Ms.….Siderova, is it?"

"Yes. Leah Siderova." With great effort, I stilled my tapping heels and jiggling knees.

Detective Sobol assured me. "Now, Ms. Siderova. Nothing to worry about. Start at the beginning."

I told him everything. Again. Not, of course, about anything that happened during the dreadful rehearsal we'd attended earlier. But everything that happened afterward.

As if I hadn't already explained the situation, he said, "Why were you late to your appointment?"

Sobol's persistent reiteration of questions began to get on my nerves. "I told you this three times already. After eight hours of dancing, I forgot about my costume fitting. I went to the café around the corner for some coffee."

He looked up quickly. "What's the name of the place?"

"Figaro. Café Figaro."

Detective Sobol hitched his chair closer to mine. "You said the room was empty, and you thought Ms. York might be on the roof deck. Why didn't you check to see if she was there? Why did you just sit here?"

I started to feel nervous. My voice was shaking, and I could barely get the words past my teeth and tongue. They both seemed to have gotten bigger, as if they no longer belonged in my mouth.

"Why did I sit here? Bobbie—she hates it when anyone interrupts her cigarette break." Although I was telling the truth, I felt embarrassed, as if Sobol had caught me in a complicated lie. "I was tired. I wasn't thinking, really, of anything except that."

"How long did you wait? What did you do while you were waiting?"

I crossed and recrossed my aching legs. "While I was waiting? Nothing. I—I lay down on this bench. My feet hurt."

Sobol looked at my feet. Bruised and swollen bunions poked through the gaps in my sandals. An oozing blister on my left big toe stained the pink fabric an ugly shade of brown. I bent my knees and tucked my feet under the bench to hide my shame.

Sobol leaned forward. "At least tell me approximately how long you were here. I need some kind of time frame. Think."

I pressed my fingers into my temples. "I don't know. Maybe ten minutes. Not more than that."

Sobol's insistence on times and places was understandable, but I couldn't come up with the precise information he was so determined to obtain.

He was now so close to me I couldn't see past him.

"If you had checked the roof, you couldn't have missed seeing Ms. Bonneville much earlier than when you claimed you did. Which means you sat here with a dying woman for ten minutes and didn't call an ambulance."

I covered my face and tried not to cry, but the rush of tears came anyway. "I could have saved her. I didn't see her—didn't hear her until it was too late. I'll never forgive myself."

He threw me another inscrutable look and backed off. "Let me get you a glass of water. I know how difficult this must be for you."

I was grateful for his consideration. Officer Helen Diaz kept me company while I waited for Sobol to return. He was gone so long, I thought he'd forgotten about me.

When he did return, his voice dropped its unemotional tone and became warm. "Tell me about your relationship with Ms. Bonneville. I understand you two were rivals, so to speak."

I started choking on the water. So to speak? *Who* spoke?

"I don't know what you're talking about." My voice held so little conviction I wouldn't have fooled a five-year-old, let alone a New York City homicide detective.

Sobol tapped on his notebook with his pen. "I think you do know, Ms. Siderova. Leah. Can I call you Leah?"

What kind of a stupid question was that? Were we at a cotillion? Everyone called me Leah. And as I'd mentioned, Sobol and I were about the same age. At first he spoke to me as if I were a child. Then he spoke to me with the kind of deference you reserved for your maiden aunt.

With great sympathy, the detective said, "It appears Ms. Bonneville complained you were hostile to her. So, it's understandable she upset you. And totally understandable she made you angry. Listen, I know there's nothing worse than dealing with nasty coworkers. Forget about it. You should hear some of the talk around the precinct. Maybe you want to tell me about what happened between the two of you?" He smiled, but not for a minute did he cease scrutinizing my every move.

I lowered my head and took out the pins that held my hair in a bun, hoping to release the vise-like pressure across my brow. "I'm not—I didn't—you're wrong about what you're thinking."

"What am I thinking, Leah?" Sobol sat motionless.

"You're thinking I'm guilty. And that's crazy. There is nothing in the world that could get me to physically hurt another human being."

Sobol opened his mouth to speak, but the sound of loud angry voices interrupted him. I rose to my feet and saw a crowd of people arguing furiously with two cops who stood guard at the threshold of the room's double doors.

I didn't care about Sobol or anything else. I needed a sympathetic face and voice and shoulder. I did an end-run around the cops and rushed to join my fellow dancers.

They recoiled, as if my tears were drops of toxic waste and they were worried about radioactive contamination.

Bryan was the first to speak. His voice was anguished. "What did you do?"

I didn't understand at first. I started to tell him I called nine-one-one as soon as I saw Arianna, but then I realized that wasn't what he meant. He wasn't asking what I did *for* Arianna. He was asking what I did *to* her.

This was so insane, I started laughing. Bryan turned white, and his knees sagged. Friedrich Holstein, our new boss, rushed to support him. Madame Maksimova, my ballet coach and mentor, after a horrified look at Bryan and Friedrich, opened her arms to me, but Detective Sobol intervened. He shepherded me back to my perch in the costume room and suggested the precinct might be a better place to continue our little talk. I opened my mouth to decline the invitation, but a wave of nausea prevented me from protesting.

Officer Diaz followed me to the bathroom, perhaps to make sure I didn't escape through the tiny window that looked as if it hadn't been opened since disco died. Or maybe the police wanted to prevent me from committing suicide, which would deprive the people of New York their right to imprison me.

I didn't want to speak—since anything you said could be held against you in a court of law—but I couldn't stop myself. "This is crazy. I'm the last person in the world who could do such a thing. I'm sure the detectives know that, right?"

Officer Diaz didn't smile at me, and she didn't disagree. But she did watch me closely, without making eye contact. And then the truth sank into my feeble, fevered brain. The cops didn't think I was nice and normal. They thought I was a killer.

I checked the mirror to see if I was still me. A streak of blood stained my forehead. I bent over the sink to wash and realized my hands had rusty red blotches. No wonder Bryan and Friedrich and Grayson wouldn't let me get near them. I looked like the last survivor of a zombie apocalypse. Only Madame Maksimova had opened her arms to me.

I bolted back into the stall of the bathroom and vomited the grande skinny latte that had been my only meal of the day. So, the diet was going well. It was the rest of my life that was swirling down the drain. Given Diaz's unsympathetic attitude, I decided not to mention the events that transpired earlier that day. They probably wouldn't have understood.

I rode to the police station in the back of a cop car with no sirens, but with swiveling lights on top. Watch out, New York. Dangerous criminal inside.

Chapter Three

I do not try to dance better than anyone else. I only try to dance better than myself.
—Mikhail Baryshnikov

O n the way to the precinct, I pondered how much, if anything, I should tell Detectives Sobol and Farrow. Not a single event in the previous eight hours foreshadowed the horror in the costume room, because the day Arianna was murdered was approximately the same as any other day in a large ballet company.

The first thing I did after company class was check the schedule, which had its own complicated rationale—so complicated, in fact, that novice dancers spent every free minute examining its ever-changing, penciled-in additions and deletions. But for all its muddled logic, by no stretch of the imagination did any item on the calendar foreshadow violent death.

In the square marked *New Ballet/Bryan Leister/Studio 4B*, I was pleased to see my name was included in the bold-faced group of principal dancers. Arianna's name was there too. And Zarina Devereaux, a guest artist from the Rive Gauche Ballet, was slated to join us the following week.

I remembered that long before the start time, the studio was full. A select number of high-end donors sat in chairs along one side of the room, while on the opposite side Bryan was deep in conversation with the pianist. Ten of our youngest dancers whispered excitedly, as they flicked nervous glances at Friedrich. Grayson Averin, the odious dance critic who had reneged on his promise to write about me, and had featured Arianna instead, sat at a makeshift desk. He wrote at a furious pace, slamming the keys on his laptop as if he had a longstanding grudge against them. Grayson didn't acknowledge anyone's greeting, but he doffed an imaginary hat to Arianna as she pirouetted past him. That was ballet for you. Every dancer was one injury away from becoming irrelevant.

Despite the presence of a photographer, who roamed the room capturing every casual and choreographed moment, Grayson paused often to take pictures on his cell phone. His social media skills were legendary, and he counted more influential followers and friends than most of the artists he wrote about.

I sat on the floor in the back of the studio and chatted with two friends, Daniel and Horace. We pretended not to notice the photographer as we stretched our aching limbs into aesthetically pleasing shapes, but we were quite conscious of being watched. Clearly, Grayson had carte blanche, and none of us wanted to be an object of mockery on his Instagram or Twitter feed, let alone in his newspaper column.

Although Bryan was rehearsing the corps de ballet and wouldn't be working with the principal dancers for another forty minutes, Arianna served as his model, demonstrating the steps for the larger group. The photographer followed her around as closely as if she'd magnetized him.

I wasn't jealous of Arianna. Did I need to explain that to the police? Would they understand that because her style of dancing was so different from mine I didn't envy her? I made up my mind that if the detectives asked me about my relationship with Arianna, I could honestly say we had no relationship. But if they asked me what I thought of her, I would lie. Because the truth was, the longer I watched her, the more I loathed her—her clever cruel mouth, her faux innocent looks, and her dexterity at stepping on, elbowing, and otherwise unnerving the other dancers.

Olivia, one of the youngest dancers, caught my eye. She moved with extraordinary lightness and grace, and her style was well suited to Bryan's choreography. She was also quite beautiful, but in a ballet company, extreme attractiveness was the norm. Her eyes were dark and intense, with heavy fringed lashes, the kind of eyes that made her look as if she were on the verge of crying, even when she was laughing. Unlike the long-legged recruits in

American Ballet Company's new army of tall blonde lookalikes, she was tiny. She looked like she could be my kid sister. I hoped she would get a good part. Arianna noticed her too, and when she thought no one was looking, she stuck out her foot and tripped Olivia.

I jumped to my feet, but before I could say anything, Daniel grabbed my arm and pulled me back.

In a low voice he said, "Cool down, Leah. You fight your battles and let Olivia fight hers. She's tough. She'll be okay." He looked me over. "And so will you."

I resented Daniel's callousness, but, after a few minutes, I saw that he was right. Although several corps de ballet dancers were unnerved by Arianna's presence, Olivia quietly held her own. Not for the first time, I wished I still had Gabi, my longtime best friend, by my side. She'd know how to deal with Arianna's aggressive physicality. But Gabi was now a wife, a mother, and a teacher of ballet. I'd have to fight this battle on my own.

Bryan dismissed the large group of dancers after quietly conferring with Friedrich. They were talking about casting, of course, and which lucky dancers would get a few extra minutes on stage, or, best of all, a featured sixteen-bar solo. Although Friedrich told them they could go, only those who were scheduled for another immediate rehearsal left. The rest ranged themselves in the back of the room. Daniel, Horace, and I had spent many minutes watching them. It was their turn to watch us.

I wrapped a black chiffon skirt around my waist to match the rest of my all-black outfit. Very slimming, and it definitely made me look taller. A few feet away, Arianna preened in her pale pink leotard and tights. She also wore pink leg warmers. Their bulk stopped slightly above her knees and emphasized the delicate strength of the rest of her body.

She was the perfect picture of a ballerina, with a heavy sweep of bright blonde hair, blue eyes that startled in their vividness, long limbs, and a fragile neck, and shoulders. As she rose en pointe, her feet arched in beautifully articulated curves. Her legs stabbed the floor and the air with precision and grace.

With sugary concern in her voice, she purred, "Leah, I'm so happy to see you trying to dance again. We were all worried that after your knee surgery you wouldn't be able to make a comeback. My mom said she had the same surgery and was never able to dance again."

Arianna inherited her mother's cold ambition, as well as her talent for ballet. I respected both attributes. I preferred that Arianna keep her knife out of me, but I understood her as well as only another dancer could. I needed this ballet to keep on top. Arianna needed it to get there. We each knew both those things. Hell, everyone in the room knew it.

"There have been a lot of advances in surgery since your mother was a dancer," I informed her, loud enough for others to hear. "And I'm definitely ready to return to the stage."

"That's great. Of course, when my mother tried to return, she was also juggling *my* ballet lessons, so it was a lot easier for her to retire. But you're not married, are you? No kids to distract you?"

Arianna knew perfectly well I wasn't married. I couldn't have been more unattached if I were an uncoupled caboose at an abandoned railway station. I pushed away memories of my most recent boyfriend, who ditched me during our European tour. To his credit, he did me the favor of a telephone breakup. It could have been worse. He could have texted me. Or I could have found out via a Facebook update, which he executed minutes after telling me he couldn't commit to someone who couldn't commit.

"I'm so excited about Bryan's new ballet!" Arianna enthused. "He told me all about it while we were working together, and it sounds amazing."

I stayed neutral. "When was that?"

Arianna widened her already wide blue eyes. "A bunch of us rented a place in Montauk the last two weeks of the summer." She gestured toward Daniel and Horace. "Those guys were there and a few girls. It was super amazing. Lazy days on the beach and barbecues every night. But Bryan worked every morning, listening to the music and planning the choreography. We spent a lot of time together."

I squelched a rising tide of irritation. "Sounds lovely. What was Tess doing while you and Bryan were working together?"

Arianna laughed. "Who knows? Bryan didn't seem to care what his girlfriend was up to." She put air quotes around the word "girlfriend," which was so annoying I didn't trust myself to say anything further.

Arianna kicked her leg in a grand battement, missing my fragile knee by less than an inch. "Did you know Bryan and I are going to be on *Good Morning America*? We're dancing part of his new ballet for the studio audience. And, of course, all the millions of viewers. Super exciting. And then there was that great picture of us in the newspaper. So cool, right? My parents bought, like, fifty copies!"

At least I knew now why Bryan had been too distracted to call me back. It wasn't his new friendship with Grayson Averin. He was so busy bonding with Arianna he didn't have time for me. Or Tess, the woman he'd been living with for the last year.

Arianna put her face close to mine, as if she were my friend. "I know Bryan thinks you won't be able to keep up with his new choreography. But he's too nice to tell you himself. That man is too kind for his own good."

Arianna's malice was unnecessary. She so clearly held the upper hand. What was the point of all that cruelty? I was no threat to her. My fingers trembled as I adjusted the ribbons on my pointe shoes. Arianna, from ten inches away, and with apparent mindlessness, flicked her foot so the point of her shoe kicked in my direction. Each time she did it, she got closer to nailing me.

There were many things I couldn't do: drive a car, sail a boat, or pilot a plane. And there were many things I feared—most notably bugs, rodents, and high places. But where my own body was concerned, I'd always been in control. And I'd never backed off from a challenge. I got up, shook the tension from my hands and feet, and tested my knee with a few easy jumps and turns.

For the next two hours, Bryan put us through one grueling dance combination after another. I did not, by so much as a flicker of an eyelash, indicate I was exhausted or in pain. I breathed only as heavily as the rest of them. But my lungs were exploding and my toes, which had lost toughness during all those post-op weeks of enforced rest, were ten individual licks of fire. I resigned myself to losing at least one toenail, which sounded horrific.

It was very unpleasant, but not bad enough to make me, or any other dancer worth her tiara, stop dancing.

Bryan was unusually tense and impatient, and he sighed mightily when I paused to change my worn pointe shoes for a pair that would give me more support. He had a split personality. Outside the studio, he was charming and easygoing. Inside, he was distant, aloof, and sometimes unreasonably exasperated. But, at that first rehearsal, he was downright surly. He'd said when he was working he got impatient with himself, but he came across as impatient with us. After I flubbed the pirouette sequence—twice—he shook his head. This energized Arianna so much she pulled off one quadruple pirouette after another, while I continued to struggle with doubles. I made up for my deficiency by moving as fluidly as possible.

I sneaked a look at Grayson, who watched the rehearsal and typed without looking at the keyboard. The presence of the dance critic shouldn't have made any difference to me, but it did. I knew the rest of the dancers felt the same way. There was a different air in the room with him there. Rehearsals were always intense, but depending on the choreographer, they were usually somewhat informal. Unlike in class, we actually talked during rehearsals. But Grayson made all the dancers feel as if we had to impress him, and there was very little of the kind of dialogue that made the creative process so intimate and so enjoyable.

I didn't know Friedrich well enough to discern if there was any difference in our new director's attitude. Perhaps his surly expression was the way he looked all the time. As for Bryan, once he began working, he was oblivious to the rest of the world. The roof could cave in and he wouldn't notice.

Although I appreciated Bryan's dedication and concentration, I wished he'd been more sensitive to the fact an outsider was listening and recording all that transpired. Especially when he called out, "Leah! You've got it all wrong. At that tempo you might as well be doing the crypt scene in *Romeo and Juliet*." He bent down and plucked several loose threads from my skirt. "And I think you're molting."

I gathered the threads and circled the room in order to give myself ten seconds to catch my breath—and to look over Grayson's shoulder at his

19

computer screen, which went dark before I could see anything other than a glimpse of his Twitter feed. He turned briefly, when I dropped the shredded bits of skirt into the garbage can next to him, but, for the most part, he had eyes only for the perfect Arianna.

After the rehearsal, Bryan talked at length to Daniel and Horace. I dallied in the back of the room, waiting for him to finish. While I busied myself reading nonexistent text messages in one corner of the studio, Friedrich walked over to Arianna, who had stationed herself in the opposite corner. I watched them in the mirror. They were dancers, and even though Friedrich gave up performing when he became a ballet director, his body still telegraphed volumes. So, of course, did Arianna's. That was how I knew my boss was sleeping with my rival.

I wasn't the only one closely observing them. Grayson appeared mesmerized by their conversation. Overall, there was a wary, watchful undercurrent in the air. Every dancer in the room was checking out which way the wind would blow this season. If Arianna hadn't been so nasty, she would have acquired at least a dozen best friends from the corps de ballet. Young dancers would willingly follow General Custer into battle if they thought it would improve their chances to move up to bigger roles.

Yes, talent and ability and hard work, all that crap did matter. But at our level? There wasn't a girl in the company who couldn't whip through those thirty-two fouetté turns in *Swan Lake*. Each year the company turned down dozens of dancers who could accomplish all that and more.

A lump sprouted in my throat, a consequence of the day's suppressed emotion. I swallowed it and hurried toward the exit. From across the room, Friedrich told me to wait. Arianna followed a few feet behind him and stopped when he did. She pretended to look for something in her dance bag as she eavesdropped.

Friedrich looked at his clipboard and told me, as if reading someone else's notes, "*Es ist gut*. Very nice that you are back in class, but this ballet is too much for you, *ja*? Arianna, she started rehearsing with Bryan over the summer, and we have Zarina Devereaux joining us as a guest artist. Perhaps you get one or two matinees later in the season. But for now, you will understudy Arianna and Zarina."

As a matter of survival, I'd long ago mastered my natural tendency for inconvenient tears, but I checked the mirror anyway, to make sure no sign of weakness escaped me. My cheeks were red and my eyes were a bit glassy, but that was only because I was winded from dancing so hard. Friedrich seemed to be waiting for a response, but if so, he would be standing there until hell froze over. A few awkward moments passed before he resumed his conversation with Bryan.

"Too bad," said Arianna. "Better luck next time!" She turned her back to me and swung her bag over her shoulder, clipping me on the side of my head. The woman wasn't simply verbally abusive. She exerted a calculated physical intimidation as well.

I didn't visibly lose my temper. But I also knew I couldn't allow Arianna, or anyone, to treat me with such disdain.

Instead of moving away, I circled around so we were again face-to-face. She stepped back, but I narrowed the gap between us and got close, so close I could smell the perspiration behind the perfume.

"Stay away from me." I stared straight into her eyes.

She appeared startled. I didn't know what she expected from me, but clearly it wasn't retaliation. This woman was used to getting her own way.

Arianna stammered a bit—the first chink in her armor. "You—you can't—"

"I'm warning you. Stay away from me."

"Or what?" She stuck out her chin and looked down her nose.

I opened my mouth, but no words came out. She'd called my bluff, and I had nothing. But when she laughed at my powerlessness, I grabbed her arm. "If you even come near me again, I'll—I'll cut you down."

My voice stayed dispassionate, but there was a roaring in my ears.

She jerked her arm from my grasp and turned her back. This time I was ready for her. Before her bag hit me, I grabbed it. Caught off balance, she stumbled and fell.

Horrified, I reached to help her to her feet, but she smacked my hand away.

"Don't touch me! Keep away from me!"

21

The room was suddenly quiet. Bryan and Friedrich rushed to Arianna's side.

She rose slowly to her feet, pretending a weakness I was certain she didn't feel. Bryan and Friedrich stared at me, as if I'd suddenly sprouted horns and a tail.

"It was an accident! She hit me with her bag..." I looked around the room, trying to find a witness who would corroborate my story, but every face was studiously averted.

After a minute or two, Friedrich clapped his hands. "Back to work, everyone."

The pianist resumed playing, and the dancers picked up where they left off.

Arianna followed me to the door. Before I exited, I turned to face her once again. Her mouth, which had trembled after my meaningless threat, curved downward in a nasty, close-lipped sneer. She whispered, "You're pathetic. You're finished, and you don't even know it. But everyone else does. And you can try to push me around all you want. Nothing can help you now."

She walked over to where Grayson was sitting. She whispered in his ear and he nodded. Even at that distance, I could see her whole body glowed with triumph. Her blue eyes sparkled, and even her sweat shone. She'd won, and we both knew it. Everyone in the room knew it.

Everyone except the murderer.

Chapter Four

You have to love dancing to stick to it. It gives you nothing back...nothing but that single fleeting moment when you feel alive.
— Merce Cunningham

Detectives Sobol and Farrow walked me through a noisy, shabby, dirty outer office and into an interrogation room. It had a cracked linoleum floor, four plastic chairs, and a chipped table with faint brown stains. The table was pushed against the wall, and I had no barrier to hide behind. No one came to apologize for this massive blunder on the part of New York's Finest.

The grim nature of my surroundings extinguished the faint I hope I still had that I would wake from this nightmare. The studiedly casual demeanor of the detectives was familiar from many cop shows, and I stopped talking, except to make a phone call. Not to my mother, although with the expertise she'd garnered researching her mystery books, she might be helpful at some point. No, this situation demanded I call Dad.

My father answered his phone immediately. "Leah, darling. Are you alright? I heard the news about that poor young dancer. But I heard they took someone into custody already."

"Dad, I'm at the Twentieth Precinct. I'm the person they took into custody." I tried, without success, to keep my voice from rising to hysterical heights. "I need a lawyer. Like, now."

Bless my father. Jeremy Feldbaum, a philosophy professor who spent most of his adult life debating Kant's moral imperative, asked no questions, and spared me his shock and horror. "I've got it covered, my darling. Sit tight and *don't say anything*. I'm on my way. I'll call Uncle Morty right now. And don't worry about calling your mother or your sister. I'll take care of that."

My spirits, which had risen slightly after hearing my father's voice, took another swan dive when I heard Morty Feldbaum was coming to the rescue. Uncle Morty specialized in landlord-tenant relations and spent most days drumming up business at Housing Court. Although he often bragged about his ability to broker deals with the "scum of the earth," I wasn't sure how practiced he was with criminal investigations. If the problem was nonpayment of rent, then Morty was your guy. But felony murder? His name wasn't the one I'd have on speed dial.

As soon as I finished my phone call, the detectives reentered the room. Farrow offered me a cup of coffee while I waited for Morty. When I refused, he left to get a cup for himself, and I was alone with Detective Sobol. We sat in a few moments of silence. "I bet you dancers get to travel a lot. Italy, Germany, France. Never been to Paris myself, but I've always wanted to go."

Startled at the change in subject, I answered without thinking. "American Ballet Company dancers travel a lot, but when we do, we don't get much time to sightsee." I stretched my aching legs. "We visited Paris a few months ago, although the trip didn't end well. I injured my knee after the last performance. I'm just getting back to dancing now."

Sobol shook his head. "That's a damned shame. Must be tough to have to stop dancing after you've been doing it so long." He handed me a picture of a dark skinned man with high cheekbones and a charming smile. "What do you know about this guy?"

I froze. The photo was of Charles Colbert, the slain ballet master of The Rive Gauche Ballet.

My mouth was so dry I had to unstick my tongue from my teeth. "Colbert. His name is Charles Colbert. And yes, he was the director of the ballet company in Paris. I—I didn't know him well."

Sobol took back the photo. "You were in the theater the night he was killed. And you worked with him the previous year as well. You must have gotten somewhat close after all that time together."

I clasped my hands to keep them from shaking. "No! We—it was a professional relationship. I never saw him outside of work. And—and when he was stabbed, I'd already left the theater."

I knew what was coming next. Sobol handed me a picture of a blonde, impossibly beautiful man, with classically regular features. I could barely look at it. "I know even less about Valentin Shevchenko."

The detective sounded amused. "Really? I heard he was quite popular with the ladies."

I refused to meet his gaze, horrified I had selfishly talked about my knee when the more compelling reason the Paris season ended badly was that two men had been murdered.

Detective Farrow wandered back in as I fumblingly tried to make up for my idiotic comments. He tapped a plastic spoon against his cardboard cup. "You have to admit, this is quite a coincidence—two attacks on ballet dancers in Paris and another one in New York. I understand you were in the theater when Mr. Colbert was killed. What went down that night?"

I jumped to my feet. "I wasn't the only one who was there! The—everyone in American Ballet Company was there too. And really, I honestly don't know what happened. My knee started hurting more and more, and I left early. So, I don't know too many details."

Detective Farrow paused, his cup halfway to his mouth. "Sure, sure. I get it." He gestured to the chair I'd vacated. "Why don't you sit back down? Shame about your injury. When you left the theater, did you go to the hospital? See a doctor?"

I opened my mouth to answer when Morty charged in. Despite my misgivings about his competence, he was surprisingly quick and effective. "Is Leah charged with a crime?"

Detectives Sobol and Farrow looked at me, looked at Morty, and looked at each other. Sobol shook his head slightly, and the next thing I knew, I was "free to go." Before I left, Farrow asked me if I had any plans to leave New York, which I felt was an unnecessarily dramatic touch. Where would I go? Rehearsals for the fall season had barely begun. It wasn't as if I could phone it in.

I looked straight ahead as we walked toward the exit. Although there was plenty of noise and activity around us, I was conscious of stares and whispers at each desk and cubicle we passed.

As Morty and I exited the building, a crowd of people surged toward us, and in an instant we were surrounded. Reporters shouted questions and photographers yelled and cajoled, "Look this way! Hey, Leah! C'mon, baby! Give us a smile!"

One of the reporters, whose face was shadowed by dark glasses and a brown porkpie hat, got so close his breath fanned my neck. I had a terrifying flashback to when I was twelve years old and a gang of kids came swarming out of a schoolyard and stole my backpack.

But this was no schoolyard. I couldn't run and couldn't yell, and the thrust of microphones and cameras in my face terrified me. Morty had disappeared. I turned my back on the scrum, determined to hole up with the police department until the coast was clear.

From nowhere, Morty's arm plucked me free from the jostling mob. He was calm and seemed pleased.

He faced the press, and, with a grave and important air, said, "We have no statement at this time." He resisted my efforts to pull him away. Instead, he straightened his tie, put one arm around my shoulders, and stood still. The photographers went wild. I wanted to turn away, but Morty's iron grip kept me next to him.

The reporters continued to shout questions at us. Under his breath, Morty told me not to smile and not to say anything. Told me to look serious but not scared.

From our position at the top of the steps, I saw Barbara, Dad, and Ann, Dad's second wife, arrive at the same time, but not together. Three separate cabs pulled up to the curb, and three times Morty signaled them to wait. He seemed unmoved by having my parents watch this horror show.

There's no point in saying things couldn't get worse. They could always get worse, and at that juncture they did. Wrenching cramps gripped my stomach, and I feared I was going to throw up or pass out. I couldn't help but grab my middle. My legs began to wobble.

In an undertone, Morty commanded, "Stand straight. Look like you have nothing to hide."

Nauseated and dizzy, I gasped, "Uncle Morty, I think—I'm…feeling sick…"

The next thing I knew, I was stretched out on a plastic sofa that smelled like sour milk and disinfectant. Above me, my parents and Ann swam into view. In the background, Sobol and Farrow hovered. I still didn't remember fainting in front of all those people, but any time I wanted to, I could view ten thousand pictures of me, passed out on the steps of the Twentieth Precinct, humiliating photos that would live forever on the internet.

Everyone spoke at the same time until my father commanded, "Stop! Give Leah a few minutes to breathe. We'll figure this out together, and not inside a police station." Dad nodded a quick apology to the detectives, to indicate his distress at having to exclude two complete strangers from an intimate family discussion. My father was an extraordinarily polite man.

My mother was so pale I feared she too would faint. But she stayed resolute. She put her arms around me, and the scent of Joy perfume and cigarette smoke immediately calmed me down. She asked Farrow if there was a back exit. There was, but that too was being watched.

My father took charge, and the next thing I knew, we were bundled into three different cars. The driver of my car introduced herself as the editor of Dad's latest treatise on philosophy. She didn't bother with small talk and instead described her work on moral dilemmas. With the press in hot pursuit, I found it difficult to concentrate, but since she was a philosopher, she easily managed both sides of the conversation. Fifteen minutes later, we arrived at the Rare Book and Manuscript Library at Dad's university.

The head librarian was waiting at a side entrance. She unlocked the door as each of us arrived, acting as if there were nothing more commonplace than accommodating five people fleeing the media.

The librarian led us through an underground maze that terminated on one end of the quadrangle. Mindful of the crowd of students, we spoke in whispers. Barbara suggested we go to her apartment, but Morty vetoed her plan. He wanted dinner. I'd recently thrown up a skinny latte and a quantity of bile, and I wasn't in the mood to eat, but I also didn't want to leave them, or have them leave me.

Uncle Morty's suggestion that we go to Broadway Bistro elicited glares from the rest of us. The restaurant was quite close to the scene we'd just fled, and we were still shaking with relief from our escape. Worse, its proximity to Lincoln Center made it a favorite with my colleagues, who, for all I knew, had already tried, sentenced, and hanged me in absentia.

Dad took my arm. "Follow me." We walked a few blocks to Palmyra, an Italian restaurant located below street level.

Barbara inspected the place with a censorious eye, but even she couldn't find fault with the restaurant.

Every fiber of my body was thrumming, possibly because I'd put my phone on vibrate. Many of the numbers that popped up weren't on my contact list, but one very familiar name appeared again and again.

I handed the phone to my mother. "It's Melissa. Please, talk to her for me. I'm talked out." When I was a successful dancer, I was capable of dealing with my perfect and perfectly wonderful sister. After falling so low, the burden of her sympathy would have been unbearable.

Barbara didn't argue. She took the phone outside and rejoined us after a surprisingly short conversation. She then turned her attention to the menu and carefully perused the options. "Have a salad with grilled chicken. Dressing on the side. This is no time to let yourself go."

"Barbara. For heaven's sake! Leave her alone. She can eat whatever she wants. I think she's too skinny, anyway." Dad tapped at the menu. "Have the lasagna, darling. You need your strength."

And people thought dancers obsessed about food. We were no crazier than the rest of world. Or at least the part of the world that was bound by the Hudson and East Rivers.

My father's wife, Ann, suggested a protein shake and herbal tea. My mother sniffed at this suggestion and observed that the items Ann recommended weren't on the menu of the restaurant we were sitting in, or, indeed, any restaurant she would deign to patronize. Ann took this opportunity to inform Barbara of the benefits of flax seed for sensitive, irritable, high-strung neurotic women. Dad cut short Ann's discourse on nutrition by ordering a bottle of Malbec, Barbara's favorite wine.

Morty gave us his food order and left the table to take a phone call. He reappeared ten minutes later, with a worried look on his face.

Dad appealed to his brother. "Walk us through this, Morty. What the hell is going on?"

Uncle Morty, sweet Uncle Morty, spoke in a reassuring tone. "Let's not get ahead of ourselves. At this point, Leah hasn't been charged. So, it's early days. Worst-case scenario, we plea down to first-degree manslaughter. Under the circumstances, I don't think she'll get the maximum, but maybe ten years? With good behavior, she'll be eligible for parole in seven and a half. And who knows? We might get lucky."

I choked, and my mother thumped me on the back. When I recovered my breath, I said, "But I didn't do it! This is crazy! Uncle Morty, what did you tell them?"

Morty ignored the question. "Leah, how old are you now? Thirty-two? Thirty-three? You'll be out before you're forty-five. Go to trial, and you could get twenty to life. Big difference. Think about it."

My father had always been affectionate toward his younger brother, but mild-mannered Jeremy Feldbaum looked ready to strangle Morty.

Dad's face was fiery, but his voice was cold. "Leah is innocent. My little girl isn't pleading guilty to anything. Maybe we need another lawyer."

Morty was practiced in dealing with the high emotions and fierce drama of landlord-tenant relations in New York City. "Do you want your little girl in prison for the rest of her life?"

Barbara responded by transforming herself into the Wicked Witch of the West. She leaned forward and pinioned my uncle with a lethal stare. "You're overlooking one very important fact. If Leah didn't kill Arianna—"

"Of course I didn't!" I didn't cry, exactly. But floods of tears dripped, and I couldn't stop them. I dried my eyes with a white napkin that turned dirty gray from whatever mascara had survived the previous onslaught.

Barbara softened her tone. "Yes, darling. I know. You couldn't hurt a fly. But as I was saying, if Leah didn't—I mean, *since* Leah didn't kill Arianna, someone else did. The police have to find that person."

29

The total logic of this silenced all of us, except for Morty. "The police think they've found the murderer. Detective Farrow, at least, wants to move quickly. The other one's not so sure."

Barbara still didn't seem to believe him. "No one could be that dumb."

Morty sighed. "Leah told me she held onto the murder weapon, even though the nine-one-one operator told her not to touch anything. She was the one who was found with Arianna. She has no good explanation of why she was in the room nearly an hour past her appointment. She says she was waiting for the costume lady, which means the period of time between the actual stabbing and when Leah was there is extremely narrow. I've got a friend at that precinct, and I talked to him while Leah was passed out. He told me that before she died, the victim said Leah did it. That's a helluva big matzoh ball sitting in the middle of some very hot soup."

Despite my horror, I sensed Morty, while still upset on my behalf, was pleased with his metaphor. This was probably because my father was the undisputed brains of the Feldbaum brothers. Dad went to Brown and did his post-grad at Yale, while Morty barely made it through Southwestern Texas College of Law.

From between clenched teeth, Barbara said, "She has no motive."

Morty shifted in his seat, looking as uncomfortable as if the bread he'd been gnawing on had bitten him back. He turned away from Barbara and looked at me. "One of your, uh, friends told the police you threatened to stab Arianna in the back."

Diet Coke went up my nose, and I started choking. "I never said that! That's a lie!"

Morty was insistent. "Other people heard you."

I gulped for air, which was suddenly in very short supply. "Then they're all lying."

Morty munched on a breadstick and then pointed the remaining half at me. "What are you telling me? That there's some kind of conspiracy against you?"

So this was what paranoia felt like. Or maybe not. Paranoia was when you imagined people were conspiring against you. My nightmare was real.

Morty persisted, acting as if he were the DA on a third-rate cop show. "Did you or did you not hit Arianna during the rehearsal?"

Ann gasped. "You hit her? You hit the dead girl?" My stepmother drew together her eyebrows and pursed her lips. "What possessed you to do such a thing?"

Dad elbowed his wife and took my hand. "I know you would never deliberately hurt anyone. Can you remember exactly what happened?"

I put my hands in my lap so Dad wouldn't feel them shake. "I didn't hit her. She hit me. I was trying to defend myself. And yeah, I might have said something like, 'I'm going to cut you down,' but I wasn't serious. And I didn't mean it literally, for heaven's sake. I meant I was going to cut her down to size."

Morty and Ann wore the same disapproving expression.

I turned to my mother. "Barbara, you have to believe me. If you don't..." I could say no more.

Barbara broke in. "The police must be totally incompetent. No one who was going to commit a murder would announce it to a roomful of people. Tell them, Morty."

Morty paused in his demolition of two pounds of lasagna. "Leah was passed over as lead ballerina in some new ballet. The police think that's plenty of motive."

My mother turned even whiter than her usual pallor. "What's this about, Leah? Did that bastard Bryan pick Arianna instead of you?"

My mother's investment in my career had never been less welcome. "That's not important right now. Let's not get distracted by details. You were on the right track with what you said about the real killer being out there. What are we going to do?"

It didn't take Barbara long to come up with an answer. She stabbed a slice of cucumber with vindictive force and said, with a determination that was the legacy of generations of ancestors who'd survived pogroms, "Of course, we figure out who did it." The tension around the table eased a bit and then shot back up again when she added, "Then I kill the guy."

Dad choked and spilled his wine on Ann's yoga pants. She didn't look happy, but as Barbara pointed out later, she could buy another pair for $9.99.

Dad looked long and meaningfully at Barbara. "This isn't a game. Or a plot for one of your books. Our daughter's life is at stake here. Maybe we hire an investigator?"

Or another lawyer.

Barbara lowered her lashes and looked at me out of the corner of her eye, and I could tell she'd had the same idea.

After that, no one said much. I couldn't handle any more talk about the murder, and all other subjects became too frivolous to discuss with me at the table. Morty's appetite was undiminished, and Ann consumed her allotted grams of protein and carbohydrates, but Barbara, Dad, and I didn't fare as well. Barbara poked, jabbed, and otherwise abused her vegetables, but she didn't eat any of them. She filched a meatball from Dad but gagged on the second bite. My father pushed the food around on his plate, but not much of it went into his mouth. Both my parents did better with the wine.

The party broke up early. Dad paid the bill, and Barbara hailed a cab. After giving the cabbie meticulous directions on the route she wanted him to take, she turned her attention back to me. "Why didn't you tell me about Bryan's ballet?"

"Uh, I was kind of busy."

Barbara folded her arms. "Fair enough. But let's talk about it now."

I stared out the window. "You talk. I can't worry about Bryan's ballet when I'm terrified I'm going to go to prison for a crime I didn't commit."

Barbara pulled me to her. We didn't need words to understand each other. I kissed her goodbye at Eighty-Ninth Street and headed west on foot. The wind picked up and swirled bits of garbage into little eddies. As I waited for the traffic light to turn green, a car careened around the corner, spraying me with pebbles and dirt from the adjacent construction site. At every turn, the city I loved seemed determined to hurt me.

Chapter Five

If you cannot get rid of the family skeleton, you may as well make it dance.
— George Bernard Shaw

I'd never felt so lonely, not even after my latest boyfriend broke up with me. When Matt left, I was upset but not surprised. He wanted a wife, a baby, and a house. I wasn't ready for all that, or maybe he wasn't the husband I wanted. He'd been nice enough about it, and I supposed I knew the end was coming. By the time I returned home from Paris, he'd already moved in with Gwyneth. I saw them together occasionally, at brunch on a Sunday morning, or eating dinner at our neighborhood burger joint. At first, I was too busy to feel the pain of his absence. Another boyfriend was surely just around the corner. But as I traversed Eighty-Ninth Street, I realized several months had passed. No new boyfriend. No new ballet. And for all I knew, no future. Other than ten or more years at Bedford Hills Correctional Facility. Seven, with time off for good behavior.

I climbed five flights up to my apartment. My shoulder was sore from carrying my heavy dance bag, my feet were a swollen mess, and my surgically repaired knee wailed with each step. After the third floor, I climbed one step at a time, using my right leg to get to the next step and dragging my weak leg after. The rest of my body registered its routine complaint from a full day of ballet, and I had to rest before the last flight up. Breathless as I finally reached the top floor, I collapsed as soon as I got inside. The climb wasn't easy, but it was better than returning to Barbara's apartment, where I'd spent weeks recuperating from my knee surgery.

The apartment was just as I'd left it. Six cans of diet soda in the fridge, an unwashed coffeepot in the tiny kitchen, and a lineup of drying tights and leotards in the bathroom. Home.

Apartment 5B was billed as a one-bedroom, and, technically, there was a bedroom. You walked into a tiny living room and to the left was a sliver of a kitchen, with exactly enough room for two very slender people to sit at the round, café-style table. To the right of the living room was the bedroom, which had a smaller footprint than most SUVs. For New York City, it was a bargain. The living room windows looked out on a brick wall a few feet away, and the bedroom faced the street, but the ceilings were high and outside the kitchen window was a leafy expanse of trees—a rarity for a tenement building.

My cell phone kept buzzing with text messages. One was a text-caster message from American Ballet Company. Friedrich cancelled the usual company class, and he scheduled a mandatory company meeting instead.

I wondered if I should go to the meeting. I was afraid—afraid of facing colleagues I'd thought of as friends. If even Bryan rejected me, what would the rest of them think? Ballet friendships could be both shallow and ephemeral. We were always on the move, and because one's career was so short, the turnover was high.

The second, third, and fourth text messages were from my sister. Melissa had also left two voice mail messages. I texted her I would call in the morning. Then the chimes of a Chopin waltz floated from the phone. I almost fainted with relief. It was Gabi, the best of best friends.

I was so emotional, my fingers fumbled to answer the call. "Gabi. I'm so happy to hear from you! How are you?"

"Don't be such an idiot." Gabriela blew a Bronx cheer into the phone. "I didn't call to talk to you about me. Sid, *mi amiga mas querida*, what the hell is going on? I leave you for three weeks and all hell breaks loose!"

Gabi was the only one who called me Sid. She started doing it after my parents got divorced, when Barbara changed our last name from Feldbaum to Siderova. She thought, quite correctly, that her parents' Russian surname would look better on a Playbill and a book cover. The change felt false to

34

me, but Gabi made it special and fun instead.

"Oh, Gabi, things couldn't be worse. I wish so much that you were here. I really needed you today."

Gabriela was visiting her family in Argentina. Until three years ago, she was a principal dancer with American Ballet Company. She navigated complex choreography and treacherous company politics with grace and good humor, right up to the day she kissed off her dance career. At her emotional farewell performance, she got fifteen curtain calls, and I got to bring her one of many bouquets of flowers. I tried not to cry when I handed her the roses, but since a million other people were sobbing up a storm, I ignored my usual interdict against public tears.

Gabi quit dancing because she wanted to get married, get pregnant, and, to quote her, get a life. She did all three in record time.

In soothing tones, she assured me, "I'll be home soon. And don't worry. We got through middle school together. We'll figure this out too."

I met Gabi in the seventh grade, on my first day at the New York Arts Academy. My parents wanted me to attend a progressive school on the Upper West Side, a place that offered plenty of personal freedom, but a very heavy academic load. When I was thirteen, I rebelled. My new school had a shortened day that accommodated aspiring actors, musicians, and dancers. Somehow, I persuaded my scholarly parents to let me make the move.

Most kids started at the school a year earlier, in the sixth grade, and on that first day, as I saw friends greet each other, I got more and more nervous. I considered running back to my old school, where I had the safety of my sister and her group of friends. Then Gabriela Acevedo sat next to me, and it wasn't long before we were as close as if we'd grown up together, which I guess we did.

And that was that. We shared top billing at American Ballet School's graduation performance. We apprenticed together immediately after school, got into the company the same day, and danced together for her entire career. Then she got married, and ten months later she had Lucie.

"Talk to me," Gabi entreated. "I'm worried about you."

I tried to sort through the events of the day so I could present them to

Gabi in a way that made sense. She listened to the whole story without comment, other than an occasional murmur of sympathy or distress.

Finally, she said, "Do you think what happened today is related to the attacks in Paris? Can you think of any connection between Arianna and Charles Colbert? Or Arianna and Valentin Shevchenko?" She sighed deeply. "Maybe the killer had a grudge against Russian dancers who look like blonde Greek gods. And maybe after murdering Valentin, the killer decided dark, gorgeous Parisians were also a threat." She hummed a bit, one of her more endearing habits. "Or maybe both guys jilted the same girl, and she killed them."

Detectives Sobol and Farrow also asked me about the night Colbert died. I gripped the phone with sweaty palms and tried to stay calm.

"If a girl killed both guys, why would she then go after Arianna?"

Gabi paused to consider my objection. "Maybe Arianna was the girl both guys were after, which drove some poor ballerina into a crazed fit of violence."

I told Gabi, as perhaps I should have done more coherently to the detectives, "I hardly knew either of them. Colbert was stabbed after the performance, when everyone—or at least most people—were at the gala. But I wasn't even there! Or at least, I wasn't there when they discovered the, the body. My knee hurt like hell, and halfway through dinner, I went back to the hotel. No sane person could think I was involved. As for Valentin, he died of some obscure poison. I heard the Russian government was involved. As far as I know, no one is linking the two deaths as anything other than a freak coincidence."

Gabi clicked her tongue in sympathy. "This is twice that you must have just missed the murderer. You could have been killed."

A cold sweat broke out on my forehead, and the phone slipped from my fingers and fell to the floor. Somehow, this hadn't occurred to anyone else.

My heart beat so hard and so fast I felt it pounding through my shirt. I said a hurried goodbye to Gabi and pressed my hands against my chest, trying to still the painful throbbing. What to do? I checked the internet and confirmed my symptoms were life threatening. I swallowed two aspirin tablets, a Wikipedia-approved treatment, and headed to the emergency room. I slipped the phone into my handbag and, on shaky feet, began the long descent to the street.

Calling an ambulance felt unnecessarily dramatic, and I figured if I couldn't immediately hail a cab I'd call for one. I ignored pleading noises from my phone and concentrated on putting one foot down and then the next. After two flights, a burning pressure in my throat forced me to rest. Leaning heavily against the bannister, I finally answered Gabi.

"Sid! Sid! What's going on? Why didn't you answer me?"

Over the swelling in my throat, I wheezed, "I can't—can't breathe. Going to—get to doctor." I sat on the steps and gasped, "Hospital."

"Stay where you are. I'll call Barbara. She'll go with you."

"No." I swallowed hard and tried to control my breathing. "I'm—I can—I can do this. My mother's been through enough for one day."

Gabi's voice had a forced calm to it. "Please. Let me call her."

I covered my face with my hands. They were cold and felt good against my sweaty face. "No."

Her voice got so loud I had to hold the phone away from my ear. "Then call nine-one-one. They'll come get you."

Gabi's advice wasn't unreasonable, but I didn't trust anyone to maneuver a stretcher around the tight corners of the steep stairs. What if they dropped me?

I promised Gabi I'd call my mother, and I stuck the phone in my back pocket so it wouldn't fall into the black hole inside my handbag. Step by step I got myself into the lobby and out of the building. Once outside, I gripped the wrought iron bannister at the top of the stoop and peered down the street. To my left, a couple was out walking their dog. Farther down the block, the usual group of teenagers leaned against parked cars, blowing smoke rings and drinking beer out of paper bags.

Nothing out of the ordinary, unless I counted a shadowy figure across the street. He wore a hat pulled low over his face and stood in a pool of darkness, halfway down the basement stairs of the tenement building across from mine. Was he watching me? I couldn't tell. He had a furtive look about him. I cautioned myself against paranoia. The guy was probably awaiting entry into an apartment he was illegally renting through Airbnb.

I couldn't make out his face, but something about the set of his shoulders looked familiar. Since I was in no shape to meet anyone, I turned away and pretended not to have seen him. He was probably a regular at the diner or the supermarket, one of those people you met almost often enough to greet.

The pressure in my throat and chest persisted, but the cool night air made it easier to breathe. I decided against an Uber and instead took cautious steps toward Broadway. If I didn't feel better by the time I reached the end of the block, I would hail a cab.

At the corner bodega, Mr. Kim waved me in. "New shipment came in yesterday!" He pointed to tiny packets of sugar-free candy. The candies were so good I suspected they weren't dietetic, but they were so small I figured they wouldn't do too much harm. Some entrepreneurial do-it-yourselfers from Brooklyn had started making them a few months ago, and while the recipe was excellent, the supply side of their business wasn't as good. I was addicted to the black licorice-flavored candies, and whenever he got a delivery, Mr. Kim stockpiled them for me.

After stacking several boxes on the counter, Mr. Kim looked more closely at me. "Whatsamatter? Eat some candy, missy. You don't look so good." Every female under the age of ninety was "missy" to Mr. Kim.

I was afraid the chewy candies would get stuck in my throat. But to make him happy, I popped one in my mouth. They really were good. I ate another and then one more for good measure. Feeling better with each bite, I left the store feeling more optimistic than when I walked in.

Before I left, Mr. Kim advised, "Go home, missy. Storm coming." He walked me outside and looked at the sky. "I think I close early. Slow night."

I laughed at him. "When was the last time you closed early? Not as long as I've been living here."

Gusts of wind knocked at the containers of flowers and fruit that lined the exterior of the store, and a few apples rolled into the street. Mr. Kim grimaced as he ran after the fruit. "Yes. But there is always a first time. Early night for me!"

I did a mental check of my physical health and realized if candy mitigated the symptoms of my incipient heart attack, I wasn't sick enough to go to an emergency room. Absent a gunshot wound or cardiac arrest, the average patient could spend upward of five hours waiting to see a doctor at most New York City hospitals. If I still felt sick in the morning, I could make an appointment with my doctor, which would have the added benefit of keeping me away from the ballet studio, which was now a crime scene.

The strong breezes felt good against my sweaty skin, and since I was still too anxious to fall asleep, I decided to walk around the block. Whenever I was restless or lonely, I roamed the streets of my neighborhood. They were like friends that never let you down.

The smell of rain was in the air, and sudden bursts of wind snapped at awnings and tree branches. It was a quiet night, with more cars than people on the street. I hunched my shoulders against the wind and walked past the diner, the shoe store, and the pharmacy. As I turned the corner, I sensed, rather than saw, a figure behind me. I turned around to see who it was, but temporary scaffolding outside a new apartment building blocked my view. Hyper-alert, I quickened my pace and listened for footsteps.

Someone behind me was pacing his steps to mine. I was afraid to turn around. Afraid to run. Afraid to scream, because what if the person following me was a perfectly innocent bystander and I ended up making a spectacle of myself?

Only mortal peril would induce me to call nine-one-one for a second time in one day. The memory of finding Arianna's body was still too raw.

I sought refuge in a store, but the Laundromat was closed. Ditto the craft store, the gift shop, the bookstore, and two very expensive boutiques. The rest of the block consisted of tenement buildings. I risked a glance behind and saw a man with his hat pulled low. He had his hands shoved into his pockets.

Why? Was he carrying a gun? A switchblade? A vial of acid? People were crazy. You never knew what they were capable of doing to single women walking by themselves down deserted streets on dark and stormy nights.

I walked faster. The footsteps kept pace. I sped up again, but the pounding in my ears and head kept me from hearing if I'd lost my stalker. I turned the last corner and broke into a run.

I didn't go inside my building. No one who had grown up in New York City was going to risk fumbling with keys if a predator was nearby. Instead, I headed toward the safety of Mr. Kim's bodega. My stalker yelled out to me, but I ignored him and didn't stop until I was back in the store.

Mr. Kim didn't wait to hear what happened. He took one look at my face, grabbed a huge flashlight, ran into the street, and yelled, "I'm calling the police!"

In doing so, he startled a middle-aged customer, who was waiting to buy a pack of cigarettes.

A moment later, Mr. Kim returned. With a pleased look, he announced, "Don't you worry, missy. I scared him off." He offered to take me back to my apartment, but I refused. He had no one to take over at the store, and, even though he claimed he was going to close early, he never did. He loved to tell his customers how his store stayed open all through last year's massive blizzard. His bodega became a center for collections to help people devastated by the storm, and he still felt proud about his contribution.

Worried, he told me to call the local precinct, but I'd had enough of the police for the rest of my life. Also, I suspected that after the stress of the day, I'd overreacted. After all, what really happened? I thought I heard someone follow me. Someone I couldn't identify, because I'd been too afraid to confront him or even look at him. I imagined the bored-but-patient looks I'd receive if I tried to report this crime that didn't happen.

Mr. Kim and I compromised. He'd watch me walk back to my building. If I yelled for help, he could be there in two seconds.

Mr. Kim, even with his flashlight, wasn't a scary-looking guy. He was short and spare, with thin gray hair and thick dark eyebrows. Most days he wore an expression of mild benevolence. Nonetheless, he was my hero. He stayed on the street, watching me, until I got to the vestibule of my apartment building, when I waved him off.

Before I put my key in the lock, I checked to see if I was being followed. At first, I thought the loitering stranger was gone. But he had simply changed locations. He was ten yards away and advancing in my direction.

I snapped my key in the lock and slammed the door. He yelled my name, but unless he was a master at picking locks, I was safe. Although I feared giving myself a heart attack, I made it up the stairs in record time, only to come close to fainting again, when, for the second time that day, a disembodied voice called to me.

Chapter Six

There is a bit of insanity in dancing that does everybody a great deal of good.
— Edwin Denby

T he spectral-sounding voice belonged to a very corporeal Gabi, whom I'd pocket-dialed during my mad rush up the stairs. I updated my friend on the status of my non-heart attack, or as the Mayo Clinic put it on their website, my myocardial infarction. I didn't tell her about the mysterious stalker because I was still trying to convince myself I was overreacting. Talking about it would have made it more real. And far more terrifying. It wasn't until later that I wondered how the guy knew my name.

I poured a glass of wine, even though the standard cures for anxiety rarely worked for me. When I was upset, or nervous, or angry, ballet soothed me better than alcohol. I blocked out the real world, and I concentrated on one of the many dances I'd committed to memory. I didn't even need the music. I had every note memorized, even the really difficult and dissonant pieces.

While Gabi made comforting small talk, I concentrated on the exact sequence of jumps in Act II of *Giselle.* I abandoned Leah Siderova and left all her problems behind me, and I let myself sink into the role of the heartbroken village girl. Memories of the haunting music dulled the ache in my brain, and, without moving from the sofa, I hopped around in arabesque and crossed the stage in a series of feathery jumps.

Visions of orange jumpsuits and gray prison cells kept interrupting images of that ethereal ballet, in which the ballerinas wore long white tutus and danced in an enchanted forest. Then the magical setting slipped away, and I saw myself sitting down to carbohydrate-centric meals with terrible coffee and no Diet Coke.

In a distant corner of my mind, I heard Gabi regaling me with the humorous oddities of Lucie's bedtime routine. As gently as I could, I broke in. "Sorry, girlfriend, you know I love your daughter, but I've got a lot on my mind. I've gotta go."

Gabi ignored my attempt to hang up. "Maybe I was wrong to tell you to put everything out of your mind. Maybe you should do the opposite. Go back to before you found Arianna. Think of it as a movie. Or a ballet. Take it frame by frame, step-by-step. Sid, my sweet, you may have seen the murderer and not realized it at the time."

To humor her, I forced myself to relive each moment of the day, which culminated in Arianna's death. "Bobbie York was the first to arrive. She could have been hiding on the roof, waiting for me to show up and take the blame. Maybe she killed Arianna."

Gabi was unimpressed. "*Querida*, Bobbie has no motive. I think a better suspect is that nasty ballerina from the Rive Gauche Ballet. Remember her? The one we both disliked? She had a very public affair with Charles Colbert. And rumor has it she was also involved with Sylvain, whom the French police took into custody and then released."

I nervously paced the narrow room, which was, I imagined, approximately the size of a jail cell. "You're thinking of Zarina Devereaux. I heard about her affair with Colbert and with Valentin Shevchenko, but I didn't know she was hooking up with Sylvain as well." Remembering my brief, and extraordinarily unpleasant interactions with Zarina, I added, "I wouldn't be surprised to learn she's bonking her way across two continents. Sylvain's been making a name for himself as an up-and-coming choreographer, and Zarina likes to get her foot, and every other body part, in the door before anyone else. You have to hand it to her, she's like a one-woman United Nations of sex."

Gabi was thoughtful. "At the very least, Zarina does get around. That's something to think about."

"Unfortunately, even if I were convinced the attacks are connected, she wasn't at today's rehearsal. She's not scheduled to arrive until later this week."

Gabi sighed. "Too bad. Although, she also doesn't have any motive to kill Arianna."

I stopped short. "And I do?"

Gabi was apologetic. "No, no, of course not. But Arianna did get the role you wanted."

I paused, overcome by what Gabi said—no, overcome that Gabi was the one who said it. The thumping in my chest began again.

Gabi added, too quickly, "Maybe that came out the wrong way. Of course, jealousy is a stupid motive for anyone, least of all you. And under normal circumstances, maybe it does sound crazy. But what's crazier than three murders in three months?"

Gabi was right. Before Valentin Schevchenko was poisoned, and Charles Colbert and Arianna Bonneville stabbed to death, ballet companies were cutthroat only in the metaphorical sense of the word. But there wasn't much point in discussing this with Gabi. She wasn't in Paris when Colbert and Schevchenko died. Nor was she in New York City when Arianna was murdered.

I had to talk to someone who was at the scene of at least one of the crimes. An insider. Someone with a good memory and a sharp intelligence.

Three ambitious and cold-hearted men immediately came to mind.

I checked American Ballet Company's employee directory for the telephone number of our new ballet master and got as far as tapping the digits into my phone, but I didn't press send. Given Friedrich's chilly treatment of me, I doubted he would answer my questions unless I managed to corner him in a dark alley. Or in a court of law.

Friedrich was a lot like Colbert, his counterpart at the Rive Gauche Ballet. Both men were talented and ambitious and possessed a streak of cruelty that repelled me. They were reputed to have omnivorous sexual appetites and were infamous for promoting dancers by way of the casting couch. Unlike Colbert, Friedrich had never been physically attacked, but in the dance world, he was no less feared.

In my brief encounters with them, I'd kept my distance. Partly because I disliked them, and partly because I preferred men who had an unambiguous preference for women. I was insecure enough about my body without having to worry about meeting basic standards for equipment.

However, Friedrich wasn't the only one who might have inside information. Grayson, thanks to his position as a major chronicler of the dance scene, had a longstanding and mostly cordial relationship with members of both American Ballet Company and the Rive Gauche Ballet. Even more important was the fact that Grayson was in the theater when Colbert was stabbed and in the American Ballet Company building when Arianna was murdered.

I took a deep breath and swallowed my pride. Despite Grayson's recent coolness, he was much more likely to agree to talk to me than anyone more directly connected with American Ballet Company. As a reporter, he'd probably jump at the chance to scoop the other news outlets.

I'd never liked Grayson, even before he chose to write about Arianna instead of me. But I also didn't take his betrayal personally. If in a few months' time, I had managed a triumphant return to the stage, he'd be as eager to cover that story as he was to cover the story of my trip to the Twentieth Precinct. In short, I trusted him no less, and no more, than anyone else I knew professionally.

Grayson didn't answer the phone when I called, but moments after I left him a message, he called me back. I ignored his questions and told him I wouldn't talk to him unless our conversation remained off the record.

He reluctantly agreed but insisted we meet in person. Given his reputation, I didn't want to let that slimy worm into my apartment, and, for the same reason, I didn't want to go his place. We agreed to meet at a diner approximately equidistant to each of us.

I turned the lights off in the front room of the apartment and, from the shadows, checked the street for suspicious-looking men wearing hats pulled down over their faces. But if anyone was still staking out my apartment building, he was well hidden. Next, I checked my pulse. After ascertaining

45

I was unlikely to die of a myocardial infarction in the immediate future, I took action. From the depths of my closet, I unearthed an old-fashioned umbrella, the kind that had a curved handle and pointy steel tip. The rain had stopped, and I didn't need protection from the weather. But if the creep who followed me was still lurking outside, I would stab him. Not fatally, of course. I executed a few practice lunges with the umbrella and then called for an Uber. I waited inside the locked building until the driver texted me he had arrived.

Grayson got to the diner before I did. Through the plate glass window, I saw him chatting up the waitress, who laughed at his lame jokes. Despite his thinning hair and widening middle, he was surprisingly attractive to many women. I, however, found his drawling voice, disdainful manner, and clammy handshake loathsome.

Those qualities didn't deter other ballerinas from availing themselves of his self-serving friendship. Zarina Devereaux, the coldly beautiful star of the Rive Gauche Ballet, had engaged in a well-publicized affair with him, but it was an open secret that she loved Grayson's power as a critic more than his prowess as a lover. Grayson recently completed a book on the lives of contemporary ballerinas, and Zarina was the only dancer to earn an entire chapter to herself. After the book went to press, she ditched him for Colbert. If Grayson was hurt by her defection, he didn't show it.

When I sat down opposite Grayson, the waitress looked disappointed, but he was—or pretended to be—delighted to see me. Uninterested in pleasantries, I told him, even before my coffee arrived, "I want to talk to you about the night Colbert was stabbed. I need information, and it's literally your job to collect it."

The critic coolly countered, "And I want to talk to you about when Arianna Bonneville was stabbed. Since, as you say, it's my job to collect information."

I took the huge laminated menu from the waitress and pretended to peruse the contents. "The two events may be unrelated. Or not. But you were on the scene both times. I wasn't."

He drummed his fingers on the table. "Who are you kidding? You performed in the last ballet of the evening when the company was in Paris, and you were at the gala afterward." He pulled his mouth down in an expression of fake regret. "Sorry, Leah. Most inconvenient for you."

Grayson didn't react when my umbrella clattered to the floor, but I jumped nervously at the sound. "I left the gala early, long before Colbert was attacked."

He shook his head. "Nice try. You left the theater before he was found—not necessarily before he was murdered."

"I was in no shape to attack anyone. That's the night I injured my knee. I'm surprised you've forgotten about it, since the very next day you wrote a review saying it might be time for me to take a final bow." I tried to keep the bitterness out of my voice.

Grayson shrugged. "Sorry about that, darling. Nothing personal, of course. Happens to everyone sooner or later. If you wanted a long career, you should have become a dentist."

I held the menu against my chest as a shield against his darts. "I appreciate the sentiment, but I'll let you know when I'm ready to retire. Not the other way around. And I didn't call you to discuss your dance reviews."

Grayson nodded. "Of course not. I wouldn't have met with you if you had."

I put down the menu and clutched at my coffee cup. "In spite of what you think, I don't have a lot of information about what went down that night in Paris, the night Colbert was stabbed. Between the performance and the knee injury, I wasn't exactly paying attention to the people around me."

Grayson rolled his eyes.

I said, more forcefully, "Quit acting like I was the only American Ballet Company dancer who was on the scene for both attacks. Everyone else was there with me."

He sliced his fork into a large piece of cheesecake. "Well then, I have to ask once again, why are you talking to me? Talk to one of your ballet friends." He put his index finger to his forehead as he pretended to think. "Oh, wait. After today, you probably don't have any friends. Except for me, darling. You'd do well to remember that."

"I'm more interested in motives and alibis than in winning a popularity contest. And the dancers at the Rive Gauche Ballet weren't exactly chummy. There was an awful lot of backstage yelling when we were in Paris."

My grasp of French wasn't good enough to decipher the rapid-fire conversations I'd overheard, but I didn't need a translator to know the atmosphere at the Rive Gauche Ballet was poisonous. I assumed the usual petty rivalries were the source of the dancers' low morale, until Colbert's death demonstrated the seriousness of the company's problems.

I organized the sugar packets on the table as a way to defuse my nervousness at Grayson's unblinking stare. "Why was Colbert so angry after the performance? He and Zarina got a dozen curtain calls." I couldn't resist reminding him, "Not as many as Bryan and I got, but still, the reviews for both companies were excellent."

Grayson snorted. "Colbert wasn't happy because Sylvain, his fabulously adorable *jeune homme*, did most of the choreography. And everyone knew it. Colbert got the curtain calls, but Sylvain got his job. Rather embarrassing, don't you think, to be replaced by your protégé?"

I added Sylvain's name to the list of people who could have attacked Colbert. And then I crossed it off. "If you're right, then Sylvain had no reason to kill Colbert. More likely, Colbert would have wanted to kill Sylvain."

Grayson nodded. "Colbert felt like Sylvain had stabbed him in the back. No pun intended, of course. If it were physically possible, I wouldn't put it past Colbert to stab himself in the back and then return from the underworld in order to blackball Sylvain."

Grayson was a mine of information, but as far as I could tell, none of it helped me.

I looked away as Grayson shoved heaping forkfuls of pale yellow cake into his mouth. "Tell me about Zarina. If the rumors at the Rive Gauche Ballet are to be believed, she was having sex with Colbert *and* Shevchenko. Or perhaps Colbert, Shevchenko, and Sylvain. Maybe this has nothing to do with ambition and more to do with love. Or sex. Zarina will sleep with anyone who can advance her career."

Grayson's face turned an ugly shade of red. Too late, I remembered he was one of Zarina's many self-serving conquests.

I didn't have time for subtlety or tact. "Come on, Grayson. Tell me. Does Zarina have an alibi for when Colbert was stabbed? For that matter, do you?"

Grayson cleared his throat. "I left the party briefly to join Zarina in her dressing room, where we were, as they say, occupied. So yes, we both have quite ironclad alibis."

Like many secretly insecure men, Grayson wanted to brag about his sex life, but I didn't have the stomach to listen. "Okay, let's forget about Zarina for the present. Tell me about Friedrich. What was his relationship with Colbert? They're both directors of major ballet companies. And they both choreograph. Were they rivals? Or friends?"

Grayson yawned. "No idea. And I can't speak for any alibi Friedrich might have, since I left early. Right after Zarina and I, uh, finished." He laced his fingers across his belly. "I hate to love 'em and leave 'em, but I had to post my review of the performance."

If I had known Grayson left so soon after I did, I probably wouldn't have bothered to meet him. Still, I persisted. "No one seemed upset or angry or suspicious? Is there anything that happened in Paris that seemed similar, or relevant, to what happened to Arianna?"

Grayson idly pressed the crumbs of his cake into his fork. "Nothing comes to mind. Sorry I can't be more help. But that's in the past. Let's talk about today. You could take this opportunity to tell me your side of the story." He took out a notebook and a pen and, for good measure, placed his phone on the table to record our conversation.

I crossed my arms. "No comment." I forced myself not to look at my lap, where my cell phone was recording our conversation. I refused to go on the record with him, but he had made no such stipulation to me.

Grayson snapped his fingers in the direction of the waitress, taking his frustration out on her. She hurried over to refill our coffee cups. I placed my hand over my cup. If I had any more caffeine, I wouldn't sleep for the next two days.

Grayson grabbed my hand and, when I tried to pull away, he tightened his grip. "My sources say you're the prime suspect in Arianna's murder. If I were you, I'd be more concerned about what happened today than with what happened months ago. Unless you know for a fact the same person committed both crimes." His eyes bored into my head. "Speaking as a friend, my darling girl, I'm trying to help you out here."

I jerked my hand out of his damp grasp. "You're not trying to help me out. And stop calling me your darling. You're looking for a juicy story. But your credibility is going to take one hell of a hit if you blame me and then the police catch the real killer."

Grayson didn't hesitate. "It's all news, dear Leah. The rights and wrongs don't matter much. And anyway, I was a witness to your threats to kill Arianna. I don't need you to confirm what I already know. And the attack on Colbert? Who knows? Maybe you had the hots for him and he dumped you." His mouth curved upward in a grin, but his eyes were as cold as ever. "Or maybe you had the hots for me. Plenty of women do, you know."

He grabbed my hand again as I put money for the coffee on the table. "It's on me, darling. I'm available whenever you are, and I'm very discreet when I need to be."

I had a sickening feeling that the entire meeting had been a horrendous miscalculation, but I couldn't resist defending myself. "You know I wasn't serious when I said—when I said that to Arianna. I was trying to get her to back off. For heaven's sake, she clocked me in the side of my head." Shivering in the over air-conditioned diner, I said, more to myself than to him, "Maybe someone in the room heard me and figured he could get away with murder by blaming the attack on me."

As I waited for Grayson to respond, I stared at a clock that hung over the wait station. It ticked off ten seconds before he sighed without speaking. And then ten more seconds silently elapsed. I felt as if ten hours passed.

Finally, Grayson said, "It's all over social media—no one's talking about anything else. The whole dance world is buzzing. Twitter is lit up like a Christmas tree. It's not just online chatter, either. My phone has buzzed fifteen times since we started talking. And a bunch of people emailed me. Everyone knows I've got the inside scoop at the company. And while you may not trust me, you should be careful whom you talk to. Not everyone is as nice as I am."

Though my legs were shaky, I got up from the table. I couldn't keep still. "Yes, yes—but what are people saying about me?"

"They're saying what we both already know. That you threatened to kill Arianna. And then you did it."

Chapter Seven

Dance first. Think later.
— Samuel Beckett

G rayson's terrifying words propelled me out of the diner and into previously uncharted social territory. Under normal circumstances, New Yorkers didn't barge in on other people's apartments without advance warning. But in the brave new world I now inhabited, ordinary rules no longer applied. I was fighting for my life.

On my way to the subway station, I whirled around and brandished my umbrella at every passing breeze, but no one threatened me, and the only damage I did was to my self-esteem.

As soon as I boarded the train, an annoying voice inside my head told me to go back home. That voice of restraint and good manners sounded a lot like my mother's. Barbara's imaginary advice continued to bedevil me as we advanced from station to station, as it had for most of my life. In fact, I was so busy justifying the trip downtown I nearly missed the Fourteenth Street stop. Of course, I left the umbrella in the subway, leaving myself without a weapon. The next step in my descent into craziness was probably going to be talking to myself out loud. At least in New York City I'd still blend in.

The streets were busier downtown than they were uptown. The Apple store was packed, the Chelsea Market was in full swing, and restaurant goers and bar hoppers spilled into the street. A group of people more chic than I ever was or ever will be crowded around velvet ropes in front of a dark building, which was the not-so-secret location of the latest hot dance club. I checked the time. Although it was too late for an unannounced visit to anyone other than your very best friend, it was way too early for the fashionable and famous to go clubbing.

The hopefuls who lined up on Fourteenth Street knew this, but they waited anyway. There was no sign in front of the building where the heavily tattooed and pierced crowd gathered, an indication of the exclusiveness of the club. You probably had to go through an alley and up a fire escape to find the place. Gaining entry to the latest trendsetting venue was New York City's version of a competitive sport. You needed persistence, courage, and stamina. Kind of like mountain climbing or big game hunting, but with better clothes, shoes, and drinks.

My destination was a brand new building close to the High Line, one that towered with moneyed aggressiveness over its neighbors. I surveyed it with some apprehension. Twenty-four hours earlier, I wouldn't have invaded anyone's privacy. But twenty-four hours earlier Arianna was still alive, and my biggest problem was replacing salted caramels and Italian biscotti with shredded kale and mineral water.

The façade of Bryan Leister's apartment building contained enough glittering stone to rival New Hampshire's status as the Granite State. And judging by the number of apartments, it probably had more residents than most New England towns. I wondered if people in other parts of the country were more open-minded than New Yorkers about uninvited guests.

I came there to talk to Bryan, but I also wanted to talk to his well-connected, trust fund girlfriend, Tess Morgan. Tess and Bryan were at the summer house share in Montauk with Arianna, and they might have some insight into Arianna's personal life. I wasn't especially friendly with Tess, but I did know her family moved in the same exalted social circles as Arianna's. Without a personal introduction I could never gain access to that rarified milieu.

Unlike the doorman at my mother's apartment building, who wore a burgundy uniform with gold braid and a matching cap, the guy who ushered me inside Bryan's stone-cold palace wore an Armani T-shirt, close-fitting black jeans, and loafers with no socks. I stepped into a lobby that refracted soft light from angled glass and steel walls. The translucent floor was lit from underneath, which made me briefly dizzy, and I stumbled a bit as I made my way to the reception desk.

Behind a tall, brushed steel barrier sat the most beautiful man I'd ever seen. He surveyed me without any reciprocal enthusiasm. I was sure that he, like so many waiters and waitresses and receptionists, was waiting for his big break, as either an actor or model. Echoing the doorman's sartorial aesthetic, he was dressed in a tight T-shirt, rippling muscles, and a three-day scruff of a beard.

He took a deep breath and closed his eyes. I was still there when he opened them. "May I help you?"

His attitude was less willing than his words. For one lunatic second, I regretted not wearing something more fashionable, even although I didn't own the kind of clothing that commanded respectful attention from nasty receptionists. Then I remembered why I was there, and it wasn't to make a good impression on the building staff.

I lifted my chin and did my Katherine Hepburn imitation. "Yes. I'm here to see Bryan Leister."

"Hmm. Leister, Leister. Yes, alright. And you are?"

I didn't answer right away. I wasn't sure I wanted to give the receptionist my name. Maybe I should pretend to be someone else. But who would impress this jerk? Anna Wintour? Meryl Streep? Stella McCartney?

I rejected total paranoia and the flickering warnings of a panic attack. "Leah." I fantasized for a moment that I, like Madonna, Bono, and Mr. T, needed only one name.

My interlocutor turned away and murmured into his headset, as if state secrets might be revealed by an audible repetition of my name. The guy looked a lot less beautiful the longer I stood there.

"Mr. Leister will come down. You may wait there." He extended his arm and pointed to a black leather bench.

I sat down but couldn't sit still. I'd never been a cell phone fiddler, but I needed some release of tension. I avoided Facebook and Instagram and checked the stock market, although I had no stocks. I stared at Words with

Friends, even though real friends were in short supply and I couldn't put together a three-point answer if I had the entire alphabet at my disposal. I started a game of Solitaire but quit after thirty seconds. Too ironic.

The bank of elevators was at right angles to the seating area. I got up to check the digital display as each car progressed from floor to floor. If I, like Bryan, had hooked up with a trust-fund baby, I too could have been mechanically whisked home at the end of the day. But when I saw how the handsome gatekeeper eyed me, perhaps worried I'd break into one of the mini-mansions above, I decided to be happy with my tenement walk-up.

When Bryan finally arrived, he didn't look pleased to see me. His eyes were red, and his mouth was pressed into a thin line of displeasure. Perhaps I woke him. Or maybe he was catching up with the latest binge watch on Netflix and I interrupted at an inopportunely suspenseful moment.

He crossed his arms and said, in a very low voice, "What are you doing here?"

I'd heard more inviting openings, but I was desperate. "I'm sorry to barge in on you like this, but I didn't know who else to call. I'm trying to get information about Arianna. I'm in trouble, Bryan, and I need your help."

"I can't help you. Please leave." He hardly opened his lips as he spoke, as if grudging me even those few words.

"That's it? That's all you have to say? Bryan, we are—we were—friends. I need you."

"I can't talk to you. There's a police investigation." Bryan slipped his phone out of his pocket and stared at the screen. "It's late. Get some sleep and we'll talk tomorrow."

"Okay." I stood as if I were leaving. "I'll go. Just give me five minutes."

He shook his head and turned away from me.

I planted myself in front of him. "You owe me, Bryan. You'd be nowhere if I hadn't convinced the best dancers in the company to work with you for free. And it was me people came to see when you started out."

Without turning his head, Bryan moved his gaze from the doorman to the receptionist/would-be model. Even though he lived there, he looked as if he were casing the joint.

He muttered, "Do you mind telling me what the hell you were thinking, barging in on me? You woke Tess out of a sound sleep."

I checked the time. "Why does Tess go to sleep so early?"

Bryan rubbed his eyes. "I dunno. Something to do with work. She's at a hedge fund now, and she's gotta get up early to talk to—what? London? Tokyo? I forget."

This vagueness wasn't like Bryan, who was obsessively organized. His tone was dismissive. Another bad sign for his relationship with Tess. He added, with more emotion, "I don't even know why I agreed to see you."

"Maybe because we've known each other for five years and we're friends, and I'm in a bad spot. Maybe that's why?"

Bryan stared at his feet. "No. That's not it. Anything you have to say to me you can do at the studio. I don't need to be dragged into your mess."

I tried to get him to meet my gaze. "What is going on with you? I seriously feel as if I'm in the *Twilight Zone*. Bryan, it's me. You can't think I had anything to do with Arianna's death."

He turned red. I'd like to think I shamed him into decency, but I wasn't too good with reading people's emotions. Especially guys.

In desperation, I reached for his hand. He pulled it away but gestured toward the door, indicating I should follow him. The doorman, deep in conversation with the receptionist, didn't bother to usher us out.

The earlier storm had left the city even hotter and muggier, and I struggled to keep up with Bryan. If his muscles were half as tired as mine, we wouldn't have too long a walk. I slowed at Beaulieu, a café with French press coffee and tiny, jewel-like pastries, but Bryan kept going. I walked more quickly as we approached Zanzi-Bar, which was famous for its large wine cellar and avant-garde cocktails. A few months earlier I had a drink there, the memory of which still made me gag. The cocktail was a peculiar shade of yellow and arrived in a swirl of smoke. I was afraid to even taste it, but my date, a creep, insisted I would love its sophisticated bite. He was wrong. I preferred less aggressive drinks and less pretentious men.

After we turned the corner, Bryan took my elbow and steered me farther west. I was sweating again, and the breeze from the Hudson River felt good.

Bryan didn't say anything, but it seemed as if he had a destination in mind. I was fine with whatever location he chose, as long as he wasn't planning on tossing me off a pier.

Chapter Eight

How can we know the dancer from the dance?
— W.B. Yeats

On a lonely stretch of sidewalk, beyond which there was nothing but the West Side Highway, Bryan led me through the doors of the Aband-Inn. The bar was so dark my eyes had trouble adjusting, even though the street outside wasn't well lit. We sat in the back, where the high seats of a vinyl-covered booth sheltered us from view. It wasn't pretty, but it was a lot better than the lobby of his building, where the seating area was designed for maximum visibility and discomfort.

I couldn't figure out if I was in one of the few places that resisted the glamorization of the rest of Chelsea or in a destination spot too cool for me to recognize its retro-chic appeal. The greasy feel of the table and the chalkboard menu settled it. The bar had to have been a holdover from the bad old days, when New York's Meatpacking District sold meat and not high fashion. The Aband-Inn offered exactly four menu items: hamburgers, cheeseburgers, French fries, and onion rings. Crumbs from all four dusted the edges of the booth's seats.

There was no table service. Bryan picked up a can of Diet Coke and a beer from the bar and slid them onto the table.

He stared at a point six inches to the right of my head. "I heard what you said to Arianna. Everyone did. Everyone's talking about it. Friedrich was furious you had a fight with her in front of the donors and the press." Finally, he looked at me. "I know you're in trouble. But I can't help you. I have my career to consider."

My mouth went dry, and I took a sip of soda. "Of course you can help me! I'm frightened the police think I killed Arianna because I happened to say something stupid. I could never hurt anyone, let alone kill someone. For God's sake, you were there! I was angry—understandably angry—but not homicidal."

Bryan didn't answer.

The thought popped into my head: *Permission to treat as a hostile witness.*

I leaned forward, over the greasy table. "Try to concentrate. I swear I'll leave you alone after tonight. The police asked me a bunch of times if I was jealous of Arianna. Someone told them she beat me out for the lead role in your ballet. Was that you? Did you tell them that?"

Bryan leaned back. "No. I could have, because it's true, but I didn't."

"Then who did?" I refused to give up. "Friedrich? Was it Friedrich?"

Bryan shrugged. "I honestly don't know. The police already knew what happened between the two of you by the time I spoke to them. All I did was tell them where I was and who I was with. They asked a bunch of questions about Colbert, because all of us who were in the building when Arianna was killed were also in Paris when Colbert was attacked. They wanted to know where you were. Of course, I couldn't lie about it."

"What did you tell them?" I grasped his wrist, but he immediately pulled away.

"I told them the truth. That I could provide an alibi for about a dozen dancers, but not for you. Not in New York. And not in Paris, either. I have no idea where you were when Colbert was murdered."

I pulled a napkin from the metal holder and mopped my wet forehead. "You know I left the party early. You know that. You said goodbye to me."

Bryan again looked into his beer, but he didn't drink it. "You said you were leaving. That doesn't mean I knew where you went. And anyway, you can tell them yourself. You don't need me."

He was probably right about me not needing him. I thought Friedrich was the one who cut me out of Bryan's ballet, but maybe it was Bryan's idea. In the nightmare that had become my reality, anything was possible. "Was

Arianna scheduled to dance your ballet on opening night?"

"Don't know yet. But I do know Friedrich wants Zarina Devereaux to have the lead role. Arianna was going to alternate with Zarina. But he didn't want you, other than as a substitute."

"Why? Why wouldn't he want to at least give me a chance?" I clenched my teeth and fixed my gaze on the table. Anything to keep from showing pain.

I could have saved myself the trouble of controlling my expression, since Bryan barely looked at me. He sounded annoyed, as if I was being unreasonable. "Friedrich and Zarina know each other well. It's not personal."

I stayed silent, waiting for him to continue.

He waved his hands dismissively. "Maybe they know each other a little too well and that's why he was so hot for her to guest with the company. But then Grayson Averin contacted Friedrich and told him he wanted to do a story on Arianna and me. You know, like a hot, young choreographer hooks up with hot, young ballerina. He had a whole narrative planned." Bryan's mouth twisted into an arc of pain, and his eyes grew glassy with unshed tears.

I felt as if we were conversing in two different languages. What narrative was Bryan talking about? Who was directing this horror show? In the only narrative that interested me, I was being cast as the villain, instead of the victim. And I didn't like the way the story was heading.

Anxiety kept me from realizing, until much later, that what I felt at that moment was a sense of loss. And it hurt. Hurt in the way hunger did, in that you could forget about it for a while, but it didn't go away. In the competing narratives of rising star versus international star, there was no room for me.

In the last few years, I'd become closely involved with Bryan through his ballets. I loved dancing with him, and I believed in him. His choreography was so inventive, so intensely sensuous and beautiful, that even on makeshift open-air stages, audiences were moved to tears, laughter, and applause. The continued success of our collaboration was partly grounded in our agreement to avoid becoming romantically involved with each other. We mostly kept to our promise, despite a fair amount of sexual tension during late-night rehearsals.

Dancing in Bryan's ballets made me think I knew him. But as my mother, who inhabited her own fictional world, often told me, ballet wasn't real life. I guess I already knew Bryan was using me to get ahead, to get noticed. That hadn't bothered me before, because I was using him too. That sounded cold and shallow. But on some level, using people was what artistic collaborations were about, however intimate they became.

I stopped thinking about Bryan as a friend and a colleague and put him in the category of possible suspects. Or possible witnesses. The fact that he wasn't willing to help me didn't mean I couldn't use him to get the information I needed.

I kept my voice steady. "Let me get this straight. The police think I killed Arianna because of a stupid casting decision?"

Bryan let a small smile escape. He couldn't help himself. Like all artists, he was in love with his own creations, certain that the universe revolved around his imagination.

I patted my mouth over a mock-yawn. "I know what you're thinking, and please, don't flatter yourself. Even if you end up creating a blockbuster hit, you're not that crucial to anyone's career or life."

Bryan sat straighter.

With nothing to lose, I poked another hole into his balloon of self-importance. "You must know that the greatest choreographers in the world have staged ballets on me and for me. And when I wasn't dancing in a new work, I was starring in a classical ballet. Which means your little fifteen minutes of fame wasn't going to make or break me. I was happy to help you out when no one was willing to take a chance on you, but you're not that significant a figure in the dance world."

He narrowed his eyes. "Then why are you here?"

"Because you might know something, or you might have heard something, that could help me. It's no secret Arianna beat me out for a role I thought should have been mine. And the police seem to believe this fact gives me a credible motive for murder."

I sipped at the icy soda. "If I can't come up with an alternate solution, those detectives, Sobol and Farrow, may succeed in pinning this on me. They'll be heroes. There was a lot of negative publicity in Paris when the French police failed to identify the murderer. The stakes are even higher now."

Bryan seemed unmoved. "You haven't said one thing to prove you're innocent."

"That's because I am innocent. I haven't prepared an alibi or an excuse because I never imagined I'd need one. Now I do."

"I can't help you with that. I'm not going to perjure myself to help you."

I suddenly understood the rage that propelled people to violence. I was incapable, under any circumstances, of killing anyone. But my fingers itched to dump Bryan's beer over his head and smash the empty bottle into his smug face.

"If you don't help me out, I will make such a scene in here you won't be able to show your face below Forty-Second Street without someone calling the cops and wrestling you to the floor."

Bryan didn't answer, but I was pretty sure he was thinking of how much he wanted to dump my Diet Coke on my head and smash the empty can into my face.

He didn't call my bluff, so I kept at him. "After my knee injury, I returned to New York while the rest of you continued with the tour. That left me totally out of the loop. And to make matters worse, a lot of my friends left the company. I guess Friedrich fired them—or forced them out—same as he wants to do to me."

Bryan rolled his eyes. "Nothing new there. A dancer's life is short. You know that."

"Yeah, I don't need you to tell me the facts of life. But I don't know any of the new dancers. And you do. I don't know who's hooking up and who's breaking up. You can trust me. I would never betray any confidences. I wouldn't do that. I swear I'll leave you alone after tonight."

I tried to keep my voice down, but it was difficult. Every time I spoke above a whisper, Bryan made little shushing noises and shifted in his seat as if preparing to make a run for it. I slicked away cold beads of water from the outside of my soda can in order to give my fingers some employment, other than nervous tapping on the tabletop.

He didn't answer right away. But the muscles in his clenched hands relaxed a fraction of an inch. I sensed he was beginning to waver. He still didn't want to help me, but he did want to get the hell away from me without attracting attention.

It was hard to tell if anyone was taking an interest in our conversation, since the line of high-backed booths blocked my ability to see any of the other customers. The only visible employees were behind the counter of the open kitchen and behind the bar, and neither gave us more than an occasional bored glance. A grizzled group of stoned bikers gazed at a televised Mets game with as much intensity as if they expected a divine presence to begin coaching third base.

I turned back to Bryan. "For the last time, who had it in for Arianna? I watched her while you rehearsed the corps de ballet, and she was nasty as hell to the girls, elbowing them and trying to make them look bad. She was mean to me too, even after Friedrich told her she was in and I was out. I can only assume she was cruel and spiteful to a lot of people."

Bryan shook his head at me. "No matter how you felt, or what you did, that doesn't make it okay to talk about her like that. Not good, Leah. Not good at all."

He was right.

But I was also right. "I know I sound like an unfeeling bitch, but you're an oblivious jerk. You think I like talking about Arianna this way? I don't. But I like even less my lawyer's suggestion I cop a plea. Yeah, Bryan, you don't have to act all surprised. Especially since I think you pointed the cops in my direction. So, this is your chance to make it right. I need to know if Arianna beat up on any other dancers. What about that new kid in the corps de ballet? Olivia, I think, is her name. Arianna gave her a hard time today."

"Yeah. Olivia Blackwell. Nice kid. No connection to Arianna I know of."

"Who, besides me, has a motive?"

"No one. And no one, except you, ever had a problem with Arianna." Bryan said this without flinching and without deliberate irony.

I wondered if he was in love with her. Only a man in love or extreme lust could think well of Arianna. "You're a liar, and not a very good one. I apologize if speaking ill of the dead offends you, but that woman was pure ice. I can't imagine Arianna's made many friends in the company."

Bryan said, in a choked voice, "She was beautiful. Everything about her was—perfect. Flawless." He buried his face in his hands.

Bryan's misery restrained me from pushing him too hard. Which was a good thing, because I felt like shoving him off a cliff and into a river filled with flesh-eating piranhas. Since that last option wasn't open to me, and since I needed his flesh-bearing bones to continue to choreograph beautiful ballets, I gritted my teeth and agreed with him. "Yes, she was. Beautiful, I mean. Every guy in the company—no, make that every guy in New York City—had to have been in lust with her."

The stern lines of his face softened. "Of course. She could have had anyone in the company."

"Did she have one? Or more than one?"

Bryan got extremely interested in one of the brown spots on the table. He didn't look away from the blotch, which bore a remarkable resemblance to the state of Florida. "Yeah."

"Friedrich? Was he, er, involved with her? And is that why he gave her top billing over me in your new ballet?"

Bryan put his hands on the table and half-rose out of his seat. "That's it, Leah. I've said all I'm going to say."

I almost choked as I realized Arianna's killer might have been involved in the murder at the Rive Gauche Ballet. "Fine. Let's forget about New York for a minute. What about Paris? Was Arianna in a relationship—or at least, having sex—with Charles Colbert?" Thinking about what Gabi had suggested, I added, "Maybe the killer got jealous, killed Charles, and then went after her."

He crossed his arms and stayed silent.

"Why are you being so secretive? Did she have you too?"

He sat back and clenched the beer bottle. He didn't answer me. Which was all the answer I needed.

I wondered if it were possible to run out of tears. My eyes had been spilling buckets, but fresh supplies kept coming.

Bryan shot a quick glance at me. "Leah, I'm sorry. Really. I am sorry. But I've gotta go." He started to rise but then unexpectedly sat back down again. For the first time all evening, he looked directly at me. "I owe a lot to you. I know you gave up vacation time and plenty of money you could have made as a guest star with other companies in order to work with me. I'm not ungrateful. But I have to think of myself and my future."

I ignored his pathetic excuses and focused on what I needed to know. "Arianna was at the summer house share in Montauk. With you and Tess. What went on?"

There was more I wanted to say, but that damned crying got in the way. I didn't want to draw attention to myself, but trying to stifle sobs was noisier than actual sobbing.

Bryan looked horrified and not especially sympathetic. "All right already. Stop crying. I'm, uh, I'm sorry. You're right about one thing. I don't think Arianna has—had—too many close friends in the company, other than Horace. People were jealous. You know how it is."

"Horace? I thought Arianna was hooking up with Daniel. Or was it Friedrich? It's a miracle she had any time to dance."

"I said they were friends. Doesn't mean they were lovers too. There is no reason to believe she was hooking up with any of them. No one could help admiring her. It doesn't follow that she returned the favor."

My heart started racing again. Was this the real reason Bryan had been avoiding me? Was he protecting someone other than Arianna? As long as I'd known him, Bryan had involved himself only with female partners, but that didn't mean much. In different ways, Daniel and Horace were very good-looking. Daniel was dark and intense, like Charles. Horace came from the same genetic stock as Valentin, long-limbed, blonde, with finely cut features. Of course, both had beautiful bodies.

On the other end of the equation, how many people was Arianna sleeping with? Friedrich was a definite possibility. And Bryan didn't deny hooking up with her.

Before I could continue, Bryan stood and tossed a twenty-dollar bill on the table. I followed him but didn't make a scene.

Before he hurried away, I grabbed his arm. "Can I trust you've been honest with me?"

Bryan shrugged me off. "Maybe I should be asking you the same question."

Chapter Nine

Every dance is a kind of fever chart, a graph of the heart.
— Martha Graham

ryan easily outstripped me as we exited the bar. I didn't try to keep up with him. Despite a lifetime of strenuous exercise, I was once again short of breath. My only consolation was that if I died, he'd think it was his fault and he'd feel guilty for the rest of his life. With any luck, he'd be visited by panic attacks that made my present predicament look like a commercial for Ambien.

As I made my halting way down the street, it occurred to me that I hadn't ever been sufficiently sympathetic to my sister's occasional bouts of anxiety and depression. To me, Melissa's woes were a relatively cheap tax on lifelong perfection. I sent her a mental apology. The real one would have to wait, since it wasn't fair to apologize as a prelude to talking about myself.

I turned up a side street, away from the roaring trucks and honking cars, and ducked into the recessed doorway of an antiques store. In New York, the street scene could change from block to block, and the dingy piece of real estate I'd chosen for relative privacy felt miles away from the chic stores on Fourteenth Street. A few blocks from where I stood, Theory, Tory Burch, and DVF stores seduced shoppers. The line of dark brownstones in front of me felt threatening, although the combined market price of the buildings probably totaled more than the GDP of a small country.

The beautiful people hoping to gain entrance to expensive clubs were absent from this block, although the street wasn't completely deserted. A pack of teenage boys passed, shoving and jeering at each other as adolescent kids did. They were followed by a group of girls, who stopped and stared at me as they lit their cigarettes. One of them gave me an insolent, hard-eyed look. She murmured to her friends, and they blew smoke in my direction and laughed. In their wake, three more pedestrians passed by. All looked mean. All looked menacing.

Five more minutes and I'd go mad with anxiety. And loneliness. Still, I hesitated over my contact list. I was reluctant to burden the people I loved with another panicky phone call. My parents had been through enough for one day. I worried I'd give my father another heart attack.

Calling my mother was similarly unappealing. If Barbara saw my name on the incoming call, she'd probably need a triple dose of sleeping pills to recover. That, mixed with the wine she'd drunk, might be enough to ensure my parents would once again share the same address. The problem was, it would be Lenox Hill Hospital.

In the window of the store where I'd sought refuge from the hard-driving city, the gilt hands of a grandfather clock told me it was too late to call Gabi again. It was 10:00 in New York, which meant it was 11:00 in Argentina.

Despite a nearly unbearable desire to connect with a friendly voice, I knew a friendly voice wasn't what I needed. I needed to talk to someone who disliked and distrusted me. And no one seemed to dislike and distrust me more than our costume mistress, Bobbie York.

My fingers hovered over her name and phone number. Perhaps I should wait until morning.

I couldn't wait. I made the call.

Bobbie had rigged her phone so that instead of a ring, the caller heard a tune from the opera *The Magic Flute*, the one sung by the Queen of the Night. It was a beautiful piece of music, though as I heard the upper reaches of the song I was uncomfortably reminded that the character who sings it had a decidedly wicked side, and a good chunk of the opera described what had to be one of the worst breakups in history.

The call played out to the end of the musical phrase, at which point a recording of Bobbie's gravelly voice took over. Defeated, I hung up without leaving a message. I was headed toward the subway when I remembered Bobbie and her husband lived in the ground floor apartment of a brownstone a few blocks away. Having already barged in on Bryan, I figured I'd make a night of it.

Deciding on a mission was energizing, and the brisk walk helped me forget the worrisome fluttering in my chest and stomach. Ten minutes later, I was in front of Bobbie's house. No lights were on, but, for the first time that day, I was in luck. Music from the Reverie Hotel across the street drew my attention. And to the left of the entrance stood Bobbie, leisurely blowing cigarette smoke into the night air.

Before I could approach her, she tossed her cigarette into the gutter and reentered the bar of the hotel. I followed a few steps behind. If she had been with a group of people, I would have given up and gone home, but a quick survey of the room revealed that her only companion was her husband. Peter York sat on one of the cushy love seats that dotted the lounge area of the bar. A beautiful long-legged cocktail waitress bent over him, taking his drink order with as much respectful attention as if he were delivering the Sermon on the Mount. Like the doorman and receptionist at Bryan's building, she was probably an aspiring model or actress. Bobbie stopped short and put her hands on her hips. Even from the rear, I felt her rage.

Bobbie walked toward Peter very slowly, pausing at the end of the long, curved zinc bar, where a crowd of Wall Street frat boys held court. They ignored her but stared at me, in the half-insulting, half-pleading way men did when a single woman walked into a bar. I conjured up my Medusa impersonation, and that did the trick. If I needed backup, I had dozens of stinging rejections ready to fire, but they weren't necessary.

I hung back and waited for the waitress to remove her cleavage from Peter's face and then patiently strolled around the perimeter of the room until I was sure Bobbie had finished castigating her husband.

After Bobbie took a few healthy gulps from her purple drink, I approached them. The lounge was divided into cozy seating areas, each one fitted out with a love seat, one or two chairs, and a low table. The whole place looked like someone's living room, or the showroom of an expensive furniture store—that was, if the living room or store were filled with expensively dressed customers, a stylish wait staff, and the latest music.

Our conversation didn't start well. Bobbie jumped out of her chair when she saw me sit down across from her. She snapped, "What do you want? Because, whatever it is, if you don't get the hell out of here, I'm calling the police. I don't want to find you within ten miles of me ever again."

I had too much at stake to take offense, although, if I wanted to, I could have pointed out I hadn't—as yet—been charged with a crime. And even if I had been charged, I was innocent until proven guilty. On a more practical level, since she was the costume mistress and I was a principal dancer, she was contractually obligated to get close enough to stick her nose in my armpits, if that was what was needed to get the costume properly fitted.

None of the above was at all germane to the information I needed from her. "I know what you think you saw today. But you're wrong. I would never hurt Arianna. Never. But someone else did. Please, talk to me for a minute. That's all I ask."

Bobbie gave a nasty laugh. "I'm leaving." She looked at her husband. "Peter, let's go."

Her husband looked regretful, but he didn't dare cross Bobbie. Even calm she was a formidable woman.

I shook my head in disgust. "I guess you were the one who called Friedrich and told him I did it. Nice move, Bobbie. You're a freaking genius. Way to go."

She noisily blew her breath through her lips. "Are you crazy? I didn't call Friedrich. I called nine-one-one."

I tried not to seem too eager. "Okay, of course, of course. So…since you didn't call Friedrich or Bryan, who do you think did? Was there, uh, anyone else around besides you and me? Did you see anyone exit the building when you walked in?"

She pursed her lips and slowly shook her head from side to side.

I pressed her again. "Fine. Either you didn't see anyone around—or you did see someone and you don't want to tell me who it was. At least tell me how long you were gone." I held my breath as I waited for her answer.

Bobbie banged her glass on the table. "I'm warning you, Leah. You better not be trying to pin this on me."

Bobbie was one paranoid woman.

I said, far more patiently than I felt, "Of course I'm not accusing you! That's as crazy as you accusing me."

An ugly note crept into her voice. "Arianna didn't say my name. She said yours. I asked her who attacked her. Remember that? She said Leah. Not Bobbie. Leah."

I looked away from Bobbie's contorted red face, trying to stay calm and reasonable. Peter appeared transfixed by our conversation. He sat without speaking, moving his head from side to side, a dumb spectator at our deadly game of tennis.

I tried to reason with Bobbie but kept an eye on her husband. Peter and I had always gotten along well, and perhaps he would intercede on my behalf. "You weren't close enough to understand why Arianna said my name. She wasn't saying I killed her. She just—she saw my face and said my name. She was asking me to help. And I wish with all my heart I could have."

I held onto my bottom lip with my teeth. I wouldn't let Bobbie see me cry. It was bad enough I'd wept through most of my conversation with Bryan.

Bobbie didn't answer me. She gestured sharply to her husband, who leaned forward, ready to do whatever she asked. Bobbie gave him a second impatient wave. "Go home. I'll handle this myself. Not that you've been any help."

He shrugged and walked away. From behind the bar, another gorgeous cocktail waitress sang out a sweet-toned farewell to him, calling him by name. This didn't improve Bobbie's mood.

She watched him exit before turning back to me. "After all the years we knew each other—you've got some nerve coming to me now."

I clasped my shaking hands. "We may have known each other for years, but I don't know what you're talking about or why, after all these years, you've decided I'm the enemy."

Bobbie picked viciously at a hangnail. "At the fundraiser last year you were hanging onto my husband, egging him on, kissing him at the auction

71

after he paid a fortune for a signed pair of your smelly pointe shoes. And now you want my help?"

The surreal, nightmarish feeling that had surrounded every moment since I found Arianna on the floor of the costume room got stronger. Despite Gabi's warnings about Bobbie's jealousy, I was unprepared to defend myself against her accusations. Flirting with Bobbie's husband was as crazy as murdering Arianna. One was absurd, the other tragic. Both were untethered to reality. I was more likely to flirt with Uncle Morty than Peter York, and the chances of either event occurring were approximately a billion to one.

Bobbie breathed heavily into her drink. I suppose she was waiting for me to defend myself, but I had other ideas, and discussing my nonexistent flirtation with Peter wasn't one of them. "Let me tell you about my conversation with Bryan."

Bobbie plucked a maraschino cherry out of her cocktail, examined it, and popped it into her mouth. She waved the stem at me. "I'm pretty sure I know Bryan better than you do. He's utterly devastated by Arianna's death. I thought he was going to pass out. He could barely walk. Grayson and I had to put him in a cab."

I paused to think about this. I forgot that Grayson remained at the studio after Bryan's rehearsal, which explained why the story went so public so quickly.

Bobbie finally volunteered some information. "Grayson is doing a movie about the making of a ballet. I'm in it."

For the first time that night, she looked happy. And who could blame her? After many years in the shadows, she finally had the chance to perform. While dancers, conductors, musicians, and composers received the applause of the crowd, costume mistresses toiled far from the bright lights.

I smiled encouragingly. "That's terrific, Bobbie. I look forward to seeing it. But yeah, not to change the subject, we were talking about Bryan. I just left him. We were at the Aband-Inn."

"Huh. The Aband-Inn?" She smirked. "Of course, you know what that means."

As much as I wanted to keep Bobbie talking, the throbbing music beat a painful tattoo in my head. "I have no idea what going to the Aband-Inn means. I'm not in the mood for games."

She gave a bitter laugh. "That's where he hides out from Tess and all of Tess's friends."

I wondered again about Bryan's relationship with Tess, and with Arianna. "What's going on between him and Tess?"

Bobbie sounded angry, and I couldn't figure out why she would care about Bryan's sex life. I decided to play dumb. If nothing else, my ignorance would let Bobbie feel superior to me.

I wrinkled my brow, as if in deep thought. "Bryan and Tess are engaged to be married."

Bobbie laughed with no discernible pleasure. "What Tess doesn't know would fill the Grand Canyon. Bryan fell in love with Arianna. It started in Paris. Tess saw which way the wind was blowing when they were all together at Montauk. Apparently, it wasn't a pretty scene."

I said, with a casual tone I was far from feeling, "Why do you care? Does it make any difference who Bryan is bonking? Or whether he and Tess break up?"

Bobbie got even sharper. "I don't give a damn about Tess. It's Arianna I cared about. And her death sure as hell makes a difference—not just to me, but also to the whole company. I happen to know that it was Arianna's family connections that got the ball rolling with all this media attention. The more press we get, the more money we get, the bigger the budget for new ballet costumes and more staff for me. She was going to ask her family to invest in Grayson's movie project. Well, goodbye to all that."

Bobbie's assessment sounded suspiciously complicated and unlikely. "How do you know the Bonneville family set up the deal with Grayson and the rest of the media? Grayson's always followed the company pretty closely. Maybe the Bonneville family had nothing to do with the recent publicity."

She stuck her face uncomfortably close to mine. "I have my sources. Goodbye, Leah. It was nice knowing you."

I didn't try to stop her. Instead, I fished in my bag and fumbled for my notebook and a pen. Very retro, but as the daughter of two writers and the sister of a third, I've been trained not to leave the house without a notebook, at least two pens, and a novel. Because God forbid you should have to rely on an electronic device. Until I was arrested, my parents could think of no more shameful situation.

I started scribbling. Perhaps Bobbie was right and the decision to cut me out of Bryan's ballet was a consequence of the Bonneville family's deep ties to the media and not Arianna's sexual manipulation of Bryan. Or Friedrich. Or both of them. Given the high stakes and the fragile finances that keep every dance company afloat, I couldn't discount the possibility that either man had taken advantage of Arianna, rather than the other way around.

I put down my pen. Bobbie's information, such as it was, didn't appear to help me.

Nonetheless, in the flickering light of a candle, I jotted down every detail she'd told me. Just in case something she said turned out to be important.

Chapter Ten

Those who dance are considered insane by those who can't hear the music.
— George Carlin

Almost every article of clothing I owned was black, which made my closet look like an inanimate funeral procession. This situation wasn't unusual for New Yorkers, as a whole, or for ballerinas, in particular. And yet, despite the preponderance of mournful hues, I wasn't sure what to wear to our company meeting. I settled on black jeans and a black sleeveless top with a high neckline. I wore black sandals with stretchy bands across the instep and a two-inch heel. Stylish, but respectful. Modest, but not guilty. Only a cool bath could feel good on my aching feet, but the open shoes were wearable and bearable.

The usual morning ballet class had been cancelled, but I couldn't afford to skip a day of practice. I packed my bag with new pointe shoes, a fresh towel, a sweatshirt, and clean leotards, tights, and leg warmers. Makeup, hairpins, Band-Aids, sunscreen, sewing kit, Excedrin, and Advil never left my tote. I worried that taking a ballet class might be construed as heartless, but, as Barbara would say, this was no time to let myself go.

In my darkest times, like when Matt left me and started dating Gwyneth, dancing was my refuge. When I was feeling a tiny bit sorry for myself, and I couldn't stop thinking about him and the way he broke off our relationship, ballet classes provided a respite. Rehearsals were like an emotional vacation.

After a full day at the studio, I was too tired to worry over the fact Matt had left me, and my previous boyfriend dumped me almost as unceremoniously, and the breakup before him was so freaking painful I could never think or talk about it ever. It was inevitable that someone, like my mother, for example, would think there was something wrong with me, since my last three relationships ended because the guy wanted out. Of course, I never told Barbara any details of my romantic life. But I think she knew.

The absence of romance in my life was more complicated than a few failed relationships. I could pretend that my devotion to dancing was more important to me than any guy. But that wasn't the whole story. The truth was, I wasn't in love with any of them. I liked them. I enjoyed their company, and the sex was always good. But love, the way I understand love to be? No. Not even close. Nothing that matched the love I felt for ballet. I needed to dance. I didn't need a boyfriend. And yet, losing Matt hurt with a deep ache that continued to linger.

In the ballet world, I am—or at least I was—at home. I was never that comfortable, that certain of myself, with a guy. In all of my relationships, I felt as if I had to look good. I was never confident enough to relax and be myself. I never cried in front of any of my boyfriends, not because I tried to be strong and tough, but because my face got swollen and blotchy when I cried. I always wore makeup, even on days when we stayed in. I always wore heels, because I feared looking too tiny.

I wished I could say my former boyfriends were idiots and cads. But they weren't. So yeah, maybe I suffered a few pangs when they left me and found someone new and got married and moved to Park Slope. But you'd have to chloroform me before I'd move to a place in the Slope. Of course, Matt still lived a few blocks away, but the last time I bumped into him, he and Gwyneth had that look—the one that said we're-gonna-get-married-and-find-a-nice-place-in-Brooklyn-and-give-birth-to-gifted-children.

I was in the middle of applying makeup when these unsatisfying recollections about my past took hold of me, and I realized, while I was gazing empty-eyed into the mirror, the clock was ticking away. I swiped some lipstick, grabbed my dance bag, and took the stairs as quickly as I could.

Across the street, a guy who looked like the previous night's stalker lurked in an alleyway. I strained to see his face, but he wore his cap low over his eyes. Was he the one who followed me? I couldn't tell. He seemed to be waiting for someone. Me?

I'd worn sunglasses and a hat to disguise myself from crowds of reporters. But somehow, I felt more menaced by this single figure. I fidgeted back and forth, peeking through the window of the vestibule and worrying I'd be late. I was about to call an Uber when a bit of unexpected good luck came to my rescue. A UPS truck pulled up right in front of my apartment building, and stuck behind the truck was an empty taxi. I ran out of the building, threw myself into the backseat of the cab, and crouched down so low my head was beneath the window.

My driver was more concerned with the position of the delivery truck than he was with my nervous behavior. He held his hand on the horn until the UPS guy emerged, none too happy at the noise the cabbie was making. After he left the last of the packages, he gave us both the finger.

We escaped into traffic that wasn't too terrible, and, thanks to my driver's suicidal approach to changing lanes and scooting through yellow lights, I arrived at the American Ballet Company studio earlier than I'd thought possible.

Unfortunately, I wasn't early enough. Dozens of reporters and television news teams choked the sidewalk, much to the distress of people trying to enter the office buildings that flanked the studio. Early morning shoppers, who were probably intent upon buying half-price pineapples in the street-level grocery store had to strong-arm reporters who stood between them and piles of produce. I had the cab driver let me off a short distance past the mob, hoping to avoid notice. As I drew closer, the media hounds spotted me. With the determination of a pack of hyenas battling over a withered carcass, they converged upon me.

Without Morty, I was totally exposed. The hat and sunglasses fooled no one. I fought through the crowd, and a police officer opened the door to the lobby and ushered me in. Much shaken, I punched the button for the elevator. In the cloudy mirror that sat at right angles to the elevator door, I saw a white, haunted face that looked vaguely familiar. Minutes passed before I realized I was looking at my own reflection.

My face was so bleached, so old. Overnight my lips had thinned, and two tiny lines etched themselves into the space between my eyebrows. Eyeliner and mascara and under-eye concealer didn't mask my sunken, puffy eyes. I looked older than my mother, whose beauty "interventions" included Botox, laser treatments, and the occasional minor facial surgery.

Horace and Kerry entered the lobby, and a guilty awkwardness hung in the air when they caught me studying myself in the mirror. I reached out to Horace to hug him. He didn't hug me back. Instead, he awkwardly patted my shoulder before pulling away. Kerry looked at me as if I had sprung, alien-like, from Horace's stomach. My own stomach flickered with pain. If this social isolation continued, in about three days, I'd be as skinny as I'd always said I wanted to be.

My mother had warned me that if I didn't take control of explaining what really occurred in the costume room, I would be the victim of a thousand rumors, thanks to Bobbie York's skewed interpretation of Arianna's last words. Word.

I ignored Horace's attempt to distance himself from me and tackled him head-on. "I don't know what you've heard or what people are saying, but I had nothing to do with Arianna's death. Nothing. This is all a colossal mistake."

Horace didn't respond. He pressed the button for the elevator and avoided looking at me, but once I started talking, I couldn't stop. "You have to believe me. Arianna was dead when I got there."

Horace raised his brows at me, and he and Kerry exchanged a meaningful look.

When I saw their reaction I realized my dreadful mistake. "I, uh, I misspoke, because, like you, I'm devastated by what happened. So, to be clear, Arianna wasn't dead when I got there, but she was stabbed—and dying, before I found her. I didn't see her right away, but as soon as I did, I called nine-one-one."

Kerry shot a glance at Horace before challenging me. "Bobbie is the one who called nine-one-one. You're the one who let her die."

"No! I mean, Bobbie may also have called for an ambulance, but I called first. I called as soon as I saw Arianna." Stuttering in my eagerness to set

78

the record straight, I continued to explain. "Maybe Bobbie didn't realize I'd already made the call."

As soon as the words were out of my mouth, I wondered anew about Bobbie. Did she really think the ambulance arrived ninety seconds after her phone call? She's a lifelong New Yorker. She couldn't have thought an ambulance would arrive that quickly, unless the EMTs were shopping in the ground floor grocery store.

I appealed again to Horace and Kerry. "It was terrible. Traumatic and terrible. But I didn't hurt her. I could never do such a thing."

Neither dancer responded. I put a hand on Horace's arm, but he shook me off. He backed away and held his right arm stiffly in front of him, to keep me from further polluting him.

Then he gently pulled Kerry behind his back, to protect her from me. "Listen, I've got nothing to say to you. We all know you threatened her. And Bobbie told us what Arianna said when she was dying. Just stay away from us. Far away."

"No! Bobbie misunderstood! She was hysterical. Arianna didn't mean what…what Bobbie said. She got it all wrong." I should have been angry, but all I felt was fear. If Horace, who knew me, believed I was guilty, what would the homicide detectives think?

The ancient elevator arrived, and Horace pulled the door open to let Kerry in first. He then resumed his defensive position between me and the other dancer as I entered. I opened my lips to speak, but my mouth had dried up. I took a sip from my water bottle, but my swallow reflexes were on strike, and the liquid pooled in the back of my throat. Hot prickles ran across my chest, and itchy drops of sweat trickled down my back.

I turned to Kerry. Perhaps a woman would feel more sympathy, would be more willing to admit the possibility I was telling the truth. She refused to meet my gaze and silently appealed to Horace. He put his arm around her and they stared at the elevator panel. It was as if I wasn't there.

Was this going to be my life from now on? No one looking at me or talking to me? I'd never been a very social person, but I'd never been a pariah either. Horace and Kerry took out their cell phones and stared at them so intently I took my phone out too, to make sure I hadn't missed something important.

When we reached the ballet studio, the other two waited for me to exit the elevator ahead of them. My face was burning and my voice felt weak, but I didn't back down. The elevator door hadn't closed before I turned on them. "You two are so stupid. Because one of two things just happened. Either you just pissed off a murderer. Or you were cruel to an innocent person, who will now spend the rest of her life getting even. One way or another, you're screwed."

I didn't wait for an answer. Horace and Kerry followed me at a distance and waited for me to enter the largest studio before they followed me in. I took off my shoes before I crossed the threshold, because street shoes weren't allowed to touch the floor of a ballet studio. Each practice room had a Marley floor, and only dance shoes had permission to touch its expensive surface. A pile of shoes and boots sat outside the entrance.

The air in the studio was hot and sticky. The heat, which even in mid-August felt good for the muscles, was somehow oppressive when you weren't dancing. The windows were open, and the sound of traffic, four floors beneath us, floated up in a familiar background of white noise. When a police siren screamed, I felt a sick lurch of anxiety.

The whole company was already there. Many carried cups of coffee and water bottles, and I got the feeling I was late, even though I arrived five minutes before the official start time. Only Horace and Kerry came in after me, and Daniel greeted them as if he'd been waiting for them. No one looked directly at me or told me how awful it was that I was the one to find Arianna. No one scrunched over to offer me a seat in her circle. I didn't sense hostility, exactly. It was more like a general drawing together of the herd, in order to cut off the sacrificial lamb. Well, it would take more than that to lead Leah Siderova to the slaughter. I wasn't going to go quietly. And when all this craziness was over, I would neither forgive nor forget.

I was nearly at the back of the room when one of the new corps de ballet dancers broke with the pack. She looked at me, if not with friendliness, at least not with disdain or disgust. I recognized her from Bryan's rehearsal. She was Olivia Blackwell, the dark-eyed dancer I'd admired. She gestured to the sliver of space next to her. I muttered a thank you and sat down. Friedrich stood in the front of the room, with his back to the mirror. Alongside him were the two homicide detectives I'd met the day before, Sobol and Farrow.

Friedrich was wearing flexible dance sneakers, which many teachers and choreographers favored instead of ballet slippers, and all of the dancers had either left their shoes outside the door or carried them in. But the policemen ignored ballet protocol. They were wearing shoes. Heavy shoes. Shoes that said even though the detectives were on our turf, they were in charge.

I didn't want to stare at them. But I couldn't look away.

Olivia ignored the people around us and asked me, quite kindly, how I was doing. It was a difficult question to answer, since we didn't know each other well enough for me to explain I was having a nervous breakdown.

Instead, I said, "You were at Montauk with Bryan and Arianna and the others, weren't you?"

She flushed. "Yeah. But only for a few days. It was a weird scene."

I felt an uptick of interest. "How was it weird? People arguing over whose turn it was to clean the bathroom? That kind of weird?"

Olivia smiled and seemed to relax. "Tess, Bryan's girlfriend, arranged for a maid to come every day, which was truly amazing. So, no problems with cleaning or dishes. And she paid for most of the rent, so it didn't cost the rest of us a ton of money. But, uh, I wasn't—I didn't—I didn't feel like staying the week."

I didn't want to come off as pushy or crazy or evil, but I felt as if I were stranded in the middle of the ocean while a lifeboat bobbed a few feet beyond my reach.

Very carefully I said, "I heard Tess and Arianna didn't get along very well. Was that the problem?"

Olivia stretched her legs straight in front of her and folded her body in half over them. I waited for her to get the kinks out.

She uncurled her torso, without looking at me. "Something like that. There was a lot of tension, and I don't like drama, so I...left."

I figured Olivia, like me, was unwilling to say anything negative about

Arianna. So, I chose a different tack. "I've seen Tess's Instagrams of her and Bryan. All those candlelit dinners at fancy restaurants and clubs. The woman makes asparagus look sexy."

Olivia laughed and then got serious. She unknotted her long, thick, stick-straight hair from the bun on top of her head and let it fall so it shielded her face from me. "There aren't so many of those anymore. After we got back, she mostly posted from some hot-yoga place in Chelsea, usually with her girlfriends."

Talking with Olivia reminded me I hadn't made many new friends in the company, even after so many of the old ones left. Sure, plenty of people squealed and kissed and hugged me when I got to the studio yesterday. But that wasn't friendship. It was what dancers did. It was as if, since we physically couldn't grow larger than the average prepubescent body, we'd mutually agreed to keep up preadolescent displays of false emotion. Which explained why none of the people who greeted me so enthusiastically yesterday had called me today. And why they'd been so quick to believe the worst of me.

And non-dance friends? Civilian friends were difficult to acquire, let alone keep. If I needed any reminder of that, I could check out my ex-boyfriend's social media posts and scroll through the metamorphosis in his social life. In the last few months, Matt and Gwyneth had attended two destination weddings. They went snorkeling in the Bahamas with a crowd of fin-clad revelers, and afterward they hoisted bottles of beer with dozens of tanned pals on a pink-sanded beach. Last week they went to a Yankees game with his softball buddies. Over the weekend, they guzzled champagne at her sister's engagement party. Not that I cared. I wouldn't want to do those things anyway. I never thought about Matt. I simply hadn't had time to electronically delete him.

Detective Sobol interrupted my conversation with Olivia. "First of all, Detective Farrow and I want to extend our deepest sympathy to all of you. Mr. Holstein has told us that this ballet company is like a family, and we're very sorry for your loss. At the same time, someone killed Ms. Bonneville, and it's our job to question you and to find out who that person is."

Sobol didn't look at me, but one by one, everyone else in the room did. As if from very far away, I heard him continue to speak, but I couldn't make out the words. My heart thumped in an uneven rhythm and perspiration trickled down my back and my forehead. My chest grew too small for my lungs, and I opened my mouth to gulp extra oxygen.

From every corner of the room, censorious eyes accused me, until the outlines of their faces slipped out of focus and a hazy fog clouded my vision. The burning pain in the back of my throat spread across my chest and was infinitely worse than what I'd suffered the night before. I stumbled out of the studio, not caring who was watching.

I got to the office and fell into a chair. Wheezing, I told the woman behind the desk, "Help—doctor..." I couldn't get any more words out. My heart was bursting out of my chest. I couldn't breathe, and the lack of oxygen made the room swim in nauseating circles.

Ms. Crandall looked at me and nearly stumbled over her own feet. Her fingers stabbed the buttons on the desk phone. Sounds came out of her mouth, but the roaring noises in my ears prevented me from hearing what she said. It didn't matter. I couldn't have answered, even if I wanted to.

A shadow loomed to my left. It was Detective Sobol. I think he spoke to me, but I wasn't sure. I wrapped my arms around my middle and rocked forward and back, trying to quiet the upswing of nausea.

For the second time in two days, an ambulance made its screaming way to the entrance of American Ballet Company.

Chapter Eleven

I would believe only in a God that knows how to dance.
— Friedrich Nietzsche

Ms. Crandall, the office manager, must have texted or called Bryan, because he and Friedrich emerged from the meeting, followed by several dancers. They drew back and watched as the medics checked my blood pressure and heart and then wheeled me into the elevator. The only person to offer to go with me was someone I barely knew—Olivia, my underage fairy godmother.

I refused the company of my lone sympathizer. It wasn't fair to burden a near stranger with my problems. She didn't insist, but she did run back to the studio to retrieve my dance bag and shoes, which she placed by my side.

The ambulance attendants wheeled me into the elevator. Detective Sobol must have taken the stairs, for he was waiting outside. He helped the medics push past a throng of sidewalk shoppers more interested in organic grapes than an oxygen-deprived dancer on a stretcher. The reporters were still there, and they got dozens of pictures of me being shoved into the ambulance like a pizza pie into an oven.

Uninvited, Sobol sat beside me. The stretcher was secured to the interior of the vehicle, and I was strapped to the stretcher. Although this setup rendered me virtually immobile, every time we swerved, Sobol winced and clutched the frame of the stretcher, as if to cushion the jolt. He acted worried. He probably didn't want my death from a heart attack to interfere with his murder investigation.

Sobol asked me again and again how I was feeling—a rather inane question, given the circumstances. I didn't answer. If ever good manners needed a holiday, it was then. My heart pulsed in my throat and I squirmed my hands out of the straps so I could press my chest and quiet the throbbing. I shook my head so a few strands of hair covered my face. I did it to shield myself from his gaze, but he defeated me by delicately brushing the hair aside.

I turned my head away from him and tried to forestall further attention. "Leave me alone. Please don't—don't touch me."

Sobol looked at me out of those deep dark eyes. "I was trying to help."

I loathed him so much I could barely look at him. "You can help by leaving me alone."

"Ms. Siderova, I'm sorry. Really sorry."

I tried to answer, but once again my breath got too short to sustain speech. The detective shut up for the last part of the ride. We lurched through the crowded streets of the Upper West Side and ended up at St. Luke's emergency room.

Sobol stayed by my side. He asked me a few more times how I was feeling. I told him I was fine, hoping he would go away.

Two medical attendants hauled me from the stretcher and into a hospital bed in a huge crowded room. Flimsy curtains separated the beds, but the medics left the curtain in front of my bed open. I had no privacy. Sobol stayed with me. He didn't deliberately intrude, but he didn't leave, either.

He fidgeted with the edge of the curtain. "Can I get you anything? Water, or something?"

I still couldn't swallow, but I agreed to some water in order to get rid of him. Why was he still there? Did he think I was going to make a run for it?

The sights, and especially the sounds, of the other patients terrified, sickened, and saddened me. The heart monitor behind me softly beeped, and the unseen patient in the bed next to mine moaned and groaned. Although the day was hot, the room was frigid, and all I had to keep me warm was a thin sheet. A resentful attendant in rumpled blue scrubs, that looked none too clean, handed me a clipboard stacked with medical forms.

"Wait—nurse? Can you get me a blanket? I'm freezing."

85

The nurse said yes but shook her head from side to side, as if she'd actually said no. Sobol returned with a cup of water. He asked if I wanted him to get me a blanket. I sent him on another mission of mercy.

The black pen that was attached by a string to the clipboard was indented with what looked like tooth marks. On top of everything else, I worried that the thing was crawling with germs from previous patients infected with antibiotic-resistant illnesses. My brain felt sluggish, my body exhausted, and I puzzled over the existential questions. Who was I? Why was I there? What medications was I on? Did I smoke? Do drugs? Was I allergic to anything? I checked "No" next to most of the questions. No allergies. No rheumatic fever. No recreational drugs, unless you considered a passionate devotion to coffee, Excedrin, and Advil an addiction.

I put the medical forms aside and texted my mother. Barbara arrived seven minutes later. She was one of those New Yorkers who could get a cab any time she raised her forefinger. I'd seen her work her magic in the rain during rush hour, even as thousands of drenched and stranded commuters waved their arms in vain. It was another parental gift I hadn't inherited.

Barbara put the clipboard and pen aside and wrapped me in her arms. I closed my eyes and concentrated on the smell of her flowery perfume, her coconut sunscreen, and the herbal sachet she folded into the drawers of her dresser. The muscle spasms that jerked my body didn't make her loosen her hold, but the sight of an attractive man caught her attention. Sobol stood a few respectful feet away.

With some hesitation, Detective Sobol said, "Leah. I mean, Ms. Siderova. I'm sorry, but I couldn't find any blankets. Do you want my jacket?"

Despite her distress, Barbara smiled at my attractive and attentive companion. I could see her trying to place where she'd seen him before. Before Sobol could respond, I clarified the situation for my mother.

"Barbara, this is Detective Sobol. He's the homicide detective who took me into the precinct yesterday. Detective Sobol, this is my mother, Barbara Siderova."

Sobol extended his hand to my mother.

Barbara stiffened, and her nostrils narrowed, as if Sobol had offered her a dead fish instead of an attractive hand. After a brief pause, her lifelong devotion to good manners resurfaced. "Detective Sobol. I appreciate your taking care of Leah. I'll take it from here, so please, don't feel as if you have to stay."

"I appreciate that, ma'am, but I did have a few questions for your daughter."

"I'm sure you do, Detective. Do you want to ask them in the emergency room of a hospital?"

"Well, it's just a—"

"Excellent. Then tomorrow will do just fine."

Detective Sobol made a halfhearted gesture of protest. Barbara put her hands on her hips and positioned herself between him and me.

It wasn't a fair fight. Sobol surrendered unconditionally, helpless in the face of the immutable fact that hell hath no fury like an Upper West Side mother in full protective mode.

Barbara stood guard and watched Sobol leave the emergency room. Then she took approximately ten seconds to locate two blankets. She wrapped one around my shoulders and tucked the other around my legs.

But even Barbara couldn't commandeer the staff of an emergency room in a busy New York City hospital. As she fumed, two people came by and asked me the same questions I'd answered on the medical forms. The sullen nurse returned, wrapped a blood pressure cuff around my arm, and frowned at the result.

She was about to leave when Barbara said, "Care to share that information with us?"

The nurse didn't seem impressed. She frowned again. "Normal."

My next encounter was with a doctor who looked too young to apply for admission to a sorority. She pressed an icy stethoscope against my chest and back. "Normal." Not much else happened until the attending doctor arrived.

I was sure I'd had a major cardiac event, but Dr. Mitchell insisted I was in excellent health. I wasn't so distressed that I didn't immediately notice he was very good-looking. Nice dark curly hair with a half dozen sexy grays mixed in.

The outer corners of his blue eyes slanted down, which made him look sad and sympathetic. I didn't find tall men appealing, but he wasn't so tall that if I were standing next to him I would have to crane my neck to see his face. He seemed unaware of his good looks, which I found hard to believe. Every single woman with a pulse had to be angling for his attention.

Dr. Mitchell smiled at me. "You're fine, Ms. Siderova. Nothing to worry about. Have you been under an unusual amount of stress? Panic attacks aren't uncommon in stressful situations."

I pretended to think. "Stress? Um, maybe a little bit. But my symptoms weren't from stress. My heart was pounding so hard I could feel it in my ears. I was sweating. I had chest pain and shortness of breath. Those are the classic signs of a heart attack."

Dr. Mitchell looked resigned. "The internet, right? You've done your homework, and those are the symptoms of a heart attack, but you're going to have to trust me. You're the healthiest specimen I've seen in weeks. You're absolutely fine. Healthy as a horse."

If there was anything I was not, and was not going to be, it was absolutely fine. And I didn't appreciate the equine reference. "Maybe it was a mini-stroke."

He shook his head. "I can refer you to a behavioral therapist for an evaluation and treatment, but many people suffer a single episode and then have no subsequent attacks. It's up to you."

He excused himself and returned with several sheets of paper. The top one was titled *Anxiety and You*. Dr. Mitchell handed the papers to me. "If you have a primary care doctor, you might want to talk to him or her."

I thanked him and got up to leave, feeling both embarrassed and disappointed that my life-threatening symptoms had dissipated. If I'd been admitted to the hospital, I could have avoided the stresses that put me there.

Although we seemed to have come to the end of the conversation, Dr. Mitchell lingered. "I see here that you're a dancer."

"Yeah."

It wasn't often I was that terse, but something about his sympathetic manner made me feel weepy. It was mortifying enough that Dr. Gorgeous diagnosed my heart attack as a panic attack. I didn't want him to add clinical depression to the rest of the anxious and pathetic package that was now me.

Barbara gave me a Mother Look. The kind of look that said When a single, good-looking doctor started a conversation with you, you shouldn't act like a tongue-tied school kid.

Ever helpful, she added, "Leah is a principal dancer with American Ballet Company."

Dr. Mitchell smiled. "Then I do know you. I took my daughter to see you dance in *The Nutcracker*. She's a big fan of yours."

Barbara was disciplined. She revealed not the faintest whiff of disappointment. Perhaps he didn't wear a wedding ring for fear of germs, but the absence of any indication of his married status seemed underhanded.

Upon learning the doctor was out of reach, I recovered my equanimity. "If you give me your address, I'll send your daughter an autographed photo, or a program." I didn't mention that my next appearance might be in prison garb.

It was Dr. Mitchell's turn to look embarrassed. He took out his phone. "If you can wait a minute, I'll get you the address. She and her mother just moved to a new apartment."

Instead of exchanging glances, my mother and I looked at the same point on the wall. We didn't always need actual contact when there was no doubt what the other is thinking. I could almost hear Barbara's exclamatory thoughts. *A doctor! Good-looking! And single.*

I mentally answered her. *I wonder how long he's been divorced. I hope it wasn't too recent.*

Barbara shrugged at the spot on the wall. After my thirtieth birthday, she got a lot less picky.

Chapter Twelve

Never give a sword to a man who can't dance.
— Confucius

Perhaps it was premature for Barbara to begin planning my wedding to Dr. Mitchell while we were still in the hospital. But this was New York City. If you'd been to a bar or a party lately, you would simply nod in sympathetic comprehension. I'd met plenty of unattached men in all income brackets who were actively seeking serious relationships. Not many had Dr. Mitchell's appeal. I was already worried future patients might distract him from my charms.

Dr. Mitchell handed me his business card. "Why don't you send it here? I'll give the photo to Elizabeth as soon as I get it. That's very kind of you."

Barbara waited until we were in the street before she said another word. At that point she hugged me and offered to buy me lunch. In Barbara's universe, this meal consists of water and black coffee—no milk or sugar. It differed from breakfast in that once in a long while she ate a small salad. She ordered the dressing on the side, so if she decided to embark upon a wild orgy of eating, she could paint a few lettuce leaves with tiny streaks of unsaturated fat. We entered a diner and thoroughly examined the enormous menu before ordering salads. And coffee, even though the handout Dr. Mitchell gave me warned against it.

My physical, emotional, and legal problems didn't interest Barbara nearly as much as Dr. Mitchell's potential as a future spouse.

"Wouldn't that be something if both of my girls married doctors?" Barbara

90

couldn't contain herself. "Obviously, he admires you. Who couldn't? Before you send Dr. Mitchell that picture, I want to see it. Hmmm…head shot, or a full-body dance photo?"

I took a sip of coffee. "Barbara, he's a good-looking guy and, as you note, he is a doctor. But I wouldn't get the wedding invitations printed anytime soon, unless you're prepared to have the reception catered at Sing Sing."

"That's ridiculous. Sing Sing is a men's prison."

I couldn't even pretend to laugh. Once again, I felt as if oxygen was in short supply, and I concentrated on breathing. I didn't want another visit to the emergency room. If I ever saw Dr. Mitchell again, I wanted it to be in a romantic restaurant, not a fluorescent-lit examining room.

"Allow me to remind you there's a reason I had a panic attack. I'm panicked. I need to do something to get myself out of this insane situation. I'm worried Detective Sobol thinks I killed Arianna."

"Ah yes, Detective Sobol. He's definitely interested in you. Maybe even more than the doctor. I could tell."

I put down my fork. "Of course he's interested in me. He's interested in questioning me in connection with a homicide. Hopefully his fascination with my charms doesn't intensify to the point he wants to charge me with murder."

Barbara leaned forward and gave me a knowing look. "Darling, I know what I saw. When a man works that hard not to look at a woman, he's got more than work on his mind."

"The feeling isn't mutual. I hate him, and I hope I never see him again."

Barbara inspected her salad for hidden carbohydrates. She plucked out an offending crouton and relegated it to the rim of her plate. "I agree. I don't approve of dating two men at the same time. And a doctor is much better than a policeman."

"Barbara, this is serious. What am I going to do? Everyone in the company thinks I'm guilty. Who knows what Bobbie and the others said about me? Even my friends treated me like I had Ebola."

Barbara patted my hand. "Don't worry, my darling. I have a plan."

"Does this plan include getting a new lawyer? Or hiring a private detective?

I'm worried. And none of us has much money. I have some savings, but not a lot. And I don't want you and Dad to bankrupt yourselves."

Barbara got serious. "We have as much money as we'll need."

I tried to interrupt, but she ignored me. "We're not going to retire because we love what we do. So, what's the big deal? Our money will go to you before we die instead of after. No problem. If it turns out we need serious money, I can always remortgage the apartment. Or sell it. It's got to be worth five times what I paid for it. Dad and I had breakfast together this morning, and we went over our finances. Money won't be an issue."

Nothing about my situation felt good, but I did get the feeling my parents had gotten a lot closer in the last two days. Their relationship, after they separated, had always been amiable. But in the aftermath of my visit to the police station, the two seemed to have acquired a closer bond.

"I can't let you or Dad do that. I love you both, and I'm so grateful, but...no."

Barbara looked at me with anxious intensity. "What do you mean, no? Do you think we'll be able to enjoy life if you, not that I seriously think—but if you—" She stuttered off into an uncharacteristic silence.

"It's okay, Barbara. I get it. You don't have to say it."

Barbara blotted her eyes with a napkin. Her voice trembled a bit. "I will do anything to help free you from this threat. But it's more than that. I want to give you back your life."

I held her hand as we both struggled for composure. Under normal circumstances, the Siderova women didn't get emotional in public.

After a few moments, Barbara went back to her salad, and I tried to lighten the mood. "You write detective stories. What would Professor Natalya Romanova do in this situation?"

The heroine of Barbara's mystery series was a Russian expatriate, descendent of the tsars, and professor of medieval literature at a fictional college that looked a lot like New York University. Originally, the school looked more like Columbia, but after the divorce, Barbara revamped the setting in order to eliminate any reference to my father. I was only kidding when I brought up Barbara's fictional alter ego, but she took the suggestion seriously.

"I've heard worse ideas. After all, Natalya does always discover the murderer. I do wish I hadn't made her a professor of medieval literature. Sometimes the research is really tedious. I should have made her a professor of Victorian literature. That would have been a lot easier. Or she could have concentrated on Shakespeare. That, I know. But all those tiresome medieval texts…honestly, except for Chaucer, I find the research a slog."

Barbara has a devoted following among English teachers everywhere, but her plots weren't exactly marvels of verisimilitude. "Barbara, I know you believe your fictional detective has real-world skills, but even if Professor Romanova weren't imaginary, I don't think that solving crimes through the logic of literary analysis is going to help identify the person who killed Arianna."

A bit stiffly, Barbara asked, "Do you have a better idea? Professor Romanova is always successful at finding the murderer. Show me another detective with her insight. Look at how she solved the murder in my last book, *Chaucer and the Poisoned Chalice*."

As tactfully as I could, I said, "Barbara, I need a workable plan of action, not an imaginary plot. For starters, you know who did the murders before you start writing. We literally don't have a clue. This is real life. My life."

Barbara waved her hand. "Not so. We have clues. We just don't know what they are. Same thing when I'm writing. Sometimes I pick the wrong person as the killer. And then Professor Romanova figures it out without me."

"Not until she's encountered at least three dead bodies," I reminded her. "I'm already a wreck. I can't afford any more drama. Besides, what if it turns out I'm not the heroine of the story? If you were writing this, I could be the next victim."

Barbara had a mulish expression on her face, one I knew well. There was no arguing with my mother when she started talking about her writing. Sometimes I thought she had a closer relationship with Professor Romanova than she did with me. I knew my mother loved me, but she wasn't the maternal type. Maybe that was why I'd always thought of her as Barbara, and not Mom. She didn't mind; in fact she was pleased when someone thought she was my sister and not my mother.

I paused to check my cell phone. As if to punctuate the need for a Russian woman in my life, my ballet coach, Madame Maksimova, called. She was fluent in English, and, of course, Russian, but she retained the grand manner of ballerinas from an earlier era and often spoke in French. Thanks to her, bits of high school language classes had stayed with me long after my knowledge of the Boer War faded.

"Bonjour, Madame. Comment allez-vous?"

"Pas bien. Leah, we must talk. You come? Yes?"

Despite Madame's multilingual talents, fifty years in the United States were insufficient to erase the musical cadence of her native Odessa. Her accent was especially difficult to untangle over the phone.

"Thank you, Madame. But I'm with my mother right now. Can I come over in a little while?"

"Of course. When you come, you come. I wait. Is important."

The minute I hung up, a text message came through from Gabi. **On my way to Mme M. Come asap!**

I told Barbara I was meeting Gabi. In the time it took to click off my cell phone and return it to the little pocket inside my bag, Barbara paid the bill, tipped the waitress forty percent of the check, and headed toward the exit. My parents were serious over-tippers. It was how they compensated for the guilt they felt at leaving the working poor and joining the intellectual elite.

I felt a completely unwarranted upsurge of optimism. For reasons I couldn't explain, the involvement of two ballerinas, neither of whom had much experience in what other people called the real world, gave me hope. I felt that if anyone could see a logical way out of the mess I was in, it was my best friend and my favorite ballet teacher. They didn't have law degrees or private investigator credentials, but they were tough. And smart. And on my side.

Barbara took a taxi, and I walked to Madame Maksimova's apartment. She lived a short distance from Carnegie Hall, in a white-glove prewar building. A doorman, resplendent in gold tassels and a navy-blue uniform, ushered me into the lobby. An equally elegant elevator attendant took me to the nineteenth floor. Madame's spacious apartment was a perfect example of what city realtors called a "Classic Six," much prized by New Yorkers. Expensive when she bought it, it was now worth a fortune.

Over the years, Madame amiably married and divorced three men, each husband wealthier than the previous one, but, for the last five years, she had quite contentedly lived alone. She frequently shared her graciously proportioned three bedrooms with visiting dancers.

Worried about my financial future, Madame advised me to buy my own piece of New York City real estate, but I wasn't ready to commit. I promised her many times I would buy my railroad flat—three rooms, tiny and dark—should the building ever switch from a rental to a co-op or condo. I thought it more likely my brownstone building would be bought, razed, and replaced with a huge ugly tower.

The interior of Madame's apartment was a shrine to Mother Russia. Heavy tapestries and thick rugs colored red and gold glowed with pre-revolutionary charm, but the most beautiful thing in the room was Gabi. In contrast to her surroundings, she looked like an ultra-modern sculpture, in skinny black leggings, green fingernails, and scarlet lipstick. She sprang up and nearly strangled me with a hug.

I was breathless. "How did you get here so soon? I didn't expect to see you until next month."

Gabi shrugged. "I was bored. I hopped a flight last night."

I felt a slight return of chest pain. "I hope you didn't cut short your visit with your family for me."

Gabi laughed. "Far from it! I brought them back with me. They'll have a ball taking Lucie to the park, where they can buttonhole complete strangers to tell them how special she is." She flicked a glance at Madame Maksimova. "And we can figure out this mess."

Madame nodded approvingly. She pushed aside a tray that held an intricately scrolled silver samovar and replaced it with a cut glass decanter of sherry. She poured pale gold liquid into three glasses that glittered with iridescent light. None of the glasses matched; all were charming. Madame handed us the sherry and gestured toward a long, red velvet sofa with an arched back. It looked like it belonged in a museum, but it was surprisingly comfortable.

"So, my darling Lelotchka, talk to me. All is not well. And I worry about you now."

I pretended to sip at the sherry. "Madame, I'm worried about me. I'm also worried about you. Why didn't you teach company class yesterday? We all missed you."

Madame put her lips together and gave a very Russian-sounding exclamation. "*Pfui!* That man—that Friedrich. He had me teach schoolchildren. I, who have coached the greatest ballerinas in the world—and that includes the two of you." She paused to laugh. "But then, what you know? I go, I teach, and I find I love the children. So pretty, so nice. I love. And I find big plans for school in my head. But that is of no importance now. Again, I ask, tell me about you."

I massaged the back of my neck, which was a tight ball of tension. "I'm in trouble, Madame. My uncle said the detectives believe I killed Arianna. And everyone in the company thinks that too."

Madame shook her head. "Impossible they think that. You are artist, not killer."

Her words cracked my composure, and all the ugly sobs I'd kept inside me burst out.

Gabi threw her arms around me, and Madame handed me a soft handkerchief. I brushed them aside to get tissues from my bag, but Madame insisted on having her way. Apparently, it was against some Russian law to use paper products for tears.

Madame was silent and respectful and waited for me to calm down before she continued. "So, what is the plan?" She looked at Gabi. "How do we help our Leah?"

I explained about Uncle Morty. Madame didn't like that one bit. Then Gabi suggested hiring a private investigator. Madame didn't like that idea much better than the one about Morty.

Madame lifted her chin and straightened her already upright spine. "What we do? I tell you what we do. We figure out. No one know ballet world like we do. No one understand ballet world like we do. The…how you say it? Ballet full of intrigue—yes, intrigue. No outsider know what we know. You, me, Gabriela. We know. We work together."

I looked at my two guardian angels. "When and where do we start?"

Madame sipped at her sherry. "We each investigate our own way and compare notes. Leah, you find out everything you can about company members and where they were when Arianna was killed. Gabi, you interview with everyone not in company—donors, people watching Leah and Arianna rehearse, people who work in building. I will begin by talking again to Zarina Devereaux. I had nice lunch with her. Zarina tell me she come to America to be star of ballet."

Since Zarina's name didn't appear on the rehearsal schedule until the following week, I'd assumed she was still in Paris. I was about to question Madame concerning Zarina's whereabouts at the time of the murder but got distracted when Gabi asked us about Friedrich Holstein. And thinking of Friedrich, I was once again reminded of Colbert, the director of the Rive Gauche Ballet. Both men were dark, handsome, and intense. And both had been romantically linked with Zarina.

I looked at Madame. "Perhaps when you talk to Zarina, you can find out some more details about the Colbert stabbing. At first, I didn't think the situation there was related to this murder, but you never know."

Madame nodded. "Good. After that, I will talk to office staff. I bring them Swiss chocolates. They love me. And Gabriela, you research background and also get to internet to recheck information Leah get from dancers."

Madame gave each syllable of "internet" equal emphasis, as if going online involved a foray to a foreign country, which, for her, was a distinct possibility. She raised her glass. "Everybody got job. We meet here in two days. Is good plan, no?"

"Is very good plan," I agreed.

We kissed Madame on both cheeks and left.

Perhaps to anyone other than a ballerina Madame Maksimova's plan sounded crazy. But it made sense to me. And that was how we started—in Madame's apartment, over a decanter of sherry, and full of unjustified hope.

Chapter Thirteen

Nobody cares if you can't dance well.
— Dave Barry

G abi took the subway home, too exhausted from her overnight flight to join me in a dance class. As I waited for the crosstown bus, I scrolled through the list of missed calls, and of the first fifteen, the only personal ones were from my father and sister. Then I saw that American Ballet Company had left a voice mail. Heart thumping, I listened, hoping for sympathy, but if anyone was concerned about my well-being, that sentiment wasn't evident from the message. No, it was Ms. Crandall, the office manager, who reminded me of changes to our health insurance plan. In what sounded like an afterthought, she said she hoped I was feeling better.

I went to Studio Dance, which was my go-to place when I wasn't in a company class or rehearsal. The professional-level morning classes were popular with American Ballet Company dancers, but, for once, I was happy to take the very unprofessional 6:00 p.m. class. At that hour, the studio was filled with aging ex-dancers, office workers hoping to lose weight, and a few demented women in garish makeup, who resembled Bette Davis in *Whatever Happened to Baby Jane?* That last group tended to aggravate normal people, who attended ballet class because dancing was more fun than the gym.

I'd always been sympathetic to the crazies. In class they got in the way, in the dressing room they hogged the mirror, and in the elevator they talked and laughed to themselves, probably because most people ignored them.

But I felt a deep sympathy for these lost-looking women. I talked to them, listened to them, and whenever possible, took them out for a meal. They were lonely. Believe me, I got that.

I gave the teenage girl at the front desk my card and she logged me into the computer without looking at my face. I saw no one I knew in the dressing room. Feeling calmer at my apparent anonymity, I got ready for class. Despite the heat, I layered leg warmers and a sweatshirt over my leotard and tights. Maybe I could sweat the anxiety out of my system. And even if the class didn't lighten my mental load, it would at least help me lose those one or two or five pounds I'd gained while my knee healed.

I was halfway through the exercises at the barre when I became aware of an unusual amount of activity outside the classroom. People were crowding to peek inside. Those who scored a place at the door openly stared at me, as if I were a rare zoo animal.

It took a few minutes for me to realize the impossible was happening. New Yorkers didn't gawk at celebrities. They peered from the corner of their eyes and looked at their companions and muttered, "Was that...?" And the companion nodded discreetly and they both kept walking, pretending they weren't impressed.

At Studio Dance, although I nearly always had a group of onlookers watching me, no one ever bothered me. Sometimes I had to sign a few autographs for kids and their parents. I was always very gracious about locker room small talk, especially to young dancers who shyly approached me. But never, ever, had I had to deal with a rudely pointing crowd. Were they censuring me? Were they laughing at me? To my horror, the ones in front held up their phones and took pictures of me. It was against the rules of the studio to take pictures, but no one stopped them. My face burned with shame.

Somehow, I made it through the barre. I didn't stay for the rest of the class, and I didn't bother to undress; I took off my legwarmers and pulled my pants on over my tights. I left the sweatshirt on and got the hell out of there.

Maybe it was cowardly of me, but I didn't relish having my every move dissected by the unloving masses. A few days ago, aspiring ballerinas and adoring onlookers watched me and whispered my name and kept their distance, so as not to bother me as I got ready for my performances at Lincoln Center. Now it was open season on Leah Siderova.

Since I was already feeling humiliated and insecure, I called my sister. I figured I couldn't fall too much lower into the pit of despair, no matter what she said. Not that my sister was ever intentionally mean or dismissive. She couldn't help her own perfection, and, considering how much better she was than the rest of the human race, she was remarkably sympathetic to those of us who could never equal her, i.e., me. That too was part of her flawlessness. No one could ever accuse Melissa of anything bad, because she never did or even thought anything bad.

She answered halfway through the first ring. "Leah! I called you five times yesterday. What's going on? How are you? What can I do?"

"I'm okay, I guess. Things could be better."

She laughed. "Nicely understated. Talk to me. I want to help."

I gave her a slightly less lurid account than was strictly consistent with the truth, but it was enough to keep her gasping and exclaiming. Melissa did a good job of pretending our mother hadn't spilled every detail. My sister was very thoughtful.

I finally got to the part when I had my non-heart attack and was taken to the hospital. It was at this point Melissa interrupted, a rarity for her. She was a very patient person.

"Let me talk to David. I'll call him and get right back to you. He'll check out this Mitchell guy and if he isn't absolutely top notch, we'll get you an appointment with the best cardiologist in the field." She paused to clear her throat. "And maybe a consultation with a psychiatrist."

Before I could protest, Melissa said quickly, "You'd be crazy if all this stress hadn't made you crazy. And trust me, no one is more experienced with anxiety than I am."

I opened my mouth, but before I could get a word in, Melissa's voice broke through her muffled phone. "Benjamin and Ariel. Turn off that movie and finish your dinner."

Melissa was, as always, trying to be helpful, but the last thing I needed was another doctor's appointment. "Dr. Mitchell seems very nice. I don't need another doctor."

"Why? Is he good-looking?"

There were moments when having a sister was wonderful. And then there were others when I wished Melissa didn't know me so well. "He's decent-looking. Divorced."

"Hm. Well, you're old enough to deal with that. Any kids?"

"Melissa, if you want to know Dr. Mitchell's credentials, that's fine. But I didn't get every detail of his personal life."

Melissa, distracted by her kids' television watching, was off her game. "That's not what Barbara told me."

It figured. In the short amount of time since I'd said goodbye to my mother, she and Melissa had probably googled Dr. Mitchell, checked his credentials, and deduced his likely alimony payment. Knowing them, they had probably already negotiated a good deal on wedding invitations and were in the final stages of discussing flower arrangements.

A brief ping was all the excuse I needed. Slightly breathless, since the last part of our conversation took place as I made my way up the stairs to my apartment, I ditched Melissa.

"So sorry. I have to take this call. Talk to you soon and thanks for calling. Give Ariel and Benjamin my love."

"Wait, Leah. They want to talk to you—"

"Later, for sure. Give them a hug from me."

It was bad enough when my mother got into matchmaking mode. When my sister started weighing in on the relative merits of a man she hadn't met, I was entitled to bail. Also, as much as I loved my niece and nephew, telephone conversations with them tended to be somewhat one-sided. I longed for the day when their responses depended more on words and less on heavy, if adorable, breathing.

I debated answering the call that interrupted Melissa and me, since I didn't recognize the number. On more than one occasion, a demented balletomane had tracked down my phone number or followed me home. But the number had a 212 area code. Maybe it was Morty's office calling.

"Ms. Siderova? Leah?"

The male voice was attractive. Definitely not Uncle Morty. He hesitated slightly before uttering my name. Was it Dr. Mitchell? For the first time since the murder, my heart beat faster in a good way. And then, not so good.

"This is Detective Sobol. We met yesterday. And today, of course."

Right. The guy who sought me out for my criminal appeal. "Yes. Of course I remember you. I always remember people who hang out with me in the emergency room."

"I hope you're feeling better. I know it's late, but I was wondering if you could stop by the station house. We have a few questions. I wanted to talk to you earlier, but, uh."

I was impatient. "Yes, but uh, I had to leave in an ambulance. I'm fine, by the way."

"I know. I called the hospital, and they told me you were released."

My face burned with embarrassment. "What else did they tell you?"

"That's it. Privacy laws, and all that."

The fingers of my left hand did a complicated minuet on the table while I debated hanging up on Sobol and calling Uncle Morty.

"Listen, Ms. Siderova. Leah. No big deal. No pressure. Just a few questions."

"When are you going to make up your mind what to call me? You've called me Leah and Ms. Siderova in the same sentence about fifty times."

He laughed. "I'd like to call you Leah."

"Well, now that that's settled, what's your name? There's no way in hell I'm going to let you call me Leah while I call you Detective Sobol."

"Jonah. My name is Jonah."

"Okay, Jonah. Do we have to meet at the police station? I can't walk within two blocks of it without feeling sick. I'd hate to have to stop answering the same five questions in order to throw up. Again."

As soon as the words were out of my mouth, I wanted to snatch them back. Now Jonah would think I was a mentally unbalanced anorexic with a pathologically unhealthy relationship to both food and the criminal justice system.

He didn't sound put off by my reference to stomach problems. "I do think it's a good idea for you to come to the precinct. If you can't come now, I can meet you tomorrow."

"Not without my lawyer. And I have to work tomorrow. But if you want to talk now, in an hour or so, I'll be at Café Figaro."

I hung up. Either he'd meet me there, and I'd get a great cup of coffee, or he wouldn't, and I'd still get a great cup of coffee. My sister thought I was overly obsessed with liquids, and she could be right. But so many simple pleasures were off limits for me. Aside from food, I faced many other restrictions. I never went out in the sun for fear of premature wrinkles and spots. I rarely swam because swimming would bulk up the muscles in my neck and shoulders. I didn't bike, because cycling did the same to one's thighs and calves.

That left reading as my favorite non-dance activity and coffee, water, diet soda, and the occasional glass of red wine as my more earthly pleasures. None of this had ever made me feel deprived. I knew how lucky I was. I earned the life of a professional dancer, and that was enough nourishment for me. Even so, I dreamt of the day I could eat without calculating every calorie and carbohydrate. I had been performing these computations for as long as I'd been dancing, which had made me extremely adept at mentally adding three-digit numbers.

I chose the location of my rendezvous with Jonah quite deliberately, because, after Bobbie York's character assassination, I wanted him to meet people who knew me and didn't believe I was evil incarnate. Every member of the extended family that worked at Café Figaro loved me, and they unfailingly treated me with warmth and affection. About two years ago, I persuaded Bryan to allow the owner's daughter, an aspiring photographer, access to some of our rehearsals. I also posed for her in Central Park, in my tights and a tutu, in the dead of winter.

The kid had talent. Those photos became part of a portfolio that got her a full scholarship to the School of Visual Arts. Ever since then, it was all I could do to persuade her family they didn't have to provide me with free coffee for the rest of my life. For that reason, I didn't go there too often.

Circumstantial evidence at the crime scene precluded any easy proof of my innocence, which was why I wasn't sanguine about convincing Sobol he should be focusing his energies on more promising lines of inquiry. But at least the Pizzuto family would make good character witnesses. That was as much as I could reasonably hope for, at least until Madame, Gabi, and I got to work and came up with some results.

Although meeting with a homicide detective wasn't exactly a date, I would no sooner leave my house without fresh makeup and a new outfit than I would without my keys or purse or cell phone. These were the necessities of life, even if the destination was murder.

It was hotter in my apartment than it was outside. I was still sweaty from ballet class, a hurried walk home, and a sprint up the stairs. Five minutes after a hurried shower, I started sweating again. I tossed my black jeans in the laundry basket and slipped on a black cotton skirt embroidered with tiny white flowers. I added a sleeveless black tank top and stowed a cream-colored cardigan in my bag to ward off the ill effects of frigid air-conditioning.

I was all set, except for the shoes. They were a problem. My toes hadn't yet toughened up, and everything that touched them—even drops of water from the shower—hurt. The blister on my big toe was still oozing, and the bottoms of my feet were raw and painful.

I could either expose all that ugliness to the world, or cover up and suffer the pain.

Of course, I decided to suffer. It was what dancers did.

Before I left to meet Jonah, I pulled out the beautiful leather notebook and silver pen my mother had given me for my birthday. With this gift, perhaps Barbara was nudging me to follow the family tradition. And maybe I would. With a first-person true-crime memoir.

I came from a long line of authors. My grandmother was a staff writer at *The New Yorker* and wrote a well-regarded biography of Abigail Adams. Barbara was moderately successful at penning mysteries, and my sister was at the top of the bestseller lists. My father's textbook on philosophy was required reading for most intro courses at universities around the country. In his spare time, he penned meticulously researched historical novels. Yeah, I was the village idiot of the family.

With none of my accomplished family members around to critique my primitive efforts, I found the process of writing both soothing and productive. I hesitated only when I had to record the names of possible murder suspects. I didn't want anyone I knew to experience the pain and terror I felt at the police station. Which wasn't very smart, since the killer was sitting back, waiting for someone else to take the fall. Someone like me.

Neither Friedrich nor Bobbie had solid alibis for the narrow window of time when Arianna was murdered. They were, in a sense, their own bosses. As the director of the company, Friedrich was the only person not on the master schedule. Bobbie, as costume mistress, had similar flexibility and similar freedom.

Most of the dancers, including Daniel, Bryan, Horace, Kerry, and Olivia, had brief interludes when they couldn't verify where they were. Credible motives weren't hard to find, since any of the men could have murdered Arianna in a fit of sexual jealousy. Any of the women could have murdered her in a fit of professional jealousy. As far as I was concerned, no one was completely exempt from suspicion. How—or if—Arianna's murder connected with Colbert's was even more problematic. On the night Colbert was murdered, all of my suspects were in the theater, at a gala dinner, after the evening's performance. Colbert was equally attractive—and attracted to—men and women, and his dark good looks enabled a sex life that was, like his tenure as ballet master of the Rive Gauche Ballet, the topic of much passionate gossip.

In postulating theories about motivation, I was stymied by the fact I hadn't been friendly with Arianna. It pained me, but she was ten years younger and considerably hipper than I was. Although I was a successful dancer, which many people thought was very cool, deep down, I wasn't cool at all. For example, I was secretly terrified of social dancing. I didn't mind if I was in a dark club, where everyone around me was drunk or on drugs. No, I worried when I had to dance at weddings, which were well lit and likely to contain judgmental family members and friends not under the influence.

The standard for looking good on the dance floor was a lot higher for dancers than for the rest of humanity. Also, lacking my mother's effortless style, I fretted that I'd be over- or underdressed at nearly all social activities. I suspected Arianna had no such inhibitions. She had an air of colossal confidence, off stage as well as on.

I was happiest when I was in costume, dressed for a performance. No choices and no worries. When I wasn't on stage, I was most comfortable dressed in sweatpants, curled up on the sofa with one of Barbara's mysteries. I'd read them a million times. They were very soothing, which might explain why her sales were slipping. Most readers preferred at least some excitement.

None of the above was helpful in my pursuit of Arianna's killer. Even if I weren't terrified of approaching Arianna's family, gaining access to the rarified world of high finance her father inhabited was impossible without an introduction. The same situation prevailed in the exalted circles of her mother's social relationships. But that still left the most promising line of inquiry: Arianna's professional contacts.

Most dancers' social lives revolved around their work. We spent so much time in ballet class, in the rehearsal studio, and in the theater, we didn't have time for much else, and we tended to socialize with each other. The time Arianna spent in Montauk with Brian and Horace and Daniel might have given birth to all sorts of tensions.

Thinking about Bryan, I added Tess, his girlfriend, to the list of suspects. With some reluctance, I appended Olivia's name as well. She was so friendly and so genuinely nice, it pained me to think she could be guilty, but I couldn't ignore Arianna's targeted nastiness to the young dancer. And Olivia was at Montauk with Arianna and the rest of the group. She never clearly explained what made her leave early, and that fact, by itself, made her a suspect.

Despite a host of potential motivations I could attribute to Bryan, I moved his name to the bottom of the list. His grief was painful to witness, and he was shockingly withdrawn and shaky in the aftermath of the murder.

I circled Friedrich's name, but that was wishful thinking. If Friedrich were found guilty, my professional problems would diminish, but the facts didn't yet justify serious consideration of him as the killer. His reputation, as much as Bryan's, was dependent on the critics' approval of the new ballet, and Grayson wrote so glowingly of Arianna, it was unlikely either our new director or the choreographer would kill the source of so much good press.

No matter how arrogant Friedrich was with the dancers, he had to be feeling the pressure of his first full season. Friedrich was only the third ballet master in the past fifty years of the company, and his future was on the line. Arianna's death resulted in some very bad publicity, and I could think of no plausible scenario in which the murder helped him.

American Ballet Company was my area of expertise, and anything I didn't know Madame Maksimova could probably find out. I needed Jonah to tell me about Arianna's family and personal life. I also needed to know more about the attack on Colbert, since I had few contacts with the Rive Gauche Ballet.

More importantly, I had to convince Jonah to look elsewhere, in terms of likely suspects. At the top of my list was my mysterious stalker, who might or might not be the same guy who seemed to have taken up residence in the alleyway across the street from my apartment building. I decided to take his picture and investigate him.

According to Barbara's mysteries, people committed murder for love or money. They didn't kill because they wanted a starring role in a ballet. Anyone who thought a dancer would commit murder in order to secure a starring role in a ballet was stupid.

Chapter Fourteen

Dancing is poetry with arms and legs.
— Charles Baudelaire

The owners of Café Figaro were first-generation immigrants, and everything about the place reminded me of Italy, from the sweet smell of coffee and sugar to the warm lighting, which suggested a golden afternoon on the piazza. The café was long and narrow, with tiny tables and high-backed chairs that hugged the perimeter of dark wood walls. There were no chai lattes, no plastic-wrapped food, and no curated playlist. The background music was Mozart, the pastries were homemade, and the coffee was dark and rich. Each cup was brewed by a member of the Pizzuto family, not by a bored assembly-line barista. Although the café was located too far from either Broadway or West End Avenue to garner the kind of foot traffic that small businesses depended upon to survive brutal New York City rents, word-of-mouth had guaranteed it was nearly always packed.

A quick glance from the doorway informed me Jonah wasn't yet among the crowd of latte lovers. There was no apologetic update on my cell phone, and I turned to leave. I waited for no man. But Mrs. Pizzuto greeted me so warmly, I decided to stay long enough to drink some coffee.

Every seat was occupied, so she took a reserved sign off a tiny table in the rear and sat me there. Unasked, she brought a double espresso and two fragrant biscotti.

"Thanks so much, Mrs. Pizzuto, but I can't eat sweets right now. And I don't want them to go to waste. They're too good for that."

She frowned. "You ate some last time. What's wrong? You don't feel so good?"

"Well, let's just say after eating biscotti last time I have to watch myself this week. The season's about to start. But you know I love them."

Mrs. Pizzuto sighed and turned back to the counter, but before she could return the cookies to the display case, a new customer blocked her way.

"Waste not, want not. I'll take the biscotti, Mrs. Pizzuto. They look great." Jonah pretended to fight her for the cookies.

She laughed. "Detective! You're always a good customer for my biscotti. Not like these skinny dancers."

"Love 'em, Mrs. P. The biscotti, I mean."

Mrs. Pizzuto laughed again and, with the subtlety of a circus clown, widened her eyes at me. Like my mother, she thought I should be married by now. I pretended I didn't see her.

Jonah continued talking to Mrs. Pizzuto. "So, maybe you could get me an espresso? And something for the lady." He nodded his head in my direction, apparently not noticing that a cup of coffee was already in front of me.

The whole situation annoyed me. The Pizzutos were my friends, not his. He was supposed to be impressed by my likable character, not the other way around.

The detective sat down and smiled, as if we were old friends. But even if all the gods on Olympus vouched for him, I still wouldn't be charmed. We were meeting because he was a homicide detective investigating a case in which I was a suspect.

Jonah wasn't my type, although, in the past, I might have occasionally succumbed to dark soulful eyes. Also, he wasn't too tall or too short. His jeans sat at just the right place on his hips. But given the reason for his interest in me, spending time with him was less appealing than a visit to the dentist.

I'd dated dancers, musicians, artists, and software designers. I'd dated guys who made artisanal pickles and guys who ran nonprofits. In general, I preferred the brooding artistic type. I wasn't at all interested in Jonah, except to establish that he need never see or talk to me again after this meeting.

I was peeved he'd made me wait for him, and I resolved to get the whole unpleasant episode over with as soon possible. In the scenario I'd concocted earlier, he was supposed to be waiting for me. I eyed him. "You're late."

He bit into the biscotti. "I apologize about that, but I was delayed by another case. I really prefer to talk at the station. But I couldn't resist a visit to Café Figaro. You come here often? I don't remember seeing you—at least, not in person." He pointed to the photos of me that lined the walls.

More abruptly than I intended, I said, "Let's get this over with. What do you want?" I looked at the plate of biscotti. "Aside from the cookies."

"Let's clear up a few things. I'm still a little fuzzy on the timeline you gave us. How long was it after you got to the costume room that you noticed Ms. Bonneville? And how long after that before you called nine-one-one?"

"The same as I told you the first time you asked me. I waited about ten minutes or so. When Bobbie didn't show up, I decided to leave. While I was waiting for the elevator, I bent down to tie my shoe, and that's when I saw…when I saw the bloody fabric."

I stopped talking, but Jonah kept writing in his notebook. Finally, he looked up. "Your shoes didn't have laces. There wasn't anything to tie."

My ears tingled, as if they'd been boxed. "I mean—I meant to say strap. My—the strap on my shoe. It was loose. That's what I meant. I—I didn't mean to say ties. I'd loosened the straps on my sandals."

Without any inflection, he said, "When did you loosen your shoes?"

I pictured the costume room and chose the least incriminating site for the criminal act of undoing the straps on my sandals. "As soon as I got off the elevator. My feet hurt. I told you that yesterday."

"Why did you unfasten your shoes before you sat down? Why not wait ten seconds?"

I stared at the table, so this very clever man couldn't see I was mentally cursing him for questioning me and cursing myself for lying about this unimportant detail.

I took a deep breath, but it didn't help. "I was, I must have been…the truth is, I misspoke. I mean, I forgot that I undid my shoes after I sat down. That's what I meant to say. There's nothing else to tell."

Jonah brushed a few crumbs to one side. "See, that's the problem."

I pressed on. "I don't know anything about any problems with what I've told you, other than the fact I had the bad luck and bad timing to be the first person to find Arianna. Five minutes later and Bobbie would have been in my position, and you'd be talking to her."

"The problem I'm having with your story is more complicated than that." He stopped talking to page through his notebook.

I waited, terrified of what he was going to say.

Jonah's eyebrows drew closer together and he put down his pen. "Before she went out for her coffee break, Bobbie York put a picture of Ms. Bonneville and Mr. Leister on the bulletin board. Someone with a serious grudge against the victim ripped up that picture and threw the pieces in the trash. The way I see it, you're the only person who could have done that. Do you deny it?"

Blood rushed to my face, and tears pricked my eyes. "You know I can't deny it. Ripping up the picture was stupid and childish, but that doesn't make me guilty of murder."

"No, it doesn't, but there's more. The security cameras outside the building—the ones in front of the store—indicate you spent thirty minutes in a room with a dying woman before you made that phone call. Not ten minutes. Not fifteen. Thirty."

My throat went dry, but I made no move to pick up my cup. I didn't want him to see my hands tremble. "Not possible. No way I was there for thirty minutes."

Even as I said it, I doubted my own words. Had I dozed off for that long? I'd never been completely certain. I just wanted to say whatever would prove me innocent.

Jonah leaned forward. "Listen, the hard fact remains that even if you were there for only ten minutes, you had ample time to kill Ms. Bonneville. But you had thirty minutes in that room, with Ms. Bonneville, and with no witnesses." His tone gained warmth. "Maybe you want to change your story? Or maybe you can remember some detail that didn't immediately occur to you? You two have some kind of argument?"

I banged my cup into the saucer. "No! I've told you everything."

Much colder, he said, "You have not told me everything. You didn't tell me you and Arianna were competing for the same role in the same ballet and that you threatened to kill her." He flipped through his notebook. "Several witnesses confirm that fact."

"I didn't say that!"

Jonah lifted his eyebrows, in the universal sign of disbelief.

Frustrated, I shook my head at him. "What I meant to say is I didn't say it in the way you're taking it. Do you really think anyone, other than a crazy person, would commit murder in order to get a part in a ballet? And advertise that fact to everyone in the company?"

He said more slowly, "Maybe this is about more than a ballet. What was your relationship with Bryan Leister? Maybe Bryan dumped you and took up with Arianna. Double whammy. She screwed you personally and professionally. And then you have an argument in the costume room and maybe you lose your temper?" He nodded sympathetically. "It's okay if you did. Be straight with me, and I'll do what I can to help you."

His kindness unnerved me more than his chill. I lifted my coffee cup with two hands, but a thick lump clogged the back of my throat, and I could barely swallow.

I choked out, "Bryan and I—we worked together. We were never romantically involved. I was seeing someone, not a dancer, and Bryan was living with his girlfriend, Tess Morgan. We hardly saw each other, outside the rehearsal studio. And when we did, it was strictly business."

Jonah broke off a piece of biscotti. "Are you, uh, hm. Who's the guy you're involved with? How long have you been, er, together?"

"I'm not involved with anyone right now. That guy and me...we're not together anymore. It didn't work out. We broke up."

"Why?"

I stared at my coffee. "Is that part of your murder investigation?"

Jonah shook his head. "Probably not, but we have to check every possible lead. Someone who cared a lot about you might have a motive to kill Ms. Bonneville. I'd like the name."

I choked out Matt's name. Spelled it for him. And then steadied my voice. "No one in my life is crazy enough about me—make that just plain crazy—to kill for such an asinine reason."

"So, you currently have no personal involvements at all?"

This was embarrassing. I didn't agree to meet with him in order to discuss my love life. What was I supposed to say? *No, Mr. Detective. No one cares about me. I have no boyfriend, no husband, and, apparently, very few friends.*

Would it get Jonah off my back to tell him my boyfriend found me so expendable he broke up with me on the phone? And that the coward did this when I was more than three thousand miles away? And that five minutes after he mumbled his way through telling me he'd always consider me a friend, he posted an adorable selfie of himself and Gwyneth at a romantic French bistro?

I took out my notebook to remind myself of what I wanted to ask him, and also to gain some measure of control. "I have other ideas for you to follow up on. Last year, a guy pursued me after every performance, begging me to marry him. Lincoln Center security had to post an extra guard just for me. I filed a complaint, so the police have to have him on record. But more recently, there's a guy who's been hanging around my apartment building. I'm sure on at least one occasion he stalked me. I'm afraid of him. And he knows my name."

Tiny muscles in my eyelid twitched. I was sure Jonah could see the spasms and thought I was guilty. He probably thought that even without the twitches.

Jonah put his cup down with a bang. "Why do I not know this? When was the last time he approached you? I'm not aware you filed any recent complaint."

I pulled out my sweater and wrapped it around my shoulders, in order to avoid his gaze. "I didn't call the police."

Jonah spoke with great gentleness. "I'm not the enemy, Leah. I know you don't believe this, but I want to help. And I want you to be safe."

"If that's the case, then maybe you need to expand your search. It sounds as if you only checked the cameras in the front entrance of the ballet studio.

What about the back? The killer might have come into the building from the alleyway in the rear of the building."

"Maybe. The cameras in the rear weren't aligned properly, and we only got an oblique view of the loading dock. But two guys who work in the store were there most of the afternoon, unloading produce. They didn't notice anyone who wasn't making a delivery."

"If you're so sure someone connected to the company did it, I hope you've questioned everyone."

"We have. We will. Not done yet, but we'll talk to everyone connected with the ballet company and then some."

Carefully, I let go of the cup and, to give myself something to do, fingered the vase in the center of the table. Avoiding Jonah's gaze, I leaned over to sniff at the rose inside.

I should have stuck with the coffee. My clumsy fingers betrayed me, and I knocked the vase over. It didn't break, but water spilled all over the table. Some landed in my lap, which gave me an excuse to look somewhere other than at the detective.

Mrs. Pizzuto rushed over and swabbed the table. She removed the vase and replaced it with another. I fingered a fallen petal, and the scent stirred a memory.

"Wait—there is something else I can tell you. A clue to help find whoever was in the costume room before me. I smelled perfume. It wasn't my perfume or Arianna's. It smelled like roses, I think. Or jasmine. Something strong."

Jonah jotted a few more words into his notebook. "I don't suppose you can identify the perfume."

I closed my eyes and concentrated. I knew that smell—knew it well. The scent had soothed me and perhaps was the reason I was lulled into a taking a nap.

All of a sudden, I knew exactly what perfume it was. "It was Joy. I'm positive."

"How can you be so sure?"

"My mother wears Joy. I think that's why I felt so peaceful lying there.

The room smelled like home. Roses and Joy perfume and cigarettes and coffee. About that there is no mistake."

"I'm sorry to disappoint you, Leah, but that isn't much of a clue. I'm sure most dancers wear perfume."

"Of course. But not Joy. It's quite expensive, and kind of intense. I don't know anyone younger than my mother who wears it. I don't, as much as I like it. Arianna didn't wear Joy, either. Believe me, if she did, I'd know. We were right next to each other all morning. She wore a citrusy scent. It wasn't sweet at all. So, that's your clue. Find out who wears Joy perfume, and I bet you find the killer."

Jonah said he'd look into it, but I wasn't sure how seriously he took the suggestion. He only wrote down two words in that damned notebook of his. When I was telling him about snoozing in the costume room, he practically wrote a novel.

Very casually, he said, "Just as a formality, I need you at the station house in the morning. We haven't yet fingerprinted you. It's routine. Nothing to worry about."

I got up to go, signaling to Mrs. Pizzuto to bring me the check. Fingerprinting might be routine for a homicide detective, but not for me.

Jonah rose halfway out of his chair. "Don't go. Have another coffee."

"Believe me, I'm finished."

The aisle was narrow, and he blocked my way. "Just wait a minute. Please. Why don't you tell me something about yourself? What's it like to dance professionally? Do you travel much?"

Mrs. Pizzuto was busy behind the counter. I sat down again to wait for her. "Yeah. We spend a fair amount of time on the road. Some years more than others."

Without much subtlety, he got to his real point. "The last time we spoke you mentioned you were in Paris when Charles Colbert was attacked. Stabbed in the back, as a matter of fact."

I looked at the table and saw two shredded napkins, ragged strips of torn white paper against the black marble. Apparently, the entire time we were talking a gremlin had taken possession of my fingers.

Ever since the murder, my body had acted without conscious thought. I tallied the damage: unpredictable eye twitches, breathless panic attacks, burning chest pain, and dry mouth. Since arriving at the café, I'd knocked over a vase and dismembered two innocent napkins. None of this was good. It was one thing for friends to betray you—I'd spent my life in a world where competition dominated nearly every relationship—but quite another not to be able to rely on your own strength and wit and self-control.

I balled up the mutilated napkins so I looked less guilty and, as dispassionately as possible, read to him from my notes. Madame Maksimova believed no one could understand the complicated environment of a ballet company. I had to make Jonah understand my world and my life.

I summed up the fateful night in Paris, when Colbert was attacked. "As I told you before, I left the theater before the stabbing took place."

"Where did you go? Valentin Shevchenko was poisoned, and he died the same night."

I felt as if every step I took to distance myself from the murder investigation ended up drawing me closer. All the same, I barely knew Shevchenko, a fact I repeated several times. "Anything information I have about Shevchenko I learned from newspapers and from mutual friends. Do you believe the person who killed him also killed Charles?"

Jonah didn't answer. "Why did you leave the party so early?"

I still felt like an idiot for not seeing a doctor, or at least the trainer, as soon as I was injured. My injury might not have taken so long to heal if I had. "You already know the answer to that question. I was badly hurt. My knee was killing me, and I saw no point in watching other people party on the dance floor when I could barely walk."

He tapped at his notebook and frowned at it. "The information I have says you performed that night. What happened in between your performance and the party?"

I was overcome by weariness. "My injury happened backstage, after I was done dancing. I tripped on a cable that shouldn't have been where it was. I was so revved up after the performance, I didn't immediately realize how badly I was hurt. That's it, Jonah. There's nothing else."

He put his hand on the table, close to mine, but not touching me. All the same, the gesture felt intimate. "I know you're sick of all this. Just one more thing. I promise. How did you know Colbert was stabbed after you left and not before?"

Cold chills went down my spine. "I saw him at the party. He was at the same table I was at for dinner, but now that I think of it, I don't know if he was still alive when I left. So, if you're asking about my alibi, I might not have as good a one as I thought." Before he could speak, I added quickly, "But if that's the case, neither does anyone else. I may have been in Paris, when Colbert was stabbed, and in New York when Arianna was killed, but so were the rest of the company. Including our costume mistress." Perhaps it was unfeeling to implicate Bobbie as a suspect, but I felt no guilt. She'd already done so much damage to me.

"You should think about investigating people who aren't in ABC. We've got a ballerina from the Rive Gauche Ballet who's guesting with the company for our fall season, and she was in both places as well. There's a coincidence you might want to look into. I thought she wasn't in New York when Arianna was stabbed, but Madame Maksimova had lunch with her the day of the murder."

Although Zarina Devereaux was as malicious a woman as any I'd met, after mentioning her, I felt a slight twinge of discomfort at sending a homicide detective on the trail of another ballerina.

Jonah nodded. He seemed to lose interest in the murder investigation and instead studied the photo that hung on the wall above our table.

"Nice picture. What part are you dancing?"

"Juliet."

He nodded. "Juliet, that's nice. As in *Romeo and Juliet*?"

The irony of the photograph hit me for the first time. "Yes. I specialize in doomed maidens."

"And what's that?"

He pointed across the room to another picture of me. Unlike the formal studio portrait next to us, the one he singled out was set against a bleak Central Park background. My hair was long and tangled and hung loosely around my shoulders. I was wearing a torn tutu, ragged stockings, and an expression reminiscent of Ophelia, right before she drowned. I'd always liked that picture, but seeing it through Jonah's eyes changed how I felt about it. The charming incongruities in the setup of the photo became less appealing, and I hated the haunted look in my face. I looked so fragile. So defenseless.

I couldn't decipher the detective's expression.

He shifted his gaze from the photo to me. "I come in here all the time. When I first saw you in person, I couldn't figure out why I felt as if I already knew your face. Knew you." He looked back and forth from the Central Park picture to me. "I've looked at these pictures of you a million times."

"If you knew me, you'd know I could never murder anyone. Never hurt anyone."

He didn't answer.

I got up and, over Mrs. Pizzuto's protests, put twice the price of my coffee into her palm. I didn't say goodbye to Jonah.

After all, we'd be seeing each other soon enough.

Chapter Fifteen

There comes a pause, for human strength will not endure to dance without
cessation.
— Lewis Carroll

S
tories of the supernatural abounded in the world of ballet. Old-time
stagehands loved to talk about the vengeful spirits of long-dead
ballerinas who haunted the theater and caused trouble to those who
failed to respect their legacy. These tales were passed on from one generation
of dancers to the next. No one took them seriously, but no one disregarded
them, either.

Otherworldly characters provided the narrative arc of quite a few ballets
as well, especially those of the Romantic era. In *Giselle*, the title character
dies of a broken heart, undone by her passion for dancing and her faithless
lover. And that was just in Act I. In Act II Giselle was condemned to join the
Wilis—a ghost army of girls who had suffered the same fate. After the girls
died, they became spirits and they killed all men who crossed their paths.

This was the kind of weird netherworld I inhabited in the days that
followed Arianna's murder. Although my body was fully present, in class
and in rehearsal, I became American Ballet Company's resident phantom.
No one, except Olivia, the friendly kid from the corps de ballet, spoke to
me or looked at me. It was as if I wasn't there. No, it was worse than that.
People reacted to me as if I were a Wili—they shunned me as if contact with
me might be deadly.

At first, I tried to resume normal relations with the other dancers. Not only was it terribly isolating and hurtful to be treated as an outcast, it made investigating the murder nearly impossible. Every time I said something, no matter how innocuous, faces and bodies drew back. To them I had metamorphosed into a deadly ghost, a disease, a foreign body that the organism needed to expel or destroy in order to stay healthy.

In another blow, Friedrich informed me that, in the foreseeable future, I would be an understudy only. He called me into the reception area in front of the entire office staff. "Unless something changes, you can consider yourself off the performance schedule." He fixed me with an unpleasant look. "And I cannot impress upon you enough that you are being carefully watched so nothing does happen."

The bastard took my breath away. Although, I suppose I shouldn't have been so surprised. Nearly everyone around me had made it clear Friedrich wasn't alone in his opinion.

Friedrich's cruel and aggressive attitude added more poison to the already toxic social stigma attached to me. On the few occasions I forgot myself, and behaved naturally and without reserve, people reacted with surprise and—what was worse—annoyance. It was as if the sound of my voice was enough to constitute a felony. I became the Invisible Woman.

My situation wasn't without precedent. After all, I'd been to high school and had seen how the herd could freeze out unwanted rejects. The company wanted and needed to ignore me, and it bothered them when I disturbed their unified front.

The dancers of American Ballet Company, by the way, had never worked together more harmoniously. No behind-the-scenes backbiting, no quarrels over casting, no snide remarks. Not even Zarina, the ballerina from the Rive Gauche Ballet, disturbed the general goodwill. She sailed in on arrogant wings to take the principal role in several ballets, including Bryan's new ballet, but even this didn't disturb the general air of kindness and consideration my fellow dancers extended toward each other. It was a sad fact I was the irritant that enabled all that cohesiveness. In the past, our homegrown dancers hadn't taken kindly to being upstaged by foreign stars. Loathing of me gave every dancer common ground, common currency, and a common language.

After a while, a few people did break the unwritten interdict against me and tried to give me the benefit of the doubt. But my heart and my nerves, like poor Giselle's, were so shattered by the near-universal betrayal, the kindness felt like another form of cruelty. And yet, with the same determination that made me a ballerina, I concentrated only on what was important—getting strong, getting information, and getting even.

The morning after my meeting with Jonah, I went to the precinct to get fingerprinted. He wasn't present, having delegated the job to a very junior officer. The experience galvanized me. I didn't want to ever return to the police station, and the only way to ensure that outcome was to find the murderer.

I called Uncle Morty as soon as I left the precinct, but several nervous hours passed before I heard from him.

When he did call back, he said, "They fingerprinted you."

"Yes, Uncle Morty. Tell me something I don't know."

Morty cleared his throat with nauseating thoroughness. "Unfortunately, not much has changed. We already knew your fingerprints were on the murder weapon."

Of course I knew that. But hearing it somehow made it worse. "Have they identified anyone else's fingerprints?"

Morty sighed. "Unfortunately, no. Just yours."

My excitement rose. "But that's good news! Someone else's fingerprints should have been on the weapon. I mean, like an innocent person's. Like Bobbie's—assuming she's innocent, of course. Or one of the seamstresses. The murderer wiped the scissors clean, and that proves I didn't do it!"

I waited for Morty's agreement, but it never came. "The only problem with that theory is you're the one who cleaned off the murder weapon."

I beat down the butterflies in my stomach. When I wiped the scissors, in order to get a better grip on the handles, I must have also wiped away any exonerating evidence. A tide of panic rose. "Is there any good news? I mean, at least there's nothing new to make them think I'm the killer. And clearly, they don't have enough evidence to arrest me, since they haven't yet done so."

"Let's not get ahead of ourselves. In the criminal justice system, there's no such thing as no worries."

"Is there something you haven't told me? I don't understand."

Morty sighed heavily into the phone. "You had motive, means, and opportunity. And then there's that crap in Paris. No one can corroborate your account of your whereabouts when Colbert was attacked. And let's not forget, you spent at least half an hour with Arianna before you called nine-one-one."

"This is crazy! No one at the gala can corroborate my whereabouts because I wasn't there."

Morty didn't answer.

"I'm, like, almost one hundred percent positive I wasn't there when Colbert was stabbed. I left the party and walked back to the hotel. I didn't take attendance."

Morty said, "Again, that's a problem. If your knee hurt bad enough to leave the party, why did you walk back to the hotel? Why not take a cab?"

I was shocked. "If there's one thing that is easily verified, it's that I injured my knee. Do you think an orthopedic surgeon would operate if I was faking? I've got a mile-high medical record to prove I'm telling the truth."

Morty coughed. "No one disputes you were hurt. But again, the question is one of timing. You say you got injured backstage, after the performance. No one remembers that happening except for you. It's just as likely you got hurt running from the scene of the crime. Why would you show up at a party, for even a short time, if you were suffering from a potentially career-ending injury?"

I broke into a sweat. "Is there any good news?"

Morty grunted. "No, not really. It's never looked good for you, anyway. The nine-one-one call you made complicates things."

I clenched my teeth so tightly my jaw hurt. How could making an emergency call hurt my case?

Morty seemed to anticipate my question. "The emergency operator was on the phone until the police and ambulance arrived."

"Again, I don't understand. A murderer wouldn't have made the call and then waited to be arrested."

Morty cleared his throat. "The police don't think it was a premeditated murder. They think you, or someone, seized the moment and acted without thinking. Then you felt remorse and tried to save her."

With the last shreds of my fraying patience, I said, "The operator, Morty. How does this tell against me?"

"The tape of the nine-one-one call confirms Bobbie's account of what happened. That the dead girl said you killed her."

Over and over, I told myself that the recording of the nine-one-one call wasn't enough to convict me. Morty didn't disagree. But he didn't agree either, which gave my second meeting with Gabi and Madame Maksimova extra urgency. We had to move quickly.

On my way to Madame Maksimova's apartment, I stopped by the post office and dropped off a package for Dr. Mitchell. Or, more precisely, for Dr. Mitchell's daughter. Inside I put a signed photograph, a signed program of the last time I danced *Swan Lake*, and a delicate tiara made of pale pink rhinestones. When I was a kid, I loved tiaras. I still did. Call me shallow, but there was nothing like a sparkly crown to make me feel there was still hope for the human race. I also included a brief note with my email and phone number, in case Dr. Gorgeous wanted to thank me over a candlelit dinner in a romantic restaurant.

I knew better than to bring food to Madame. Instead, I bought a bottle of her favorite champagne. The always-elegant Madame ordered her meals from the famed Russian Tea Room with the same frequency and abandon most people employed when telephoning the local pizzeria. And unlike pizzerias, The Russian Tea Room was willing to prepare whatever Madame wished. They even named their smoked salmon platter after her.

Gabi arrived at the same time I did. After the wine was poured, the kisses dispensed, and the food arrayed on delicate pink and green and silver platters, we stopped pretending this was a purely social occasion. All three of us were conscious of the business end of our planned get-together. Madame and Gabi fortified themselves with champagne, but the bubbles in my glass came from sparkling water. I didn't want anything to dull my wits.

I handed Madame and Gabi copies of the color-coded timeline I'd created over the last two sleepless nights. "As well as I could, I documented each person's whereabouts, starting from early August. At first, I concentrated only on the day of the murder, but then I figured we needed a more complete chronology. I began with the time Arianna stayed in Montauk, when she was with Bryan and a few other company members. Of the people who were there, I can find no evidence anyone's life was materially enhanced by Arianna's death, with the possible exception of Tess Morgan, Bryan's girlfriend."

Gabi asked, "Did you get any details about Arianna's relationships? With this number of people living together, there had to have been some tensions. And where did you get your information about the time they all spent together in Montauk?"

I pointed to the bottom of the page. "Olivia, a very nice kid in the corps de ballet, is my main source. She was there. She told me Bryan and Tess were constantly arguing. Bryan rented a studio in town to work on his choreography, and he didn't pay much attention to her. Tess was doubly aggravated Arianna spent all of her time with Bryan at the studio. Olivia said it was so awkward to be around them, she ended up leaving early."

Madame nodded. "But of course. Arianna follow Bryan so she get role in ballet. No shame in that." She smoothed her forehead. "Who need to be at beach? It makes the wrinkles."

Madame's skin hadn't seen the sun in something like sixty years. During the day she wore a hat, gloves, and a thick coating of sunscreen and pancake makeup. Seeing her look so beautiful inspired me to do the same which, for some reason, used to annoy my ex-boyfriend. After Matt and I broke up, he got his revenge by Instagramming dozens of pictures of Gwyneth, his bikini-clad, golden-tanned new girlfriend.

Hah. By my calculations, Gwyneth would be wrinkled and spotty by the time she was thirty. Yeah, if anyone was doing the math, Matt's new girlfriend was seven years younger than me and twelve years younger than him. Not that I'd spent two minutes thinking about it. Not even one minute.

I shrugged off memories of the distant past to concentrate on more recent events. "I need you both to check out the info on page two. There is at least one factual discrepancy I can't reconcile. According to Olivia, Tess Morgan's father has a lot of contacts with the media and that's how Bryan got all that exposure on TV and radio. But, according to Bobbie, it was Arianna's family who set up the morning news shows and the NPR interviews."

Gabi tapped the paper. "At the very least, Bryan was using one of those women to get ahead."

I shook my head. "Maybe it started out that way, with Bryan using Arianna. But when I talked to him, he was grief-stricken. To me, he sounded like a man in love."

Madame looked annoyed. She snorted, "Bryan Leister living with one girl, but in love with another? Not sound like love to me. Maybe he feel guilt, not love."

I had no answer for Madame. All I had was the memory of Bryan's red eyes and anguished tone.

Gabi took out her laptop and began a random search of the Bonneville family. "How reliable is Olivia Blackwell? And what's her in? You're assuming everything she's told you is accurate, but you don't have anyone who can corroborate the information she's given you."

Gabi's words stopped me short. I stammered a bit before pointing out Olivia's information about Montauk was surely true. She was there.

Gabi remained skeptical. "For a corps de ballet dancer, she seems to know an awful lot of personal information about people much higher up than she is." She looked away from her computer screen to scrutinize the timeline I'd given her. "There's a lot of stuff here about Friedrich. Is Olivia making this up? Or is she closer to him than she's let on? I think you need another source, because this chick may be feeding you locker room gossip and pretending it's the money. Or worse."

I reached for my ankle and stretched my leg over my head, partly to give myself time to think, and partly to release the tension in my joints. "Even if Olivia's information came from eavesdropping, or catty locker room gossip, that doesn't mean it isn't true." For a brief, uncomfortable moment, I wondered if Olivia was a lot friendlier with Arianna—or Tess—or Bryan or Friedrich—than she'd let on.

But I didn't doubt her truthfulness or her desire to help me. She was the only person in the company, since Gabi, I fully trusted.

Madame narrowed her eyes. "Bryan is maybe involved in ways we not think of as yet. Maybe Arianna make demands on him, or threaten him. Her family know the politics and they know the money. There is much we still must do to investigate."

I nodded and told Gabi, "As long as you're documenting everything, you can also note that, according to Olivia, Tess wasn't the only person Arianna infuriated during the Montauk vacation. Arianna was sneaky-nasty to all of the female dancers."

Madame tilted her head to one side. "Sneakee-nastee? What that mean?"

I knew what she was thinking. "It wasn't like back in the day, Madame, when ballerinas poured glass into their rivals' pointe shoes. Arianna did what we would call mean-girl stuff. She tripped Olivia when she thought no one was looking. She posted unflattering pictures of other dancers, and she did her best to mow them down during class. I wouldn't have said her behavior was bad enough for someone to literally murder her...but now? I'm not so sure."

Madame patted my arm. "*Tres bien, cherie.* It is a good brain you have in your head. As for me, I already talk to Friedrich about Arianna's family. The Bonnevilles, they give much money to the company, and they bring in other rich people. But the company always needs more, more, more. Was better in Russia, better in Paris. Why United States government not pay for ballet?"

Why indeed? But that was a mystery for another day, and I didn't want us to get sidetracked. "Thank you, Madame. I think you should continue to follow the financial end of things. Money is the chief obsession of every ballet director."

Gabi wrinkled her nose, as if an offending smell had invaded the room. "I think Friedrich is the killer. I hate the way he's treated you, and I'm putting his name in red."

I shook my head. "Believe me, I would love to put Friedrich at the top of the list. But it's not going to be easy to pin the murder on him. Like Bryan, he seemed smitten with Arianna. We don't have a credible motive for him yet. In fact, as far as I can tell, the evidence points away from him."

Madame picked at a flake of puff pastry. "Even cold man like Friedrich have romance. Maybe passion." She smiled slyly. "I not want to give away secrets, but Friedrich and Zarina have become close friends. Zarina say to me *very* close friends."

I rolled my eyes. "Zarina thinks every man is in love with her." Yes, I was being catty. There was no love lost between Zarina and me.

Gabi stretched her long, thin legs. "Let's not limit ourselves to the dancers. Bobbie is passionately jealous of other women, and she's the one who accused Leah."

Madame shrugged. "Is not easy for ordinary women, like this costume mistress, to compete with ballerinas. We are last remaining royalty." She reached up to the back of her head to center two tortoiseshell combs, which did make her look rather regal.

I looked over Gabi's shoulder. "If we look at means and opportunity, Bobbie is the most likely person. And yet, when I talked to her, she seemed furious Arianna had been murdered."

Gabi left off typing and snapped a few celery stalks. "Since when has Bobbie gotten so friendly with low-level dancers? When I was with the company, she didn't bother to talk to me until I was promoted to soloist. And she didn't learn my name until I became a principal dancer."

I sighed. "Don't give her too much credit. She hasn't exactly mellowed with age. But Bobbie knew that Arianna's family had done a lot—financially and otherwise—to help the company. In other words, money is the new talent."

Gabi opened a new window on her computer. "Let's go back to the Paris-New York connection. The French police originally charged a Rive Gauche dancer named Sylvain in Charles's murder. It took some time before the police judged him not guilty, because he resisted supplying any kind of alibi. After he was arrested, he admitted he was in a dressing room, having sex with one of American Ballet Company's dancers. I don't know the girl, but you and Madame might. Her name is Kerry something…"

"Blair. Her name is Kerry Blair." A long time would have to pass for me to forget how rudely that little nobody treated me.

Gabi wrote in her name. "Once this Kerry girl provided the appropriate verification, he was off the hook." Gabi gave me a skeptical look. "I'm surprised your good friend Olivia didn't tell you about it. Kerry is constantly posting pictures with Olivia in them."

I clutched my head with both hands, willing my brain cells to make some relevant connections. "Maybe Kerry and Olivia have a lot of mutual friends. As for Sylvain's alibi…is Kerry the sole proof of Sylvain's innocence? Maybe Sylvain is covering for Kerry, instead of the other way around. Or for some unknown reason, they're in it together."

Gabi quickly shut her laptop and said delicately, conscious of Madame Maksimova's sensibilities, "Kerry and Sylvain's alibi for when Colbert was stabbed is pretty well validated. There were, ah, pictures. Rather graphic selfies, quite frankly." She shrugged. "I tried not to look, but they are now…out there, as they say."

I wasn't ready to give up on Kerry. Or Sylvain. "I presume that anyone with an internet connection and the willingness to do some research can change the date and time of a photo. Sylvain and Kerry could have had sex at any point during our visit to Paris."

Gabi shrugged. "I suppose so. I'm not an expert. Although, if Sylvain and Kerry were going to fake the pictures, they probably would have chosen more flattering poses. According to *Le Figaro* and *Le Monde*, that was the first thing the French police investigated, once Sylvain admitted to his off-stage shenanigans."

Madame spoke with unusual sharpness. "When company was in Paris and Charles was attacked, Sylvain give Kerry alibi. In New York, when Arianna get killed, Horace give Kerry alibi. I am starting to think Kerry not have good alibi."

I paced back and forth from the window to the door. "How do you know Horace gave Kerry an alibi?"

Madame looked smug. "Zarina tell me all about what Friedrich say to her."

Gabi laughed. "But how did you get Zarina to confide in you? I didn't know you two knew each other that well."

Madame took a sip of champagne. She looked very pleased with herself. "I cannot dance so well now, but I am still great actress. I say to Zarina, '*Ma chérie*, no one in American Ballet Company dance like you. You are artist.' Then I tell her about all American dancers who not as good as she is. Then I ask if they have alibi for when poor Arianna was killed. I tell Zarina I do this because I am worried about her safety."

I wished I had some personal contacts at the Rive Gauche Ballet. Not that it would do me much good. I rarely spoke French after I broke up with a sexy, but not terribly brainy modern dancer from Marseille. "Madame, perhaps you could talk to some of your friends at the Rive Gauche Ballet. Find out what really went down."

"Yes. I will do. Perhaps I go. Better than telephone. I will have to take leave from work. But Friedrich not care. He not want me anyway, I think."

I was stunned. "To France? You would go to Paris?"

"Why not? Paris so beautiful this time of year. I have many friends there. And I will talk to dancers. Maybe teach guest class at Rive Gauche Ballet."

"Madame, I simply can't ask you to do this. It's not fair to you. Or to your students."

Madame took my hand. "Leah. You fighting for life. So do so. No such thing as fair in situation like this."

Speaking as if an afterthought, Madame said, "Now, we must talk about the funeral."

My mouth went dry. I wasn't going to the funeral.

Madame Maksimova removed a black-rimmed card from her purse. "Yes. Funeral in two days. We go together?"

I took a sip of water to clear my throat. "You can tell me about it. I'm not—I can't—I can't go. I just can't."

Madame looked severe. "You must go. Is the right thing to do."

Gabi weighed in. "If you don't go, it will look like an admission of guilt. Leah, you have nothing to be ashamed of and nothing to hide."

Madame and Gabi wanted to save me. They wanted to protect me. They thought if we played by the rules, I would win. So, I kept my plans to myself.

Chapter Sixteen

The only way to make sense out of change is to plunge into it, move with it, and join the dance.
— Alan Watts

My one direct link to Paris was Zarina. That lead wasn't promising, as we were never friends. More precisely, we'd always loathed each other. Nonetheless, I couldn't let a minor bit of jealousy get in the way of my investigation. Last spring, when we both danced at the Grand Palais de la Danse in Paris, she performed in a new ballet by Sylvain, and I did the Black Swan pas de deux from *Swan Lake*. I got more applause, but she got more bouquets. So, we were even. Not that either of us was petty enough to keep tabs on such trifles. But I was sure she bought half of those bouquets herself, whereas I didn't purchase the applause.

Zarina was a few years older than me, but you'd never know it to look at her smooth olive skin and bright black eyes. She had steely limbs and an equally unshakable confidence. Even her fingers radiated strength.

Undeterred by her cold attitude toward me, I accosted her in the dressing room.

She gave me a bored, blank look. *"Pardon?* Do we know each other? A thousand apologies."

I was beginning to wonder why no one had stabbed her. "Cut the crap, Zarina. You know who I am. And trust me, I don't want to be friends with you any more than you want to be friends with anyone. But you were in the theater the night Charles was stabbed. Tell me what I want to know, and I promise to pretend we've never met."

Although I spoke directly to her, Zarina kept her face angled away from me. Someone must have told her—quite accurately—she had a beautiful profile.

She ignored my reference to Colbert. "Ah, yes. I remember now. You are my understudy."

Madame Maksimova used to tell me stories of dancers sticking pins into their rivals' costumes. It all made sense to me now.

While I searched for neutral words, Zarina said, as if dredging up memories from a previous life, instead of the previous season, "You were a dancer in, hmmmm, *Swan Lake, n'est ce pas?*" She raised her eyebrows and narrowed her aquiline nose, as if she detected a noxious odor.

I resented the way she spoke of me dancing in *Swan Lake*. The corps de ballet danced *in Swan Lake*. I was the Black Swan. Not the same thing at all.

Zarina gave an exaggerated sigh. "It's not so nice for you to be my understudy, *chérie*. I guarantee it will be a thankless job." She stripped off her dance clothes and stepped into the shower. Through the rush of water, she said, "I never miss performance. French ballet training protect us. Not like American dance companies, where people all the time getting hurt. But everyone knows Americans are weak."

I wasn't a big fan of ballerina bitchiness. I did my fighting, if you wanted to call it that, in the studio. And I did it by being the best dancer in the room, not by engaging in the kind of intimidation Arianna and Zarina were so fond of. But when you needed information, confrontation was probably not the way to go. I was prepared to suck up any amount of malice in the process of nabbing the murderer.

I waited until she got out of the shower. "Yes, Zarina, everyone knows Parisian training is world-class. And speaking of the Rive Gauche Ballet, has there been any progress in identifying Colbert's attacker?"

"No, no. I cannot speak of it. *Je regrette*, I am sworn to silence."

Like most people sworn to silence, I figured she wouldn't need too much goading before spilling the latest gossip.

I shrugged my shoulders. "I figured if anyone knew what happened, it would be you. But, no problem. I'll give Sylvain a call. He's always in the know."

Zarina's dark skin flushed red. "Sylvain knows nothing! *Il est un idiot!*"

I waited. Zarina showed no signs of running off, possibly because she was naked. She toweled off before informing me, "Rive Gauche Ballet very political. Very intense. Charles rule the company because he have powerful friends—political friends. No one knows...but I..."

I was ready to throttle the information out of her. "What? What do you know?"

Zarina took out a can of hair spray and blew a cloud of chemicals poisonous enough to denude a forest. "I know things I will not tell you."

I moved a few steps away from her, in order to avoid the toxic fumes. But I kept my temper. I laughed a bit, as if I were the one in possession of important knowledge. "Yeah, that's what people say when they don't know anything." I managed to annoy her, but not quite enough to provoke her into speaking candidly.

Instead of continuing to question her, I acted as if I knew more than she did. If I were wrong about anything, Zarina would take pleasure in correcting me. "It's no secret how close you were with Colbert, uh, with Charles. At the gala last year, people were talking as if you two were getting married. That's why I was so surprised when you broke up. I guess Charles preferred Sylvain to you. That kind of rejection is pretty embarrassing, *n'est ce pas?*"

Zarina curled her fingers into claws. "He never—I never—Charles not leave me for Sylvain! That is a lie. I break up with Charles. Both men are still in love with me, of course." She picked up a brush and stroked her gleaming hair. "A few times since I break up with them—*tu vois ce que je veux dire*—hm...you understand, yes? I spend some time with them. But now I not interested in that rat, that pig. I have new boyfriend."

She held out her hand to show me an emerald ring surrounded by diamonds. "I not need men. They need me." She peered around my shoulder to look in the mirror that hung behind me, checking to see that she was still as beautiful as she was five minutes earlier.

I wasn't familiar with the phrase *tu vois ce que je veux dire,* but Zarina's tone indicated that this was how the French said yadda yadda yadda. If I were Zarina, I too would deny that my boyfriend cheated on me with a young and very beautiful man.

As if talking to myself, I said, "I wonder if the police have any other suspects. I know they ended up exonerating Sylvain." I turned back to Zarina. "Who else was implicated?"

"Je ne sais pas." Zarina shrugged. The silky wrap she tossed over her shoulders slipped off, and she bent down to retrieve it. She smoothed and folded the wrap, as if neither Colbert's murder nor Arianna's murder were interesting enough to maintain her attention.

Interrogating people in the guise of friendship wasn't for the faint of heart, especially with a subject as slippery as Zarina. "I heard you were also, uh, you know, *tu vois ce que je veux dire* with Valentin Shevchenko. You must have been upset that two of your boyfriends ended up dead. On the same night, too."

Zarina wobbled a bit in her red stiletto heels, which fit so perfectly over her misshapen feet they had to have been made to order. She shot me a look from under thick black eyelashes. "Who told you that? Your friend Madame Maksimova?"

I was startled. The last thing I wanted to do was to blow Madame's cover.

Zarina turned away from me, took a tube of sweet-smelling moisturizer from her bag, and started rubbing the cream over her hands. "You should think about who your real friends are, *chérie.* Or maybe make new ones."

"Why? What did Madame say to you?"

Zarina smirked. "Don't get so upset. Why you care? Madame is old school. Old style. France more modern, more better than you. You Americans still all the time bow down to Russians." She made an exaggerated curtsey.

I couldn't allow Zarina to insult Madame. Or me. Or American dancers, for that matter. I picked bobby pins out of my hair in order to give my hands something to do, other than throttle the life out of that miserable woman. "I can't agree with you about Madame or about American dancers. But your company and mine are very alike in some things. Both have dancers who were knifed. Both have directors who screw everyone."

Zarina applied blood-red lipstick. "I care only about myself. No one else. To think about other people is foolish."

"Really? That's not the best advice I've ever heard. Colbert was killed. Shevchenko was killed. Arianna was killed. How do you know you won't be next?"

Zarina finally turned her back to the mirror, but not to look at me. She looked over her shoulder and resumed her inspection of herself, this time scrutinizing the beauty of her rear end, which, I regretted to say, was lovely. Only a very few lucky dancers had frames so delicate they maintained softness despite their skinniness, and Zarina was one of these.

She wasn't so overcome with her own flawless self that she was completely oblivious to me. "Is it that you threaten me? Not so easy to do. But since you like so much to talk about the murder, perhaps you should tell me how Arianna die."

"I don't know how she died. I found her. That's all."

Her gaze sharpened. "Ah, but you were there. There were witnesses."

Like Arianna, Zarina was used to having her own way. But unlike the men who melted under the gaze of her black eyes, I was neither seduced nor distracted.

"Once again, Zarina, who do you think stabbed Colbert? Who killed Arianna?"

"You have the persistence, *mon amie*. But I have not the information. And now I fear I must go. *Ciao.*" She waved her hand and walked toward the exit.

I didn't give a damn about Zarina's need to be alone. Anyway, I was the understudy and had to concentrate on the same choreography she did, however painful it was to watch her take over the roles I longed to dance.

Zarina refused to look at me, so I addressed my next words to the back of her head. "I heard Colbert was giving Sylvain a hard time. After Sylvain let Colbert take credit for the choreography he did, Colbert didn't give him the principal roles he'd been promised. And that's why the police thought Sylvain was the one who knifed Colbert."

Zarina stopped short. "And I heard the same thing about you. Police think you are guilty because Arianna get the roles you wanted."

"No. Not the same thing. If the situation here were the same as the one in Paris, I'd have killed Friedrich. Not Arianna."

With a Gallic shrug, Zarina delivered her parting shot. "Perhaps Arianna was the next best thing to killing Friedrich." She paused and looked directly at me for the first time. "But no funny business with me. I can protect myself." She stepped into the elevator and blocked me from following her in. She held her hand like a traffic cop, ordering me to stop. "This car is full."

I didn't have the wit or the reflexes to lunge in after her. Just before the doors closed, she blew me a kiss.

Chapter Seventeen

All ballet. All reading. All music. That was my world.
— Natalia Makarova

The morning of the funeral I went to Barbara's house for breakfast, which, in my mother's world, consisted of coffee and mineral water. She offered me a piece of fruit from a carefully composed bowl of apples and oranges, but I had no appetite. The coffee, as always, was excellent.

Summer's heat had continued into September, and by the time I got to Barbara's apartment, I was sweaty and my black linen dress was a mass of wrinkles. I removed my wide-brimmed black straw hat, stood in front of the air conditioner, and fanned perspiration from my forehead. Because most of the time my hair was pinned into a tight bun, I liked to leave it loose when I wasn't dancing, but the heat rendered that hairstyle impractical. Without a mirror, I twisted the long heavy hair off my neck into a knot low enough to allow the hat to fit.

While I drank coffee, Barbara shouted conversation from her bedroom, reminding me at least ten times of my sister's book talk later that afternoon. With atypical tactlessness, Barbara encouraged me to look for other dance jobs. In her defense, she knew Friedrich had sidelined me indefinitely, and she knew equally well how painful that was for me.

My more immediate distress seemed to have distracted her from the larger peril I was facing. While I had spent all my free time investigating the murder, she appeared to have researched good places for me to relocate.

The San Francisco Ballet. The Houston Ballet. The Dutch National Ballet. On and on, she droned about possibilities in other cities, other countries.

I didn't share Barbara's optimism about potential employment in foreign climes. Somewhat counter-intuitively, I also didn't share her gloomy view of my future career at American Ballet Company. Some part of me, probably the stubborn part that fueled my childhood dreams of becoming a ballerina in the first place, still believed my name would be cleared. That Lincoln Center audiences would once again rise to their feet and toss flowers as I took my bow. That my fellow dancers would regret doubting my innocence. That the trending topic on Twitter would mutate from hash tags about bitter has-beens into praises for courage and grace. These fantasies were all I had to keep me sane.

Barbara emerged in a charcoal gray pencil skirt and high-collared, sleeveless shirt. Her shoes and handbag were impeccable, of course. I admired them, and she beckoned me to follow her.

She pointed to my feet. "I forbid you to appear in public in those shoes." From one of the neatly stacked boxes in her closet she brought out a pair of sky-high black pumps, with delicate straps that crossed over the instep. After a bit more rummaging, she handed me a quilted black handbag that probably cost as much, or more, than my monthly rent.

I fingered the stitching on the bag. "I'm really nervous. I don't want to go. I bet hundreds of people will be there. No one will know I didn't show up."

Barbara stared into her makeup mirror while she talked to me. "Everyone will know. You have to be strong, but more importantly, you have to do the right thing. Madame and Gabi and I will take care of you."

I stretched out on the bed and watched Barbara apply makeup. There was something soothing about this ritual, which I'd seen her do my whole life.

Barbara outlined her lips and pressed them together. "Although this is a sad occasion, it's also a chance for us to talk to people we'd otherwise have to seek out."

I sat straight up. "You can't do that! This is a funeral. We can't start interviewing people." I was astonished Barbara, the family arbiter of good taste and good manners, would do such a thing.

My mother calmly applied mascara. "Madame and I will be most discreet. You, of course, will not be involved. Leave it to us."

The prospect of Madame and Barbara interrogating mourners at Arianna's funeral wasn't pleasant, but I couldn't reasonably object. With some effort, I squeezed Barbara's narrow shoes over my bunions, and we left.

We got into a taxi, picked up Madame, and made our way to the Upper East Side church where the service was being held. There was an enormous crowd, both inside and out. Reporters roamed the perimeter of the throng. I was terrified they'd spot me, but, in this gathering of thin, black-clad women in dark glasses, wide hats, and ballet buns, I remained, at least for the moment, anonymous. A large contingent of political and media celebrities kept the photographers busy as I tried to blend into the crowd.

Bryan and Tess, Horace and Kerry, and Daniel and Olivia were at the center of a large group of dancers. Gabi showed up a few minutes later, zooming around the corner and running as lightly in her stilettos as if she were wearing sneakers. I motioned to her, but she brushed me off with a brief shake of her head. Instead of embracing me, she joined Bryan and Tess.

I understood. The other dancers would be less likely to talk to her if she showed her allegiance to me. As much as I wanted to overhear their conversation, I moved away.

At the other side of the entrance, Friedrich and Zarina posed for photographers. Madame Maksimova waited for the media attention to wane before kissing each on both cheeks. I heard her compliment Zarina on her dancing, as well as on her dress, a petal-like confection in shades of teal and lilac. In an ocean of gray and navy and black, Zarina looked like an exotic sea creature.

Madame coaxed Zarina away from Friedrich, and the two women were soon deep in conversation. Not to be outdone, Barbara cornered Bobbie and, to the costume mistress's evident astonishment, embraced her warmly. Bobbie clearly had no idea who my mother was; Barbara later explained she told Bobbie she was a major donor to the Costume Initiative. It wasn't a complete lie. Barbara did give a few hundred bucks a year to American Ballet Company fundraisers.

I was the only person standing by herself, and I was beginning to feel self-conscious. I sought sanctuary in the church, but before reaching safety, the press realized who I was, and they began a relentless attack, yelling questions and pushing cameras and microphones in my face.

To my surprise, I had several champions in the crowd. In addition to Olivia, and a few other American Ballet Company dancers who sprang to my rescue, a group of women from Studio Dance formed a barrier around me. They acted as a human shield, bulldozing reporters out of my way and shepherding me into the church. The fiercest protectors were those mildly deranged dancers from Studio Dance, the ones I'd taken to lunch and befriended when no one else would talk to them. After I entered the church, they formed a wall in front of the entrance. None of the reporters had ever faced quite so odd and formidable a group, and they retreated before this unusual obstacle.

Grayson snaked his way in behind me and motioned me to follow him behind a pillar. My skinny brigade of bodyguards kept a respectful distance, but they didn't abandon me.

The critic nodded at me in a friendly way. "Leah Siderova. We finally meet again. You haven't answered my phone calls, but I'm not one to hold a grudge."

I was even more wary of his warmth than I was of his ire. "Hello, Grayson. If you're ready to answer some questions as well as ask them, I'd be happy to talk to you. But not on the record. This is between you and me. Not you and me and your readers."

He pursed his lips. "That's a bit shortsighted of you. I'm a powerful person to have on your side. And if you ask me, you could use a few friends."

I kept my expression cool and pleasant but couldn't hide beads of sweat that dripped from underneath my hat. "I need the truth more than I need friends."

In a rather patronizing tone he said, "Of course, my dear girl. What do you want to know?"

I looked over my shoulder to make sure no one could overhear our conversation. "Tell me about Zarina. I know the two of you were lovers. No offense, but it was hardly an exclusive relationship."

Grayson pressed his lips together in a tight line of displeasure. "The lovely Mademoiselle Devereaux? Why not ask her yourself? Surely, as her understudy, you see her every day, whereas she and I are no longer quite so...quite as close as we once were."

I refused to let him put me off. "You had sex with her. And you wrote an entire chapter about her in your book, which means you know a lot more about her than I do."

His mouth arched into a smile that didn't reach the rest of his face. "My relationships with the people I interview are purely professional. Your implications are insulting."

I hastened to mollify him. The last thing I needed was for the most powerful dance critic in New York City to hold a grudge against me. "In exchange for information about Zarina, I'll answer some of your questions. For the record. No hard feelings, right?"

The critic smiled, this time for real. "You've got yourself a deal. Zarina, of course, is a divine dancer. But that is common knowledge. Surely you must also be aware of the fact that she charmed the pants off Colbert, as she so well knows how to do." He frowned. "But she never cared about him. Never. She was using him. He was crazy about her, but it wasn't mutual."

I wondered if Zarina's Russian lover was the one who'd given her the emerald and diamond ring she'd flashed at me. "Does Zarina care about anyone other than herself?"

Grayson looked offended. "Zarina is an artist. And artists don't worry about the petty values of lesser mortals."

As a lesser mortal, I couldn't admire the way Zarina used people to get ahead. More to the point, for all of his seeming candor, I had the distinct feeling Grayson was holding out on me. "You're going to have to do better than that, Grayson. I already know about Zarina's affairs. As does everyone in the Rive Gauche Ballet. And American Ballet Company."

He smirked. "I doubt you know everything." He turned to look hungrily at Zarina. "Did you know Shevchenko was mad for her? Would have done anything for her."

Not wanting to seem too eager, I kept my face expressionless. "That is something I didn't know. Did you learn about this when you interviewed him for your book? Or is Zarina the one who told you about their relationship? Either way, I'm surprised you kept that tasty bit of gossip quiet."

Grayson frowned again. "My book was about ballet. Not gossip. As for the gaps in your knowledge, perhaps you've been distracted, my dear. At any rate, there is very little more to tell, since Shevchenko is dead. French police are still investigating. Dreadful thing to happen."

Despite the heat, I went cold. "And…was Zarina a, uh, person of interest?"

Grayson looked amused. "Not at all. Remember, please, to Zarina Valentin was simply one more man so in love with her he'd have done anything to spend five minutes just looking at her."

This was too much. She wasn't that gorgeous. "Valentin was six feet of blonde male beauty who had dozens of fabulous women at his feet. I don't see him begging anyone, even Zarina, for favors. Where did you get your information? From her?"

Offended, Grayson said, "I'm a journalist. I have my sources, and I check them. She had a cast iron alibi for Colbert, Arianna, and Shevchenko. Perhaps you haven't been paying sufficient attention. Zarina always ends up on top. She, more than anyone else I know, gets her way. There hasn't been much press about the Shevchenko death, because the Russian media has done its best to squelch the story. I have my inside sources, of course. The French press reported that the secret services arm of the government did him in, after Shevchenko choreographed a ballet about a dissident journalist. Who was also poisoned in a most horrific fashion." Grayson paused. "Perhaps now you will answer a few of my questions. I believe I've held up my end of the bargain."

I nodded. "A deal's a deal. But it looks as though the service is about to start. I'll talk to you later. I'll even answer one of your phone calls."

The critic looked angry, but he couldn't reasonably protest. The pews were rapidly filling, and he hastened to secure a seat in front.

I staked out enough room for all four of us, in the back of the cavernous sanctuary. Barbara joined me briefly before flitting off again, ostensibly to use the bathroom. Left alone, I protected myself from curious stares and whispers by pretending to read the hymnal. I had no problem reserving half the aisle, since no one wanted to sit near me.

Madame slowly edged herself into the pew, in evident physical, as well as emotional, pain. She removed a handkerchief from her handbag, and the scent of roses and jasmine provided a pleasing antidote to the musty smell of the church. She inched closer to me to leave room for Gabi, who followed her in.

"Were you able to get any information?" I whispered.

Madame sighed. "Zarina talk, talk, talk, but not say much. She say Friedrich in love with her. She say Charles Colbert also in love with her. She say she had Russian boyfriend, and he too is in love with her. For now, she with Friedrich only. Unless someone better come along." Madame turned to Gabi. "I see you talking with dancers. Do you find good information?"

Gabi leaned forward. "Leah, didn't you tell me Arianna's family used their connections to promote the company?"

I nodded.

Gabi continued, "Well, no one seems to know anything about it. I mean, Bryan, at the very least, ought to know. But he claims the Bonneville family had nothing to do with all the media attention the two of them got. He thinks it's his genius choreography that got Grayson and the rest of the media interested."

This was most interesting. Had Bobbie lied when she claimed the Bonneville family used their connections to promote their daughter? Or had someone lied to Bobbie? If the latter, who was it? And who arranged for the media blitz, if it hadn't been Arianna's influential family? Bryan was very talented, but no one, other than his mother, could believe the volume of attention he received was warranted.

I turned back to Gabi. "Did you talk to Tess? Perhaps the Morgan family was the true benefactor. They have plenty of connections outside the financial community. Maybe Tess felt threatened by Arianna and thought the way to hold onto Bryan was to make herself indispensable to him." I searched for Tess in the crowd. "Or maybe Tess decided to literally kill the competition."

Gabi looked doubtful. "I was with them from the time I arrived until now. And whatever problems they used to have seem to have evaporated. He's practically attached to her at the hip."

"If Tess knew it was her family, and not Arianna's, that arranged for the media coverage, wouldn't Tess have said something about it? If only to set the record straight?"

Madame demurred. "*Pfui.* I say no to that. Tess is Bryan's girlfriend. She not going to say or do anything to imply he need help from anyone."

That made sense. But it didn't move us further along. I said to Madame, "You must talk to Bobbie. She won't talk to me. Find out if she's lying. Or if she's been fed false information."

Madame squeezed my hand. Before she could answer, the service began, and we all settled into quiet.

Barbara returned so silently I didn't register her presence until she was right beside me. She reached into her handbag and handed me a stack of neatly folded tissues. I hoped I wouldn't need all of them.

I hadn't attended many funerals and was unfamiliar with the rituals of the Episcopal church. The singing of hymns, the long prayers, and the emotional eulogies, all intended to comfort the mourners, instead inspired fresh grief. I was most moved by the flowers. They should have been presented to Arianna after a performance. Not at her funeral. I extracted a few tissues from Barbara's pile and averted my gaze from where Arianna's coffin lay. Feeling eyes on my neck, I turned around to find Detectives Sobol and Farrow, in the very last row, staring straight at me. I started.

Barbara gripped my arm and didn't let go. She whispered, "Don't react. Sit still and mourn for this poor dead girl, and then we will leave."

Fifteen more minutes passed. Twenty. Thirty.

Finally, the service ended. The family and close friends left for the burial, which was in Long Island. Madame and Gabi and a number of American Ballet Company members went in cars provided by the Bonneville family. I, of course, wasn't invited to come. Barbara and I slipped out through a side entrance, which she said she had located while searching for the bathroom.

Barbara wanted to walk across Central Park, but the shoes she'd lent me were crushing my feet, so we took a taxi to our usual diner.

I had my cell phone turned off during the service, and as soon as we'd ordered, I turned it back on. I saw that I'd missed a call from Morty. Desperate for good news, I went outside to talk in the relative privacy of Columbus Avenue.

I had to yell over the noise of the traffic and crowds. I strained to hear Morty, who spoke through a crunch of food. He was brief. "Meet me at the precinct. One hour. You're needed for further questioning."

Chapter Eighteen

Dancing is the world's favorite metaphor.
— Kristy Nilsson

Before I left the diner, Barbara reminded me, once again, of my sister's book talk that evening. I didn't tell her where I was going, and she didn't ask. She'd never admit it, but the stress was beginning to wear away at her. Even her expert skills with makeup could not hide the worry lines that had deepened since Arianna was murdered.

When I walked through the station house, I felt the burn of many stares. I could almost hear each police officer and typist thinking *So this is the jealous bitch who knifed that pretty young girl...* Bad as it was, at least it was impersonal, unlike the censorious gazes I endured at the funeral and in the ballet studio.

Morty arrived only a few minutes after I did, but those few minutes cost me. Alone, I couldn't keep calm, couldn't keep still. The two detectives watched as I fidgeted, my breath getting shallower and the twitching spasms in my eyelids growing stronger.

I vowed I wouldn't be weak, but after five minutes, I fled to the bathroom. I sat in a stall and pressed a hand against my chest to still my heartbeat. It didn't work.

By the time I returned, Morty had arrived, looking as relaxed as if he were sitting in a deck chair by the beach.

The questioning began. Sobol and Farrow poked and prodded with the determination of two prospectors bent upon extracting gold. For the most part, I heeded Morty's advice and remained silent.

146

My reticence didn't help.

"Tell me again, Ms. Siderova. Where were you before you returned to the studio?"

Apparently, Jonah and I were no longer operating on a first-name basis. I looked at Morty, who nodded his permission to answer the question.

"I bought a cup of coffee. As I've told you many times already, I realized a few minutes after I purchased the coffee I was late for the costume fitting."

Farrow looked at his notes. "Why didn't you call Ms. York? Her name and cell number are on your list of contacts. In fact, you called her later that same night."

I didn't remember telling the detectives I had Bobbie's number in my contact list, but it was true and I let it go. "Call her? I didn't think of it. I knew she worked long hours and I figured she'd still be there." Although this seemed an adequate explanation, I couldn't stop talking. "I was around the corner. If it had taken more than a few minutes to get there, I probably would have called her first."

"Still, you had to go out of your way and all. You told us your feet hurt. And that you were tired. So why not save yourself the trouble?" Farrow, staring at me, breathed doubt about my innocence into every word.

Jonah looked more at Morty than at me.

"How well did you know Ms. Bonneville?" Farrow pressed.

"Not well at all. We danced for the same ballet company, but we weren't close."

"She was a lot younger than you. Ten years, easy." This wasn't a question, and I stayed silent.

Jonah said, "You stood next to her at the morning ballet class. Why was that? Why stand next to a virtual stranger—if that's what she was. Why not stand next to someone you know?"

"I always stand there. It's my spot."

Both detectives eyed me.

I felt I needed to give a better explanation. "Most of us have a favorite spot at the barre. Arianna had nothing to do with why I chose to stand there."

"Was Ms. Bonneville's 'spot' usually near yours?"

"No, actually. Not all of us become attached to one particular location. Plenty of people choose a random place to begin class."

"How did you feel when you found out Ms. Bonneville was going to be the star of this new ballet? Mr. Holstein told us he informed you, right before the murder, that you were going to be her understudy."

The only way to keep calm was to remove myself from the situation. I counted my heartbeats and the pores on Farrow's nose, but math was never my strong suit. Instead, I mentally danced through Kitri's variation from *Don Quixote*. I needed a strong and rebellious heroine. This was no time for Sleeping Beauties.

Adopting a kindly tone, Farrow asked, "Didn't that make you angry? Resentful? You had seniority. Had to hurt. Maybe you got upset, like. Maybe you didn't realize what you were doing."

Instead of Farrow's voice, I heard the rousing introduction for Kitri's dance. *Arabesque and leap! Kick and jump and turn!* Farrow could talk all he wanted. I was no longer a murder suspect. I was Kitri, the sultry, enchanting heroine of the ballet, a passionate woman who brought men to their knees.

Most of my conscious thought—maybe ninety percent—focused on nailing each pirouette of my imaginary solo. The other ten percent thought about how much I wanted to kill Friedrich Holstein. I blamed him for putting me in this humiliating position. But, best to keep murderous thoughts to myself, even if the target of my homicidal rage wasn't the actual victim.

There was a tap on the door, and a tall woman beckoned Sobol and Farrow out of the room. The second they left, in an effort to quiet my nerves, I exhaled against my fist, as if blowing up a paper bag. The pressure in my head was so intense it was making me nauseous.

I breathed in three-fourths time. *One*, two three. *One* two three. *Chassé, pas de bourrée, glissade, pas de chat.* Without moving, I circled an imaginary stage, defying anyone who thought he could put me down.

Morty got someone to get me a cup of water and I gulped two Excedrin. "You're doin' fine, Leah. Trust me."

"I do trust you, Uncle Morty. I just don't understand why I have to keep coming back here, answering the same questions."

"It's what they do. They're looking for some clue that maybe you overlooked. Or they overlooked. So don't give it to them. Stay cool."

Morty's tactic seemed flawed.

"That doesn't make sense to me. Why shouldn't I tell them as much as possible? I want them to find the clue that leads them to the killer."

Morty put his forefinger to his lips, indicating he wanted me to shut up. He needn't have worried. I knew the room was wired. Shows about detectives were ubiquitous on television and in the movies. *Law & Order* has probably done more to inform criminals of their rights than the average cop or teacher, droning on about the Miranda ruling.

I knew better than to speak ill of the dead. But it was no secret I hadn't liked Arianna. Her ambition and her sense of privilege annoyed me. And, to be honest, it intimidated me as well. It bothered me that the police might never find out the kind of person Arianna was, because I was convinced her character played a role in her death. At least, that was what Barbara said, when she was writing her mystery books.

I was as ambitious as Arianna, and I knew the price that ballet exacted. Ambition inevitably made one selfish. It made one vain. But it also forced me to inhabit the flip side of vanity, which was a shuddering insecurity. Dancing made me so focused on my face and my body and how the world perceived me, I'd lost perspective on other aspects of what it meant to be human.

As a consequence of my devotion to ballet, I'd lost friends and lovers, but as long as I could dance, I believed I didn't need them. Sitting in that interrogation room, waiting for the detectives to walk back in, I realized I didn't like the person I was. The person I'd become. I don't think I was always so limited. But after Gabi retired, I lost her pragmatic perspective. Without my best friend, the walls of habit narrowed so imperceptibly I was suffocated before I even knew I was caught.

Sobol and Farrow returned.

Again, Farrow spoke first. "What were you wearing during your rehearsal with Ms. Bonneville?"

His question took me aback. "I don't know. I assume a leotard and tights and pointe shoes. Leg warmers."

Farrow said, "Weren't you also wearing a black skirt?"

I looked at Morty, who shrugged. "Yes, Detective, I believe I was wearing a skirt."

Sobol took a plastic bag from his pocket. Inside were several black threads. "Can you explain why threads from your skirt were found under Ms. Bonneville's body?"

"That's impossible! Someone—someone must have put them there. Or maybe they're not even mine! Or no—the murderer must have put them there. To frame me."

I grabbed Morty's arm. "That's great news! Now we know for sure the killer was present at Bryan's rehearsal." Seeing the detectives exchange a sharp look, I added, "Not me, of course. Someone other than me who was present at the rehearsal."

Jonah didn't bother to debate the point. Instead, he once again changed direction. "Ms. Siderova, several witnesses told us you threatened Ms. Bonneville a few hours before she died. You haven't adequately addressed that allegation."

My nose ran and my eyes turned red, but I didn't technically cry. Perhaps a few tears escaped, but I avoided sobs and hiccupping. "That's not true!"

The two detectives looked at me and waited.

I clenched my hands so tightly, my nails bit into my palms. "As I've already explained, I didn't mean what I said literally. I said I would cut her down, meaning I would cut her down to size. Not stab her, for heaven's sake. I never wanted to speak ill of Arianna, but if you must know, she was quite nasty. I wanted her to stay away from me."

Farrow said, "Witnesses also say you were physically aggressive. That you pushed her and she fell down. Is that typical behavior for you?"

I gulped. "I can explain. Arianna swung her bag at my head. And before that, she was getting really close to me in an intimidating way. I didn't mean to push her, or even to touch her. I was protecting myself against her."

Even I could see the irony. I felt intimidated. I felt threatened. But Arianna was the one who was murdered.

Jonah said, again without looking at me, "No one else noticed Ms. Bonneville's aggression. No one mentioned seeing that. The only thing people remember is that you attacked her. Not the other way around."

I protested, "Why don't you interrogate Zarina Devereaux? Or one of the other dancers? It can't just be me who seems to have a motive."

Farrow tilted his head, as if to focus more clearly on my face. "Trust me, Ms. Siderova, we talked to everyone. And I mean everyone. But we keep coming back to you. We'll be in touch."

Morty advised me to prepare myself for the worst. I knew I didn't have much time, and that made me brave.

Which was why I boarded the subway and made my way to Williamsburg, Brooklyn.

The subway platform was crowded, and the air was thick with the greasy scent of hot dogs and the sour odor of too many bodies. Ten minutes passed before the L train arrived, at which point I began to feel slightly nauseated from the heat and smell.

There was a concerted rush for the open doors, and although I had positioned myself well, I still had difficulty boarding the train. A group of teenagers blocked the entrance, and I had to push past them to get inside.

In the subway car, I fought my way to the overhead bar. There was a time, not too long ago, when I would casually stand without holding on, but those days were gone. I took no chances with the health of my knees—an especially prudent precaution during that trip, since the train lurched forward so violently I had trouble staying upright, even while grasping the bar.

Inside Barbara's shoes, my feet burned and stung, but the likelihood of getting a seat seemed small. I steeled myself to a sweaty and uncomfortable ride, which I feared would end in a sweaty and uncomfortable confrontation with Friedrich. I tried not to be too superstitious, but the accretion of bad luck following me, in ways small and large, made the butterflies in my stomach circle in a mad whirl of nervous energy. I was ready to seize upon any hint of a change in fortune, however minor.

And then a miracle occurred. A bona fide good sign. Better than making the light at Seventy-Second and Broadway. Better than a fast-moving line at Starbucks. Better even than finding an unused gift card to Bloomingdale's, when you thought you couldn't afford that lovely new purse. My sign of good fortune came in the figure of a bearded guy, wearing dark blue Levi's and an ironic T-shirt.

He seemed destined for his natural habitat, i.e., Brooklyn. But he didn't linger that long. Instead, he got off at Union Square, and—good sign number two—the kid toting a massive two-ton backpack didn't weasel his way into the vacant seat. I rested all the way to Williamsburg, where I exited at the Bedford Avenue station.

My parents loved to talk about their childhoods in Brooklyn, and I knew all about the formerly dangerous streets of Bed-Stuy and Red Hook, but a lot had changed since then. Brooklyn, the former home of the Dodgers, the butt of a thousand jokes, and the ugly stepsister to glamorous Manhattan, was like the skinny ugly guy in high school, who, at the ten-year reunion, showed up handsome, rich, and married to a lawyer who looked like a Victoria Secret model. And of all the neighborhoods in the ugly-duckling-turned-graceful-swan borough, none had changed more than Williamsburg.

One hundred years ago, Betty Smith wrote about the neighborhood's tenement buildings in *A Tree Grows in Brooklyn*. Forty years ago, my parents made their aspirational move to Manhattan, at a time when people admitted to living in Brooklyn, rather than bragged about it.

Things really started changing twenty years ago, when the artists who once lived in Soho and Tribeca and the East Village were priced out of the lofts and factory buildings they helped make chic. Needing cheap rent and abundant space, they migrated across the bridge.

But once again, the artists who displaced the local residents had themselves been displaced by investment bankers and trust fund kids. It made perfect sense that Friedrich had taken up residence in one of the most expensive and fashionable neighborhoods in this very expensive and fashionable city.

I didn't know the area well, and I needed online help to point me in the right direction. On the way to Friedrich's apartment, I passed one art gallery, three retro-chic bowling alleys, five farm-to-table restaurants, eight cafés, and seven bars. Approximately ten billion mothers wielding aerodynamically engineered baby strollers marched across each intersection with the confidence and purpose of Sherman making his way across Georgia.

Friedrich's building was a fifteen-minute walk from the subway stop. The farther I walked, the more the neighborhood changed. Though large swaths of Williamsburg had been gentrified to within an inch of their formerly gritty lives, Friedrich lived on an industrial street that seemed miles from the busy shopping area near the subway station.

I was surprised the fastidious Friedrich had chosen to live in so dilapidated a building. I imagined him in a converted condo or co-op, where every surface glimmered with expensive stones and brushed metal.

At the corner of Friedrich's block, I dropped a five-dollar bill into the cup of a panhandler. I'd heard you weren't supposed to give money to people on the street, and that it was better to donate to homeless shelters and the like, but the guy looked like he needed help. He hadn't chosen a well-traveled venue, and his cup was nearly empty. Also, I figured if things went badly at Friedrich's, I had the satisfaction of knowing at least one person who'd had a good day.

The stoop outside Friedrich's building was littered with cigarette butts, and the intercom was dented and dirty. It had five buttons for five different apartments, but none of them had name tags. This problem would have stymied Leah, the ballerina. But I was now Leah, the fearless investigator. Knowing Friedrich liked to be on top of everything and everyone, I pushed the button for apartment five.

A few minutes passed with no answer. I didn't see a video camera, but one could have been hidden inside the vestibule. If Friedrich saw me, he might decline to let me in. But I didn't think he'd do that. Even if he did, it would take more than one rebuff to discourage me.

I was about to leave when a garbled noise that didn't sound entirely human erupted from the box. Before I could frame an answer, and, without asking for identification, someone, hopefully Friedrich, buzzed me in.

I rode to the top floor of the building in what appeared to be a freight elevator. There was no door, only a manually operated wire screen with heavy metal bars that took all my strength to close. The ceiling was open, and I watched the grinding cables and gears with some trepidation, nervous the rusting mechanism would break and the elevator would plummet back to the first floor. As deaths went, that scenario wasn't as bad as the electric chair, but still, it wasn't the way I wanted to depart from this earth. I got into a modified second position and bent my knees in a deep plié. If the elevator went down, I wanted to be ready to jump.

The grimy lobby and creaking contraption were in stark contrast to the well-appointed elevator in Barbara's building, or the gilded elegance of Madame Maksimova's building, or the chilly minimalist luxury of Bryan's skyscraper, but as long as it took me where I was going, it was plenty nice enough for me. Even a filthy elevator that smelled of rotten apples and spoiled tuna fish was better than climbing five flights of steep stairs. I was breathless enough without that added pressure.

The elevator stopped at a small landing. I wrenched the gate open and walked toward the only apartment on the floor. The door to Friedrich's loft was ajar. I knocked and called out his name, but no one answered. I pushed the heavy iron door open and looked around before stepping inside. Wet footprints marked the floor. The sound of rushing water and the clanking of pipes were the only greeting I got. I wondered who Friedrich thought he'd let into his apartment. Whoever it was, it was someone he trusted. I called his name again but didn't identify myself.

Over the sound of a gurgling drain, he called, "That you, *mein liebling*? I'll be right out."

I hoped Friedrich wouldn't emerge naked. The situation was awkward enough without any extra thrills. Nonetheless, I didn't answer him. What if the sound of my voice caused him to slip and fall and hit his head and die? And die in the nude? It was simple kindness to allow the man to dry off and get dressed.

The sound of rushing water ceased and the door to the bathroom banged open.

Friedrich emerged and, ever the showman, struck a sexy pose. His inviting attitude didn't last long. In less time than it took to do an *entrechat quatre,* his expression changed from seductive to furious. He sputtered, "What the—"

Thankfully, he had the presence of mind to hold onto his towel. There was only so much excitement I could take in one day.

"*Geh raus!* Out of here!"

I was polite. "Maybe you want to get dressed before we talk?"

Chapter Nineteen

We're fools whether we dance or not, so we might as well dance.
— Japanese Proverb

Friedrich responded with a flood of angry German. Thankfully, I didn't understand a word. I should have been ashamed or abashed or upset, but what could he do to humiliate me that he hadn't already done?

I answered him with a calmness I didn't know I possessed. "What I have to say to you won't wait. You refused to talk to me at work. Like it or not, we're going to talk now."

Friedrich looked at his wrist, but, for obvious reasons, he wasn't wearing his watch. Or anything else, other than the towel. He walked around a room divider made of industrial piping, and I heard the sound of drawers being yanked open and slammed shut. Two minutes later he emerged, dressed in very tight jeans and an even tighter white button-down shirt. Typical male Euro-trash outfit, suitable for picking up gullible NYU undergraduate students at overpriced wine bars.

As he walked toward me, he snapped a black plastic watch around his wrist. Like the apartment, the watch seemed out of character for the fastidious and pretentious ballet master. I recognized it from the Guggenheim gift store. I expected nothing less than a Philippe Patek from Friedrich. Not a twenty-buck plastic band. But as a fashion statement, it worked. The man was cruel and heartless. But he was not without style. I'd give him that.

If I thought he was genuinely dangerous, I wouldn't have risked going to see him by myself. Nonetheless, I was uneasy about the vehemence of his responses and nervous enough that I nearly fainted when the intercom announced another visitor.

I steeled myself to meet Friedrich's date. Or maybe it was just the delivery guy from the Thai restaurant around the corner.

A loud screech from the elevator announced his visitor before she entered. And it was no delivery guy or NYU student. Zarina, prima ballerina, walked into the room.

She recoiled when she saw me, and several tense moments elapsed before she recovered from the shock of finding me in Friedrich's apartment. He rushed to her, but she shook him off.

Zarina was furious. "Explain yourself." She then let loose a volley of French.

Friedrich didn't answer. He seemed a bit stunned, although he must have been expecting her visit. Or had Zarina, like me, decided to talk to Friedrich far from the prying eyes of other company members?

In a higher-pitched tone, Zarina insisted, *"Que fait-elle ici?"*

I knew enough French and enough of Zarina to realize the conversation wasn't likely to move forward until Friedrich offered an explanation for my presence. But I was in no mood to help him out.

Friedrich looked confused, and it gave me no little pleasure to see our arrogant ballet master at a loss for words. His uncertainty was understandable. He couldn't explain my presence to Zarina, because I hadn't yet told him why I was there. Also, although he often bragged he was fluent in five languages, I could tell he was slow to understand Zarina's rapid-fire French. Friedrich's native tongue was German, and, like most of his countrymen, he was fluent in English. He was less self-assured in French. He spoke it about as well as I did, which was to say, while he wasn't clueless, he was far from articulate. His wordlessness fed Zarina's anger.

I intervened. "Zarina, let me explain."

Her command of English returned, and she told me to shut up. She paced across the length of the room, swiveling her long neck from side to side as she looked into each corner. I followed the direction of her gaze. I had no idea what, or whom, she was looking for. If anyone other than the three of us were present, there weren't many places for that person to hide. The loft held very little private space, other than the bathroom. The kitchen was open, separated from the main room by a narrow counter. Even the room divider that partitioned off the sleeping area was only four feet high.

Friedrich followed her and put a hand on her shoulder. "Zarina, you have to listen to me."

Figuring they'd be more inclined to talk if I weren't so obviously listening, I moved to the opposite end of the loft, which was long and narrow. Floor-to-ceiling windows looked out on a building that was the mirror image of Friedrich's, and, like him, the residents of the fifth-floor apartment across the street had left their windows bare. I walked a few paces to get a better view of two guys watching television and drinking beer.

The floorboards creaked and I turned quickly, remembering I couldn't completely discount the possibility one of them—or the two of them together—was guilty of murdering Arianna. If they perceived me a threat, singly or in tandem, they might decide to murder me.

Perhaps I was overreacting to the potential danger they posed. But if so, my paranoia served an important purpose. It reminded me of why I was there. Someone hated or feared Arianna enough to kill her. If I could convince Friedrich of my innocence, he might be willing to give me some insight into her life and her apparently senseless death.

I stopped worrying Friedrich would think I was eavesdropping. Better to be rude than dead. But for the moment, Friedrich presented no risk. He circled around Zarina and talked to her in a low, soft voice. The absence of rugs, curtains, or much furniture made the loft an acoustic marvel. I could not only hear both of them talking, I could practically hear them breathing. Since Friedrich was looking intently into Zarina's face, and she was avoiding his eyes by examining a light fixture on the wall four feet over his head, I was able to openly observe them.

Without moving his gaze from Zarina's face, Friedrich jerked his head in my direction. "She's leaving. You know I would never, *ach*, I would never."

Zarina snapped her fingers at him. "What I know? I know you are a liar. I

want to know what is she doing here? First Arianna, and now this—this—"
She struggled to find a word in any language that would adequately convey
her contempt for me.

Friedrich's tone changed from placating to ugly. "Don't talk to me about
Arianna. Unless you want to talk about Colbert." He seized her hand, the
one with the sparkly ring. "Or explain to me about that nasty Russian you
were seeing on the side."

Zarina said, with quiet intensity, "Did you forget about our…" Her voice
trailed off.

Friedrich gave her a warning look, and she pressed her lips together and
was silent.

I wanted badly for her to keep talking. What was it that Friedrich forgot?
Were they having a meeting, a date, an assignation, a poker game?

Friedrich said "my love" when I arrived, so presumably he'd been expecting
Zarina. Of course, he referred to everyone—male and female—as love, or
girlfriend. But the possessive nature of the words "my love" sounded more
intimate than the all-purpose darling, or *schatz*, or *amante*, or *chérie*.

Friedrich broke the impasse. "I didn't forget anything." He pointed
his thumb in my direction. "She just showed up. Probably to beg for
performance time. I'll get rid of her."

As he had done so often during his brief tenure at American Ballet
Company, Friedrich humiliated and infuriated me. I'd never begged for
anything in my life. I itched to tell him what I thought of him and ached to
punch him in the nose. But I had a job to do, and that job required diplomacy,
even if I had to swallow a thousand unfair and unwarranted insults.

Although I had hoped to get Friedrich alone, it occurred to me that having
Zarina witness our conversation might force our ballet master to speak
more truthfully than he otherwise would have been compelled to do.

Without meaning to, I'd caught both of them off guard, and it was possible
I'd get more information from them together than I would separately. The
last time I spoke to Zarina, she told me she was involved with at least
two beautiful men. Presumably, one of them was the tragically poisoned
Valentin Shevchenko. Or, as now seemed likely, Friedrich. If she'd lied about

her lovers, perhaps she'd lied about other things. Perhaps she'd lied about everything.

Eschewing diplomacy, I addressed my question to Zarina but watched Friedrich equally closely. "I need information about Arianna. And some people think you two know a lot more than what you've said about it."

Scarlet with rage, Zarina didn't answer.

I kept going. "Who do you think killed her? Assuming, of course, that neither of you is guilty."

Friedrich answered for both of them. "You. We think you did it."

Zarina looked less resolute, but she didn't debate him.

I acted more calmly than I felt. "And I think you did it. Maybe you were in on it together." I switched my gaze to Zarina. "Maybe you were jealous of Arianna. You do know she and Friedrich were sleeping together, right?"

With a fierce cry, she flew at Friedrich.

With some difficulty, he kept her from slapping him across the face, but he couldn't slow her down. "Zarina! She is crazy! I didn't—I wouldn't—And anyway, what about you and *das schwein*, Colbert?"

Screeching at the top of her lungs, Zarina broke free of Friedrich's grasp, ran to the kitchen, and started throwing random items at him. He dodged two cups, a dinner plate, and a can of beans. The two of them gave a credible imitation of a crazy foreign movie from the sixties.

Friedrich pleaded, "*Halt!* Stop! Not true, my love—I not—"

And then my cell phone rang. Zarina paused, mid-throw, to listen to my conversation.

"Where are you?" Barbara sounded out of breath.

"Why? I'm kind of busy right now." Given the circumstances, I wasn't giving away any information to my mother. Even if her call hadn't interrupted Zarina's frantic assault on Friedrich, I was very conscious of Barbara's mental state. Ever since the murder, she'd become even more anxious than her normal one-tick-away-from-panic mode.

Barbara yelped, "It's almost seven! Melissa is going to be speaking any minute now. You were supposed to meet us here thirty minutes ago. Your father is pretending to be calm, but that's only because he's got his wife, the queen of deep cleansing breaths, with him. Honestly, Leah, I don't know what he sees in Ann."

Guilt hit me hard. I was so consumed with my problems I'd forgotten about Melissa's book reading.

"I'm on my way. I got stuck, uh, on a small project. Five minutes, I promise."

It would take a New York Metropolitan Transit Authority miracle to get me from downtown Brooklyn to downtown Manhattan in under a half hour, but the truth would have been worse than the lie.

My mother wasn't so easily put off. "Where are you?"

"What? Losing you." I clicked "End" and ran out of the apartment just as Zarina opened the kitchen drawer and began tossing silverware, presumably looking for a knife. Despite the thick walls of the elevator shaft, I heard Zarina's screams all the way down to the first floor. I nearly broke my ankle sprinting to the subway. If my luck held—actually, since my luck was so bad it would be better if it didn't hold—I'd arrive at the bookstore by the time Melissa was introduced to the crowd.

I clattered down the steps to the subway and, with inches to spare, hurtled myself between the closing doors. As the train swayed and screeched, I reviewed every conversation I'd had with and about Zarina. She was at the center of every conflict and every relationship in Paris and in New York. And maybe in Saint Petersburg as well.

Chapter Twenty

I danced from the moment I could stand.
— Anna Pavlova

I entered through the back of the room where Melissa was scheduled to speak. Behind her was a large poster advertising her latest bestseller, *Classical Philosophy and Raising Gifted Children.* My father and mother were in the front row with Ann, my father's unflappable second wife. Ann, of course, was also my stepmother, although that wasn't how I thought of her. I considered her marriage to my father as a brief way station while Dad sorted through every philosophical ramification of divorcing my mother.

David Sharon, my orthopedist brother-in-law, was standing in the back. Melissa said it made her nervous to have him too close. After a fawning introduction from the owner of the bookstore, Melissa began reading. She looked a bit nervous, in her very pretty, nonthreatening way. She practiced this speaking style after people complained she seemed to think she was so much better than everyone else, to which I said, h*ello?* She was better than everyone else. Smarter, more accomplished, and more competent than the average goddess. I should know. And so, in typical Melissa fashion, she analyzed her problems with public speaking, spent hours perfecting her delivery, and ended up being so good she could have taught Dale Carnegie a thing or two. Now, the ordinary people who heard her speak wanted to be like her and no longer resented her extreme competence.

In a clear voice, Melissa said, "What can Aristotle, a man who lived more than two thousand years ago, tell us about raising gifted children? First of

162

all, he did tutor Alexander the Great, who was, well, pretty great." This line earned her some laughter and light applause.

I was so proud.

She continued, "He taught Alexander about ethics and about political theory. He taught him science and literature and philosophy. Not a bad place for the average parent—even those residing outside the hallowed halls of New York City schools—to start." Melissa paused for another round of laughter. "But putting that aside for a moment," and here Melissa put down her notes and looked directly at the audience, "for Aristotle, happiness was the greatest good, and isn't that what we want for our kids?"

At this point, the audience broke out into another round of applause.

I glanced over at Melissa's husband. David's mouth was set in a grim line, but that might have been his way of not looking so proud he was ready to burst. I was. Ready to burst, I meant. Not for the first time, I was in awe of my big sister. I could dance at Lincoln Center in front of thousands of eager and critical ballet fans. But the thought of having to speak in front of one comatose audience member gave me the shakes. Melissa looked as relaxed as if she were having a cup of coffee in Barbara's kitchen. Actually, more relaxed than that. Our mother could be...demanding.

I didn't think anyone except David saw me enter, but Melissa gave me a wide smile.

She broke off her discussion to say, "Before I continue, I want to thank some very special people in the audience. My parents, first of all, who were the best teachers anyone could ever have. And also, the best writers. You'll find my dad's books in the philosophy section of most universities. And my mom, Barbara Siderova, is well represented in the mystery section downstairs. I also want to thank my husband, David."

There was loud applause and a craning of necks, as Barbara and Jeremy half-rose in their seats to acknowledge the crowd. David didn't budge, and Melissa didn't point him out.

"Lastly, Leah Siderova, ballerina and sister extraordinaire."

I'm not sure I could describe what happened next. There was a rumble of conversation that grew louder and louder. I didn't wave or acknowledge

Melissa's encomium. That last word was hers, not mine, of course. She was the one with perfect SAT scores.

Then someone on the aisle pointed me out.

"There she is!" The people standing near me drew back. The audience in the last few rows stood up to get a better look. Scraps of conversation got louder, and the murmurs became shouts.

"She's the one."

"Yeah, I know. The one who stabbed whatshername. The kid."

Melissa tried to get the audience's attention, but they ignored her. We needed a bouncer, but all we had were two bookish employees, who looked as if they'd rather be reading. Or waiting on a TSA line at the airport.

More and more people stood up, facing the back of the room instead of the dais, where my sister stood.

Melissa said, "Okay, everyone! Now, about Aristotle and happiness. His ideas about happiness, about, er, happiness..."

I took a step or two backward, toward the exit. I tripped over someone's toes and turned around to apologize. The empty space behind me closed. Even in Barbara's high-heeled shoes, I couldn't see around the throng of people.

"Hey! Leah! Tell us what happened? You do it, Leah?" The voice was taunting, challenging.

What kind of group was this? Where were the literate, well-mannered people who normally attended Melissa's readings? I'd seen gentler crowds outside Madison Square Garden during hockey season.

It was kill or be killed. I pushed through the mob and ran. Incredibly, two giggling women pursued me. I ran past the subway and ran past the bus stop. I was at Sixth Avenue before I slowed down. When I turned around, my pursuers had vanished.

I waved wildly at an unoccupied taxi. Perspiration dripped down my back and beaded on my forehead, but my brain was frozen. Rational thought would have to wait. I gave the driver my address and reached over to turn off the automatic news feed. My hands were sweaty, and the damned button wouldn't work. The reporter's authoritative tones boomed through the car.

I wiped my sweaty hands on my pants and tried again.

A softly lit image of the fountain at Lincoln Center filled the screen. In the background, the Metropolitan Opera House glowed. The Chagall paintings weren't visible on the screen, but I knew they were there, a gift to everyone lucky enough to enter that red and gold and crystal palace. The image—so soothing to my wounded soul—made what happened next doubly painful.

A picture of me replaced the one of Lincoln Center. It wasn't a picture that made me look beautiful, or kind, or exotic. An outtake from one of the ballet company's group photos filled half the screen. My eyes were half-closed and my mouth was half-opened. To make matters worse, the picture must have been taken on a humid day. Strands of hair escaped from my bun and spiraled around my face. I looked like a demented witch of limited intelligence.

A thin blonde woman in a very short, bright purple dress announced from the other half of the screen, "Leah Siderova, ballerina with the American Ballet Company, is the prime suspect in the murder of Arianna Bonneville, who was an up-and-coming dancer with the company. Sources at the ballet company say there was bad blood between the two and that Ms. Siderova, who has had a long career at the company, was angry at being pushed out by a younger and more talented dancer."

The camera panned to the co-anchor. "What do we know about this woman?" he asked the blonde. "Are the police close to an arrest?"

In authoritative tones, Ms. Purple Dress answered, "The police aren't talking just yet. But sources say Ms. Siderova had plenty of reasons to want revenge. She was the first person taken in for questioning."

A video of Uncle Morty and me, taken outside the precinct on the day Arianna was murdered, unfolded. I looked scared and guilty.

The cheery young man said, "Thanks, Heather. And now we have an exclusive interview with Grayson Averin, noted dance critic for the *New York Times* and last year's winner of the Pulitzer Prize. Mr. Averin, are you there?"

I stabbed the off button again and again, but I couldn't get the horror to stop. "Cabbie! Can you turn this thing off, please?"

He flicked a glance into the rearview mirror. "Sorry, lady. No can do. Just press the button."

I was in Taxicab Hell. If there was a God, and He or She wanted to punish me ahead of some Judgment Day, surely the time I spent trapped in the taxi would suffice. I couldn't have felt more shame, even if I'd been guilty.

I was ready to throw myself into oncoming traffic in order to get away. But I didn't. And I stopped trying to turn the newscast off. If I wanted to defend myself, I had to know what I was up against.

The grainy image on the video feed showed a photo of Grayson. I recognized it as the publicity shot on the back of his latest book on ballet.

The newscaster said, "Hello? Mr. Averin?"

"Yes, Ned. I'm here."

"Mr. Averin, you reported on the stabbing of Charles Colbert, the ballet master of the Rive Gauche Ballet. And now, Arianna Bonneville, a ballerina with our very own American Ballet Company, is dead. Tell us about the high-pressure environment in these big dance companies."

It crossed my mind that Averin had better watch how he answered that question. He made a lot of people angry with his most recent book, *The Life of Ballet and the Ballet of Life*. Most of it was a hagiographic ode to his favorite dancers, but other parts were quite dismissive of several popular modern choreographers. And he was positively snarky about the idiosyncratic dancers who performed in those avant-garde choreographers' companies.

Grayson was a ballet purist. He adored George Balanchine, and he shared Balanchine's aesthetic about the most desirable body type for ballerinas, i.e., long limbs, long neck, long hair, big eyes, and a small head encased in an elongated ninety-pound package. To be fair, he had given me some excellent reviews over the years, but he also wrote, on more than one occasion, that I was miscast in a role that he thought was meant for someone taller. And, of course, there was his most recent review of me, in which he hinted my retirement wasn't long off. Good reviews or bad, I loathed him.

Grayson's first words were rendered incomprehensible by static. If only the rest of what he said were similarly blocked.

But loud and clear, he pronounced, "Leah Siderova is a friend of mine."

We were never friends, I silently screamed at the image on the screen. With confidence, he said, "I know her well."

Not true! You know nothing about me!

"So, it pains me to say this." He didn't sound pained at all. He sounded pleased. "She did have a very contentious and competitive relationship with Ms. Bonneville. I can't say much about her relationship with Charles Colbert, but unlike other dancers in American Ballet Company, she was not asked to take part in his new ballet. I think that says something right there—there was bad blood between them. Whether that pushed Ms. Siderova to murder Mr. Colbert, I can't say."

This was horrifying. And completely untrue—Charles had asked me to dance in his ballet, and only my knee injury prevented me from taking part.

The reporter looked serious and concerned. "We all know the dance world is in an uproar after two attacks in one year. Three, actually, if we count the poisoning of Valentin Shevchenko, the superstar of The Maryinsky Ballet."

The screen changed again, to a picture of Valentin in an airy leap above other dancers, blonde hair gleaming and muscles rippling.

Grayson answered, "Of course, the ballet world is competitive. But most dancers are generous. When the time comes for them to go, some are ready and some are not. The best become coaches and teachers. Not killers."

"Thank you, Mr. Averin. We appreciate your time."

"My pleasure, Ned."

Mournful music from "The Dying Swan" by Camille Saint-Saëns filled the taxi, as an angelic picture of Arianna slowly came into focus, her birth and death dates scrolled across the bottom.

I told the cabbie to pull over, even though I was still ten blocks from home. I didn't want to puke in his nice clean car. He took the money from the slot and turned to thank me for the tip. His eyes squinted and then widened.

"Hey! Are you that, whadayacallit? The lady that—"

As soon as I got out of the car, I threw up. It was a most effective way to end a conversation.

Chapter Twenty-One

A pas de deux is a dialogue of love.
— Rudolph Nureyev

I didn't run the rest of the way home, because Barbara's shoes had gotten so tight my swollen feet threatened to split them in half. I slunk down the darkest part of every street and kept my head low. No one paid any attention to me, because it was too late for ogling construction workers to be on the job, and they were the only New Yorkers who didn't mind making eye contact with strangers.

In the safety of my apartment, I considered various painkillers. Excedrin for my headache. Or maybe Advil for my sore muscles. But what hurt most was my heart, not my head or my feet. I mixed a shot of gin into some diet tonic water, even though I knew liquor wouldn't help much. Although I had a very low tolerance for alcohol, I couldn't get drunk. After two drinks I got dizzy and sick. Matt often teased me, saying I was a very cheap date.

Matt. Did he know? I wondered where he was and what he was doing. Was he telling Gwyneth about me? Did he confide to her, as he had to me, that I had "something missing?" As time passed, I grew to loathe him more, not less. When I told him I wasn't ready to get married, he decided there was something wrong with me, as if he were such a prize only a crazy person would refuse his offer.

Two sips into my gin and tonic, and long before I could calm down, my cell phone rang. I didn't recognize the number and didn't answer it. It rang a second time with the same number, which, upon further inspection, did look vaguely familiar, but not familiar enough for me to pick up. The mystery caller left a phone message, but I didn't check the voice mail. I didn't want to talk to anyone. Maybe a fairy godmother, but the odds of one of those calling was very small.

A text message flashed from the same number. **Hi Leah, it's Zach Mitchell. From the hospital. Let me thank you by taking you out for dinner.**

The afternoon I mailed Dr. Mitchell's daughter a tiara and a signed program felt like ancient history. In the intervening days, I'd nearly forgotten about him.

I didn't answer him immediately, because I could think of only two reasons for him to call me. One: Dr. Gorgeous didn't watch the news and lived under a rock. Two: He watched the evening news and was titillated by reports of my guilt. Maybe he was going to take secret pictures of me and sell them to a tabloid. Lurid headlines flashed before my eyes, rolling from an ancient printing press, the way they did in old movies. "The Doctor and the Deadly Dancer." Or, "Ballet Bombshell Reveals All to Shocked Doc." Admittedly, I was too skinny to be a bombshell, but tabloids weren't known for accuracy.

The phone clinked again. This time the only thing on the screen was a line of question marks. If Zach Mitchell had used emoticons, I would have ignored him. But those question marks—seven of them—they made me laugh. And I did like odd numbers.

I could have ignored him and spent the next few hours having a nervous breakdown. As I debated whether or not to answer him, the phone flashed again. **Meet me at Louie's? 77 & B'way?**

God forbid. What if we met someone I knew? What if we met someone I didn't know, but who recognized me? After that news report, was there a safe spot in New York City?

I knew the answer to that question, so I texted **Meet me here. 30 minutes.** And I sent my address. I knew meeting him was foolish. But maybe, for the next hour or so, I could pretend to be living the life I used to have.

I swooped through the apartment. Drying tights and leotards went into a bin in my closet. The morning coffeepot got a cursory wash. I showered with military brevity and ran a brush through my hair.

What to wear? Nothing fancy. I didn't want to look as if I were trying too hard. Skinny jeans and black tank top struck the right balance between not caring and not obsessing. As always, it was the shoe choice that took time.

I slipped on a pair of clogs. Even though Zach Mitchell was a doctor, and presumably had seen many horrific sights, I didn't want to test him by having him see my feet before we got a chance to know each other. Not that there was much chance we would get to know each other, but I wanted to give myself a fighting chance. It sounded crazy that I was worried about how my feet looked, but I was happy to grab at any pretext to ignore what loomed ahead of me.

In the five minutes I had left, I troweled makeup over my ashen skin and bloodless lips. Even when I wasn't terrified, I was unhealthily pale, a consequence of my battles against the sun. The one day I agreed to go to the beach with Matt, I used extra protective sunblock and a hat. Three hours and one supersized tube of SPF-50 glop later, I had what felt like third-degree burns over every inch of exposed skin. At least my feet escaped, because he insisted I hide them in the sand. For the next month, the sunburnt line of demarcation on my ankles made me look as if I were wearing red leggings with very short white socks.

I put thoughts of Matt out of my head and busied myself washing out the glass of gin and tonic. I didn't want to look like a lush, drinking by myself. I wiped down the counters and swept the floor. There was nothing left to do, and I checked the time of the last text message. More than forty minutes had passed since he'd told me he was on his way.

Where was he? Had he changed his mind? What if the cab he was in showed the same news story that sent me running? The scene I'd endured at the bookstore was humiliating, but that was nothing compared to the thought that everyone I knew, not to mention all the strangers who now knew me, saw me featured as the next candidate for *America's Most Wanted*.

As if reading my mind, my mother, my father, my sister, and Gabi called. I didn't listen to any of their voice mails but sent a group message I was asleep and would call them in the morning. Then I turned off my phone.

The doorbell rang, and I pressed the button for the intercom. I opened the door to listen for Zach's footsteps and offer encouragement. Most people needed it by the time they got to the third floor. It wasn't easy to bound up five flights of stairs, and neophytes were usually near comatose when they get to the top.

Zach wasn't winded at all.

But I was. One look at his dark blue eyes and curly dark hair and slight shadow of a beard on his narrow cheeks, and I was done for. For the first time in a long time, it wasn't anxiety, fear, or overstretched ligaments that weakened my knees.

I didn't know why, but I wanted him. Wanted him so badly I couldn't keep looking at him. I kept very still as he traversed the narrow hallway. He was good-looking. But that wasn't it. I'd had plenty of attractive lovers who wooed me and beguiled me and delighted me in bed. And that was in my off hours. When I was working, beautiful men wrapped me in sensuous—if highly choreographed—embraces.

Zach wasn't nearly as handsome or sexy as many men I'd known. But the last time I felt so irrationally drawn to a guy, I was fourteen. The guy in question was skinny Alan Lipschitz, who sat next to me in gym class and held my hand with sweaty passion. We hid together in the stairwell and he stuck his tongue in my mouth. It didn't end well, but that was a long time ago.

"Have you made up your mind yet?"

I realized my guest was waiting for me to let him into the apartment. He carried two shopping bags and a cardboard tray with four cups. I stepped aside and gestured toward the kitchen. Not that he needed a map. The whole apartment, fire escape included, didn't measure more than four hundred square feet. I peered inside one of the bags.

"I thought you might need supplies. I brought one latte, one espresso, one regular black coffee, and one black decaf. There's milk and sugar, too."

"Black, thanks."

He looked pleased. "I had you pegged as a black coffee drinker. I am too.

171

But considering the hour, I thought you might prefer a drink. I brought wine. One bottle of red, one of white, and one champagne." He put them on the counter.

"You're like Santa Claus. What's in the other bag?"

He coughed and didn't answer right away. I waited. It wasn't as if I had any other appointments. I still wasn't sure why he called me or what he was doing in my apartment. But I didn't care what brought him. Despite the love and attention my parents and Melissa and Gabi lavished upon me, it had been a long and lonely few days. Weeks. Months.

"I know ballerinas aren't supposed to eat, but on the off chance you're hungry, I came prepared." He unpacked bread, cheese, and a box of chocolates and laid them out with geometric precision on the table. I looked at the beribboned box of candy and back at Zach. For the first time in my life, I wanted to devour the man first and the chocolate second.

I took out two wineglasses. "I still don't get it. You finished your shift at the hospital and decided to bring fattening food to me?"

Zach turned to rummage in a drawer. He pulled out a corkscrew. "Red wine okay?"

"Of course. I'll pour the wine. You answer the question."

I mentally urged him to tell me that ever since he first laid eyes on me he couldn't put me out of his mind. That he was overwhelmed with desire for me and couldn't think about anything or anyone else. What other explanation could there be for coffee and bread and wine and cheese and chocolate? They were the foods of love. Of seduction.

"The excuse I was going to give you was to thank you for sending that picture and signed program to Elizabeth. She's been wearing the tiara you sent her everywhere she goes. That was very thoughtful of you."

I put down the wineglass. "You said that was the excuse. What's the real reason?" Again, I imagined him telling me I had bewitched him. That he was burning with desire.

Zach took my hand. An electric shock passed through my palm. He jerked a bit. He had to have felt it too. But he didn't say any of the things I wanted him to.

No, what he came out with was "I was on my way out of the hospital when I saw a picture of you on the news. I realized then why you had your panic attack. You should have told me you had a precipitating event."

It figured. I was swimming in visions of us in bed. But all he felt was pity. Maybe he was worried I'd sue him for malpractice.

As if I hadn't a care in the world, as if Zach were as important to me as the delivery guy from the supermarket, I said, "I didn't know doctors still made house calls. I'm sorry you had to climb all those stairs for nothing, but I'm fine. I don't need your help." I began packing up the food.

He stayed my hand. "I thought you could use a friend."

I stepped back and put my hands on my hips. "What makes you think I don't have friends? I have all the friends I need. So, thanks for thinking of me, but would you mind taking this stuff with you? I'm not hungry, and it would only go to waste."

He sat down. "I've offended you. I didn't mean to. I really do want to help."

"For God's sake, why the hell do you want to help me? You don't know me at all. And I don't know you."

I was so angry and disappointed I could have cried. But I didn't cry. Because I had too much pride and self-control to allow myself to cry in front of any man. I certainly wasn't going to break down in front of some smarmy doctor who thought all he had to do was show up at a woman's apartment and she'd gratefully throw herself at him. I walked to the front door and opened it.

He didn't take the hint. He closed the door and went back into the kitchen. This guy was way too confident. But what could you expect from men these days? Finding an unattached, good-looking man with a healthy income is like finding a Prada handbag for twenty dollars at the thrift store. It wasn't likely. It could only happen once in one's lifetime, and you'd probably have to pry it from some other woman's clutches.

In spite of his charms, I was prepared to toss Dr. Zach Mitchell back to the resale bin. If only he would stay tossed.

He leaned forward. "Please, Leah, hear me out."

"No." I walked back to the door and held it open.

He put both hands on the table. "You are the most stubborn woman I've ever met."

"Yes, I am. Please go."

He gave up. "Fine. I'll go. But first, if you ever need anything, you have to promise you'll call me. Any time."

"Why should I call you?"

"I don't know. Maybe because I want to see you again. But not as a patient."

I opened my mouth to speak. With the gentlest and briefest of touches, he put two fingers across my lips.

"I'm going, Leah Siderova. The offer still stands."

He walked out. After he left, I still felt the press of his warm fingers against my mouth.

And yet, it was Jonah's face that came to mind.

Chapter Twenty-Two

When you do dance, I wish you a wave o' the sea...
— William Shakespeare

I drank some of the wine and ate two chocolates, but I didn't enjoy them nearly as much as usual. Despite the late hour, I called Uncle Morty, who had phoned three times while Zach was at the apartment.

"Morty, did you see the news? What did you tell them? Tell the police, I mean."

"I told them I'd bring you in tomorrow morning. No cameras, no press. I'll have a car waiting. We'll use a back entrance. It's all arranged. Do you want to tell your parents, or do you want me to do it?"

I felt as if I were drowning. My limbs were heavy, as though I was moving through water, and my throat narrowed to a vanishingly thin circumference, too narrow to permit air into my lungs.

"I can't do it, Morty. I can't do it."

His voice was calm. "You have to. It's the only way. I'll call Jeremy and Barbara. We'll figure out bail. You'll be out the same day."

"What if I don't get bail?"

There was a long silence. My eyelid started twitching with a life of its own. I'd never had nervous tics before. The form my nervousness took made me feel even more vulnerable. What if other people saw the eye spasms? What if my own body betrayed me—made me look guilty when I wasn't?

My heart thumped painfully in my chest. I ignored the feeling of an imminent heart attack and reminded myself it was a panic attack—painful, but not fatal. How long could I control myself?

"Morty, I can't talk right now. I'll call you later. Don't call my parents. I'll do it."

"Sure thing. Any time. I'm here for you. Big day tomorrow, so you should get some rest. Me too. I need my beauty sleep, haha. So, if I don't answer my phone right away, I'll get back to you. Meantime, I'll pick you up at your apartment tomorrow morning. Ten, so you can sleep in. Don't forget, okay?"

I hung up on Morty. How was I supposed to respond? With calm agreement? With a promise I wouldn't forget I had an appointment to be charged with murder?

I spent the next hour saying goodbye to my life.

I wasn't very domestic, but it was the homely things I knew I'd miss. I would miss the smell from the coffee grinder and my French press coffee maker. Admittedly, my coffee didn't equal Barbara's, but it's good. Better than many a five-dollar cup from a micro-ground, locally sourced café, and I didn't have to put up with the bored and disdainful baristas.

I'd miss waiting in line at the grocery store, alongside customers who acted as if the fate of the free world depended on whether they bought food that was fair trade, organic, or free-range, non-GMO. Not for the first time, I wondered if they served coffee or Diet Coke in prison.

Most of all, I'd miss my family.

I called my father, but not to give him the bad news. That could wait until the morning. I knew there wasn't the slightest chance my parents were watching television or checking social media. Let them have one more night of relative peace.

I steeled myself to patience as I listened to a phrase from Bach's Sixth Brandenburg Concerto. Dad answered the phone seconds before the recorded message would have kicked in. He sounded out of breath.

"Are you okay, Dad?"

"Of course, darling. Completely fine and fit."

"Well, you're breathing kind of hard."

His huffing lessened. "No worries. I didn't want to answer the phone in front of my students."

"Dad, I'm so sorry! Call me back when you're done."

"Don't be ridiculous. This isn't a class. A few of my students dropped by to discuss whether or not we can experience life objectively."

I couldn't help smiling. Dad's endless parade of students, who loved to drop in on him at all hours of the day or night, used to drive Barbara crazy, but I always found their discussions interesting.

Jeremy cleared his throat. "Your mother and I called you many times after you left the reading. Melissa feels terrible about it."

My hands shook, but I kept my voice steady. "I'm fine, Dad. I'm just checking to see how you and Barbara are making out, in terms of finding a defense lawyer with a bit more experience than Uncle Morty. If you haven't found anyone, I think Gabi may know someone. I was going to talk to Madame Maksimova too. She's pretty well-connected."

Dad paused before answering. "Now, Leah. Morty may be a little rough around the edges, but he's smart and he's good. Never doubt your family."

"Of course not. So...did you get any names?"

"Yes. Claudia Espina. Best in the business. Maybe you saw her on the PBS program? She's the one who got those two kids in Alabama released from death row."

Death row. New York didn't have a death penalty, but still.

Despite the September heat, goose bumps popped out on my arms. "She sounds great, Dad. Do you have her number handy?"

"Yes." I heard the shuffle of papers, and, after a few minutes, my father recited the number to me. He warned, "She's in the Hamptons until next week. I think it's next week. Maybe the week after. She's usually back in the city by now, but she had that big case. You know the one. Those Somali immigrants? Anyway, she's going to call me back when she returns. Nice woman. Very interesting. Very smart. She's from Brooklyn—grew up in the projects, not far from us. So she's got street smarts and legal smarts."

I'd heard her name before, perhaps because she was occasionally in the newspaper and on television. I tried to keep my tone casual. "Is it possible to find out exactly when she'll he be back?"

Dad's voice sounded too calm. "Why? What's happening?"

"Nothing to worry about, Dad. Love to Ann. Talk to you soon."

"Love you."

The next task was no less painful. I called the automated message center for American Ballet Company and pressed a button that recorded my need for a personal day. Which was the truth. Not that they cared. Friedrich would probably throw a party if I called in sick for the rest of all time.

My phone pinged and chimed and buzzed with unanswered messages. Gabi, my parents, Uncle Morty, Melissa, and Madame Maksimova left multiple voice mails and texts. Well, Madame didn't text. But the others persisted. I didn't call anyone back. There was no point. They couldn't make me feel better, and whenever we spoke, I felt obliged to make them feel better.

I pulled the covers over my head and waited for morning to come.

After two restless hours, I finally fell asleep, only to wake up at 4 a.m. The sound of a bell alerted me to the fact that my voice mailbox was full. Over and over I erased messages. One of the messages was from Dr. Zach Mitchell. My finger hovered over the choices: Speaker. Call Back. Delete.

I hesitated over the Call Back option. So tempting. He did say he wanted to help.

Reality punched me in the face, and I hit Delete. Who was I kidding? My next dinner date wasn't going to be with Zach Mitchell. It was going to be with my new friends at the Bedford Hills Correctional Facility.

As had been the case since I found poor Arianna, I struggled with nausea, a headache, and a depression so deep I couldn't remember what it felt like to be happy. If I really tried, I could dredge up memories of my former life, but they felt as if they belonged to someone else. It seemed like a million years ago—and unutterably trivial—that I used to worry about my weight.

Ironically, since the murder, the flesh on my bones had evaporated. The bathroom mirror revealed purple circles under my eyes, along with cheekbones so prominent they gave me a skeletal look.

What was going to happen to me? Would I be arraigned? Would I be able to meet bail? Would I even get bail? A quick internet search taught me most people accused of murder were remanded to prison. No bail. But didn't Morty say the charge would be manslaughter, and not murder?

I felt so sorry for my parents. They didn't deserve this. They'd always loved me and supported me. And my poor worried sister, whom I'd never properly appreciated. I sent a silent apology to all of them.

Trembling, I searched various websites. The New York State Penal Code. What to expect when you're expecting to be charged with a Class A, B, C, D, or E felony. I learned about bail, arraignments, and grand juries.

Once again, I thought about the person I used to be. That pretty woman, whose most pressing problem was finding a low-calorie/low-carb salad dressing. She was as dead as Arianna.

And then I saw it. On a bail bond site, a stern warning spoke to me. It said no one should allow a loved one to spend the night in jail. It said jail was a dangerous and brutal place and should be avoided if at all possible. I knew this, of course. But the grim cast of the words terrified me beyond reason. I slammed the lid of the laptop shut.

It was then I decided to run away. If the police weren't interested or capable of finding the real murderer, I had to. Why would they continue to investigate if they thought they had the culprit?

Madame Maksimova was right. No one outside the rarified world of professional ballet would ever understand the driven souls who gravitated toward this most punishing and satisfying profession. If I were remanded to jail, I couldn't investigate.

Don't get me wrong. I wasn't exactly elated at the idea of going on the lam. I was a rule-following, law-abiding person who caved in the face of authority. But I had no choice. I simply didn't have the courage to go to jail and didn't have faith that the legal system would provide justice.

I pulled a backpack, circa high school, from the back of the closet and considered what to take with me for life on the run.

I stuffed a few T-shirts and one sweatshirt into the backpack. A pair of jeans, a pair of yoga pants, a leotard and tights, and some underwear. My toothbrush and a few travel-sized toiletries. And my pointe shoes. I couldn't completely let go of my identity. After some hesitation, I turned off my cell phone and put it in the backpack. I had no plans to use it, but I couldn't let it go. I figured I could pick up a burner phone, even though I didn't yet know what a burner phone was.

Going undercover in New York City would be difficult. Despite my recent disgrace, Lincoln Center still had a life-sized picture of me on a prominent billboard. Even worse, American Ballet Company purchased ad space on the side of buses to promote the fall season but saved money by using photos from last year. One of them was a close-up of me. Only a blind person could miss tracking me down. And then there was the little matter of my cameo role on the late-night news.

I went to the corner drugstore and used cash to purchase sharp scissors, cheap plastic sunglasses, a fanny pack, a baseball cap, and spray-on hair color. I lingered over shades of blonde and red and punk-inspired purple. In the end, although it pained me considerably, I chose pale silver—almost white, but not quite.

One of the hardest things about that whole experience was cutting my hair. I'd had long hair my whole life. But it had to go. I steadied my hand and started cutting. When I was done, foot-long strands of dark brown hair sat in a plastic bag, and my chin-length hair was gray. My head felt naked and vulnerable. Part of my armor was gone.

Under normal circumstances, I wouldn't be caught dead wearing a fanny pack—but if ever there was a fanny pack moment, this was it. I put bank and credit cards and money and tissues in the pack. I rolled a sweater around my waist and put a shirt on top of the sweater.

The added bulk around my waist concealed my figure. All I needed was a garish T-shirt and I would be indistinguishable from hordes of tourists who descended upon New York. If I needed a safe place to rest and think, I could take a tour bus or that awful four-hour boat ride around New York. I would blend right in.

What I needed was money. I figured I could do a one-time bank withdrawal, but any bank activity after ten would tip off the police to my whereabouts. After my purchases, I had about three dollars left in my purse. I doubted I could get more than a thousand dollars from the ATM, but perhaps, I wouldn't need much more.

With considerable difficulty, I composed a letter to my parents. I knew the police would see it, and I feared giving away any information. In the end, I simply wrote that I loved them and that when I found Arianna's killer, I'd be back.

I said goodbye to my apartment. It wasn't much, but it was my home. I tried not to think about whether or not I'd ever see it again. I transferred pots of basil and cilantro and marigolds from the fire escape to the kitchen. For Barbara, I cleaned and polished and swept. My mother would be very upset if complete strangers witnessed dusty woodwork or a smeared mirror.

The sky was dark with clouds. I switched off the light in the front room and peered out the window. Remembering the damning evidence of the video cameras outside the ballet studio, I worried about which apartment buildings recorded street traffic. I silently cursed myself for effecting my transformation at home. My disguise would do me no good if the police already knew to look for a woman in a fanny pack with short gray hair.

I finished packing and once again looked out the window. Despite the early hour, several pedestrians were on Eighty-Ninth Street. And a lone man, his hat pulled low over his forehead, loitered outside the building across the street. Too bad I couldn't call Jonah to report him. I was positive he was the same guy who'd stalked me before.

I saw nothing and no one in the back of the building, but that didn't mean someone wasn't on the lookout. Or was I being melodramatic? Surely New York City police officers were too busy to worry about a runaway ballerina. Nevertheless, I couldn't risk leaving through the front door. That left the fire escape.

I stuck my head outside the window and then drew back. I was afraid of heights, yes, but my reluctance to exit via the fire escape wasn't simply a case of acrophobia. Every single landing was illegally congested, and neither my landlady nor the New York City Housing Authority had bothered to keep our fire escapes up to code. Until I moved them inside, I had several plants on my fire escape, and the tenants below me had also appropriated the extra six square feet as a de facto backyard, with everything from unicycles to shopping carts cluttering the space.

The slats on the fire escape were rusty, but at least I'd had a recent tetanus shot. I'd hate to escape prison only to die of lockjaw. Worse, if the rungs of the ladder were as rusty as the slats on the landings, I could end up a pile of crushed bones.

I placed a cautious foot on the landing and edged toward the ladder, keeping close to the building. With one hand pressed against the brick wall, I reached the other to the rusty rail. From that position, I was in no danger of falling, but I was too dizzy to walk without holding onto something.

Two steps down a gust of wind blew past me with unexpected force, and my hands froze. I was so terrified I'd fall, I couldn't move. I didn't know how long I stood there, hugging the fire escape ladder and unable to go either down or up.

By herself, Leah Siderova would never make it to safety. But the Firebird—she could soar past mere mortals and, like a phoenix, rise from ashes. I hummed Stravinsky's urgent and compelling score, and the music gave me courage. Slowly, I uncurled my fingers from the rusty rails. I took one cautious step after another, gripping the corroded metal of the ladder as I inched my way down. The steps creaked with alarm at my puny weight, but they held—at least the ones from the fifth to the fourth floor did. And if I made it that far, I could make it to the bottom.

I peeked down toward the third floor and paused. The light was on. It wouldn't be good to be arrested for trespassing while trying to avoid arrest for murder. Or did Morty say manslaughter? It made no difference to my resolve. Prison wasn't for me.

I made out the sound of running water. Good! My neighbor was in the shower, and, thanks to the low water pressure in our building, he was unlikely to emerge quickly. I took small careful steps around Mr. Leonardi's unhealthy-looking begonias, small folding chair, and metal bucket, which made a horrendous noise when I banged into it. Terrified that Mr. Leonardi would think I was a Peeping Tom, I dispensed with humming Stravinsky's music and raced down to the second floor.

The second-floor apartment was empty. The landlady was renovating it, hoping to capitalize on the tight rental market.

The first-floor apartment belonged to the landlady. She spent most of the summer in her country house, but I knew she was back in residence. If she were awake, I'd have a hell of a time slipping past her. For security reasons, the ladder for the lowest fire escape didn't reach the ground. You had to ride it down. Given the state of the structure, it would wake even the soundest sleeper. I tiptoed on sneakered feet to the last leg of my trek toward freedom.

I lowered the ladder six inches, to horrific screeching of metal against metal. A light clicked on inside the apartment. No time to figure this out. No time to remember how scared of heights I was. I was seconds away from a full-blown panic attack, which would make running away extremely difficult. An inability to breathe was a definite liability when you were trying to break the fifteen-minute mile.

A male voice yelled at me and asked who the hell I was. I was shocked. I had no idea my landlady had a boyfriend. Good for her. Not so good for me. I bade farewell to West Eighty-Ninth Street with a most graceless exit down a very dangerous fire escape ladder. If I ever got to move back in, I would definitely complain.

I climbed over a crumbling wall in the rear of the building and landed in the yard of the apartment house that backed mine. I had to traverse a narrow alley to the street, which tapped into yet another of my favorite phobias. I was terrified of rats, and the alley was lined with garbage cans. Holding my breath, and looking neither right nor left, I sprinted the whole way, until I reached Ninetieth Street, where I slowed to a walk. Runners, if they weren't in workout gear, attracted attention. Anyone else was probably a criminal or the victim of a crime. I was disguised as a middle-aged tourist, out for a morning stroll, not a potential marathon competitor.

The real test would come at the end of the street. If I could fool Mr. Kim, the owner of the bodega on the corner of Broadway, I had a good chance of getting away. He told me many times he never forgot a face.

I kept my pace slow. Mr. Kim was outside the store, sweeping the street. I stared straight ahead, but, from behind the dark glasses, I watched him. He paused, leaned on the handle of the broom, and waited for me to pass. He glanced at me without interest. First test passed.

With nothing to do except go undercover, avoid arrest, find a murderer, and prepare for possible incarceration, I took my time walking crosstown. Construction workers at a large building site looked past me. No whistles, no lewd remarks, no snapping fingers, no, "Hey, baby! What's your rush?" Inside my short gray hair, baseball cap, fanny pack, and bulked up sweatshirt, I was an invisible woman.

One store after another offered the kind of comfort that would have tempted me under other circumstances. Pizza. Bagels. Cupcakes. Ice cream. Chocolate. Wine. Not to mention the relaxation that nail salons and day spas and massages advertised. Things for real people. Not phantoms.

It was at that point I got angry. The person who brutally took Arianna's life also took mine. I had to find him. Or her.

Chapter Twenty-Three

A star danced, and under that was I born.
— William Shakespeare

I still had a brief window of time before I was officially avoiding arrest. My first stop, after a quick visit to the ATM, was the Seventy-Ninth Street entrance to Central Park. The Museum of Natural History wasn't yet open, but plenty of people crowded the steps in front of the building. I pretended to examine the banner of a blue whale that hung from the arched entryway. It wasn't difficult to get into the role of a tourist. Although I'd lived in New York City my whole life, I never tired of its wonders.

I anxiously paced back and forth, ignoring the flood of people exiting the subway and the waiting tourists, and concentrating on finding one familiar figure amid the usual throng on a New York City street. I needn't have worried. Madame's morning routine never varied, and she and her dog Froufrou stood out in the crowd. In a city where half the pedestrians were bent over their phones and the other half were staring at the sidewalk, Madame kept her chin high and her back straight. She suffered from arthritis in her hips and knees, but while the pain slowed her down, it didn't make her any less graceful.

She crossed the street and headed into the park.

Keeping a few feet behind her, I waited until there wasn't anyone close by. "Madame, I need to talk to you."

She turned and looked at me blankly then summoned the smile of a woman too polite to say she didn't recognize me.

The success of my disguise made me feel a bit safer, but the loss of my former self was jarring.

I took off my baseball cap and sunglasses. "It's me, Madame. I need your help."

Madame looked shocked. She tilted her head and poked a finger into my padded middle. "My eyesight not good, Lelotchka. And what happened to your so beautiful hair?"

I feared Madame would be angry with me, or disapprove of me, or be disappointed in me. But if I didn't tell her about my imminent arrest, she'd find out from the radio or television instead of from me. "It's complicated, but the short version is I'm leaving town for a while. I don't want to be recognized, and that's why I changed my appearance. I have to find the killer, and I won't be able to do that from jail. So, I need a few things from you."

Madame looked left and right and waited until a very slow runner passed us. "Anything. I will do anything. But you must be careful! Killer is out there and may go after you."

Somehow, when Madame said the words I'd already said to myself, the result was more chilling, more threatening.

"I will be careful. I promise." I hesitated. "I am sorry to have to ask this, but could you lend me some money? I got some money from the cash machine, but I won't be able to get any more until tomorrow. And I'm guessing that by tomorrow my account will be frozen. If you call my mother, she'll pay you back."

Madame searched her handbag. "Here." She handed me a platinum American Express card. "Take this."

I was touched by her confidence. "Thank you so much, but I can't do that. Please. I will walk you to an ATM. I want to use cash as much as possible."

Madame didn't hesitate. She gave the leash a slight jerk, and Froufrou obediently turned away from some attractive-smelling grass.

Madame wanted to wait until the bank opened so she could give me more money, but I told her I wouldn't need more than a thousand. Again, she offered me her American Express card. "Just in case."

I took the card and blinked back tears. "Don't forget—have Barbara give you back the money."

She frowned. "Money not important. You important. Where you going? What else you need?"

I debated telling her the truth and ended up saying, "I'm going to New Haven. To Yale."

Madame held my arm. "What is in this place that is not in New York?"

"I'm going to see a lawyer. My father has already spoken to her about taking my case."

She kept her grip on my arm, as if fearful I would bolt. "You not have to go this moment. Why you rushing off like this? Come upstairs and I will make you nice breakfast. We can talk. Gabi will come too. You can tell me all what you want to do."

"I'd love to, Madame, but I have to get going. I, uh, I'm supposed to get arrested today."

She searched my face. "Is this running away Gabi's idea? Why you not talk to me about this plan? Does your mother know about?"

A flood of guilt washed over me. Then I reminded myself that while I could convincingly dance the role of a sixteen-year-old Sleeping Beauty, in real life, I was no kid. Like it or not, I was an adult, and I had to decide for myself the course of my life.

"Barbara doesn't yet know where I'm going." I peeled Madame's fingers from my arm and held her hand to keep her from gripping me again. "I'm not going to ask you to keep my secret. If the police question you, you can tell them the truth. I don't want to put you in an awkward position."

Madame lifted her chin. "I not tell. They can torture me. I still not tell."

I laughed for the first time in days. "That's nice, Madame, but this isn't Soviet Russia. And you were a member of the Maryinsky Ballet, not the secret police." I bent to kiss her goodbye, and she made a last effort to hold onto me.

"What I should do? I made long talk with Zarina, like you say. She have witness and she not guilty. So what next?"

I caught a whiff of Madame's perfume, and the day I found Arianna came back to me with vivid force.

"Madame, please find out, if you can, who wears Joy perfume, besides you. Someone who was there ahead of me was wearing that perfume. I'm sure of it."

She pressed her lips together. "Could be anyone. I tell you already, that not a good clue."

I smiled. "Just find out for me, will you?"

She bowed her head gracefully, as she used to do to her adoring fans. "I will do this. But that so little. I must do more. I am positive perfume will not help. Everyone wear perfume."

I had to think of something to distract her. For an old lady, her grasp of my hand was surprisingly strong. I cast about for a job to give her. "Talk to Grayson. See what information you can get out of him."

Madame looked puzzled. "The writer? He can help?"

"I don't know. But he gets around."

Madame still looked uncertain. "I will say to him...what?"

"Don't worry. Just start talking about Friedrich or Zarina. Or anyone. Invite him to The Russian Tea Room. He'll love that."

"I will do these things. I will call you after I do this and tell you all I find out."

I squirmed out of her grasp, telling her I had to catch an early train.

Madame wanted to help me, and the only graceful way to detach myself from her was to give her something to do. That was why I told her to call Grayson. But the more I thought about it, the more annoyed I was that after his television appearance I hadn't immediately confronted him myself. I'd let my insecurity and my pride and my fear get in the way. But no more.

I reminded Madame she could—and should—tell all interested parties where I was headed. Hopefully, the police would soon learn I was on my way to Connecticut. Because, while they searched Grand Central Station and the Metro North trains, I would be on my way to New Jersey.

Melissa's suburban mansion wasn't my final destination. I had to get to Paris, and I couldn't do that without my sister.

I debated the safest way to cross into New Jersey, worried about the presence of video cameras in the Port Authority Bus Terminal and at Penn Station. Neither Mr. Kim nor Madame had recognized me, but they weren't expecting to see me. Jonah Sobol, and his more belligerent sidekick, Detective Farrow, would scrutinize every passenger caught on tape. Most of my information about these devices came from television. Would the New York Police Department have face recognition software? That possibility chilled me.

I took a cab to Times Square, where I bought a burner phone, a wig with long brown hair, and a bright red leather tote. For the next thirty minutes, I had to look like myself. I locked myself in a Starbucks bathroom, where I put the wig on and removed the padding from my waist. My backpack and fanny pack and the sweater I wore under my T-shirt went into the tote. From a distance, the wig resembled my hair before I colored it gray and cut it.

Across the street from the old-world elegance of Grand Central Station I used my cell phone to call Claudia Espina, the lawyer my father recommended. I googled her name before I called her. Her resume was impressive. I got Claudia's voicemail and left a brief message. I did so only to leave further evidence I was going to Connecticut. If I had to involve yet another innocent person in a police investigation, at least the one I'd chosen was well equipped to handle herself. Claudia was one tough lawyer.

There was no point in doing things halfway. I went into the terminal and used my Visa card to purchase a round-trip ticket to New Haven. I got in line and boarded the train. Shortly before it left the station, I wedged my cell phone into the seat cushion. In the tiny bathroom, I removed my wig, padded my middle, put my baseball cap on, and prayed New Yorkers' famed disinterest in strangers would protect me from curious onlookers. I walked from car to car until I got to the end of the train.

Two minutes later, I was back in the terminal, once again a chubby, gray-haired matronly tourist in a fanny pack. With the addition of red plastic sunglasses, I didn't even recognize myself.

I called Melissa using the burner phone. Of course, she didn't answer. No one wanted to answer a caller whose name came up as blocked or unavailable. I left a message and prayed she'd listen to it. I waited five minutes and called again.

"Hi, Melissa, it's Sarah." I waited for her to register my voice.

Her tone was uncertain. "Where are you...Sarah?"

"Is anyone near you?"

Her voice was low. "I'm in the faculty lounge. If you wait a minute, I'll go outside."

I spoke in a rush. "I'm in transit, and I don't have a lot of time. I called to remind you not to forget about our meeting. We're all getting together to meet for coffee, after we drop the kids off after school. I may be a bit late, but I'll meet you at that place that serves the amazing iced lattes. If there's a problem, just text me."

Three hundred seconds passed. Also known as five minutes.

And then, the response. "I'll be there."

I shouldn't have doubted Melissa. Of course, my darling, brilliant sister remembered that our father's nickname for me was Sarah Bernhardt. Dad was endlessly amused at my childish flair for melodrama. Poor man. He could hardly have guessed his adult daughter's real life would provide enough fodder for a dozen soap operas.

Chapter Twenty-Four

Dancing is divine in its nature...
— Plato

My disguise was good, but it didn't help my mental state. Passing cop cars terrified me. Even uniformed security guards made me nervous. Hell, the sight of a random person in a dark blue shirt was enough to make me sweat. I ducked into a diner and sat in a tiny booth, facing the rear of the restaurant, where I forced myself to eat most of an egg and two slices of toast. I'd been brought up to think of carbohydrates with the same horror other people viewed heroin, and I mentally apologized to my mother for the lapse in dietary law. But my brain needed something to work with. In the ballet world, there was no such thing as being too thin, but even I could see I'd lost an unhealthy amount of weight.

Should I—could I—risk going to Penn Station or Port Authority? It was still too early for the police to have put out an all-points bulletin for my arrest. I was worried about myself, yes. But I was more worried about my sister. I didn't want to do anything that might direct suspicion toward Melissa.

As the last bite of bread hit my stomach, I got an idea. The Chinatown bus. As I knew from countless flyers, for twelve dollars, I could get a bus from Chinatown to Atlantic City. They'd even throw in sixty dollars' worth of casino credit. I called Melissa again.

"Hi, Melissa, it's Sarah again. I was thinking about our meeting today. Maybe you could get someone to pick up the kids after school and we could meet at a different place."

My sister's voice sounded guarded. Background noise suggested she might be in her classroom. Melissa said, with forced calm, "I can free up the whole day. I'd love to meet you. Should I, ah, meet you at your place?"

If ever I needed sisterly ESP, it was then. "I don't think that's a very good idea. You know how hot it's been at my place. It's so hot I can't stay there."

There was a brief pause. "Yes, it has been so hot for September."

"I've been very uncomfortable. And the AC is broken. I'm talking about the cheap machine I bought on *Atlantic* Avenue. I thought *Atlantic* Avenue would be a good place. But now I have to go back there to get it fixed. *AC* is the most important thing in my life right now."

I heard the clatter of a coffee cup. "I know the place you're talking about. It's pretty far from me—from us."

"I know. I'm sorry about that. It might take me a while to get there, so we should meet later—I'll get in touch again about the exact time. But the kids are taken care of, right?"

Melissa's voice sounded muffled. "Yes. I'm supposed to leave for Paris tonight, and my nanny is already here. But I will skip the Paris conference. Anything you need, I can do."

"Glad to hear it. Listen carefully. I have to go to the grocery store to pick up a few things. Like milk and juice. Did you know Tropicana juice is on sale?"

"Um, no. I didn't know that."

The puzzled tone in her voice worried me. "Well, there's a big sale. Right now. *Tropicana*. You know that's my favorite brand. I'll meet you as soon as I deal with getting the AC taken care of. If you want to, we can go to the grocery store together. I'll meet you by the orange juice. I have a coupon for the Tropicana."

Her voice trembling, Melissa said, "I know Tropicana. Are you sure you want to meet today? Maybe...maybe tomorrow morning would be better. I will call the organizers of the conference and tell them I can't make it. You told me you had work to finish. You know it's not good to procrastinate. Sometimes it's better to face things, no matter how bad. Because if you avoid those unpleasant…things, that could make everything worse. Much worse."

I knew this had to be tough for Melissa. Like my mother, she was eternally right and good and proper. But I was fighting for my life. And I needed her help.

"I understand everything you're trying to tell me. But sometimes putting things off is the only option. Anyway, it's not what you think. Trust me, I'm taking care of business. But first, I have a date with some orange juice."

Melissa's voice, while still very soft, was unwavering. "I'll be there. But let's have a cocktail instead of coffee. We can be bad moms and meet in the bar."

Smart woman. Neither of us had ever been to the Tropicana casino, although we had visited Atlantic City as kids. We could have wasted hours circling the place. Now, without risking further contact, I knew to meet her at the bar.

Whatever reservations Melissa may have had concerning my decision to run away, I knew she would never let me down. A rush of affection swept through me so strong it brought tears to my eyes. What did people do who didn't have sisters? There wasn't another person on the planet who, having understood my arcane references, would drop everything and drive to the Tropicana Casino in Atlantic City in order to rescue a criminal sister on the lam.

I put earbuds in my ears and kept my head down all the way to Canal Street. Chinatown buzzed with the sound of sidewalk vendors. Piles of merchandise from shops selling live fish, jade jewelry, and cheap trinkets spilled onto the street, and the spicy smell of delicious food billowed from the many restaurants.

It wasn't hard to find the bus stop. In the middle of the chaos, a group of mostly elderly people arrayed themselves in a single line. Many wore hats and T-shirts that proclaimed them the best grandma or grandpa. A few had the foresight to carry canes that opened up into chairs.

I hoped for anonymity, but as soon as I took my place in the back of the line, a cheerful chubby woman detached herself from her companions and turned to me. "First time?"

For a moment, I didn't understand the question. She was patient, and once I got over the irony of her query, I answered, "Yes. Yes, this is my first time."

She gestured toward two ladies. "We go every month. I'm Ruth. This here's Eileen and that's Miriam. You stick with us. We'll show you the ropes. It's no fun going by yourself." She clucked sympathetically at me.

The last thing I needed was companionship from three elderly women, but there was no graceful way to refuse the offer. I figured I could always ditch them later. We had a long bus ride ahead of us, and I felt awkward enough.

The women looked expectantly at me.

Ruth said, "And what's your name?"

I froze. I forgot about that part. What was my name going to be for the next few hours? I looked at the Jade Luck jewelry shop across the street and stammered, "Jay—uh—Jane. Jane Gold. My name is Jane Gold." The ladies didn't look satisfied, and I didn't blame them.

Eileen harrumphed. "Are you sure you're not a spy? And using a fake name? Like maybe Mata Hari?"

The ladies laughed, but they did look uneasy.

I wiped my eyes. "I'm getting divorced. Actually, to be perfectly honest, my husband is divorcing me. So, I, uh, I'm going back to my maiden name. It's going to take some getting used to."

All three women shook their heads in evident compassion.

Ruth said, "Bastard. You should forgive my French. What was it? Another woman?"

Either I'd so totally entered into the part of the wronged wife, or I was so emotional the smallest prompt was enough to make me cry. I wiped my eyes again. "Women. More than one."

I doubted there was anything else I could have said to them that would have more thoroughly won their friendship and their sympathy.

Eileen patted my shoulder. "Lemme tell you something, Janey. Don't you pay him no mind. But make sure you take him to the cleaners. You stick with us. You got any money? We usually take fifty dollars. Sounds like a lot, right? But you don't wanna lose more than that, unless you're made outta money. You're not made outta money, are you?"

I shook my head. But a tiny smile did relax my face. Even if I had been made out of money, I wouldn't have said so. For once in my life, I wanted to be one of the girls. Even if the girls in question were old enough to be my grandmother.

Miriam looked at my backpack. "I hope you have food in there." It sounded like an accusation.

"No, I don't have food in there."

All three became upset.

Miriam worried. "You'll be hungry! You don't want to have to buy food in Atlantic City. It's not cheap, you know. Go buy something there." She pointed to a Chinese takeout joint a few doors down.

Ruth brushed off Miriam's suggestion. "Whaddaya mean? She don't want no Chinese food." Ruth patted me on the back. "These buses, they never leave on time. Anyway, doll, we won't let them leave without you. You got time. Go to the deli around the corner. Good bagels."

"Thank you so much, but honestly, ladies, I just ate."

The three women looked at me blankly.

Ruth flicked a look at Eileen. "What about later? What you gonna eat later?"

Eileen eyed me so intently I got nervous. She scrutinized my face and then stared suspiciously at the padding around my waist. Just as I was about to get the hell out of there, she said to Dorothy, "She's skinny. It's not healthy. Poor thing."

To all this I had no answer. Ruth, who seemed to feel responsible for me, pulled out a foot-long sandwich wrapped in greasy paper. It smelled strongly of salami and garlic and pickles. "Tell ya what, honey, seeing as this is your first time in AC, I got plenty here and I'll share with you."

Rendered speechless by her generosity, I could only nod in acceptance.

A cloud of poisonous-smelling exhaust from the back of the bus blew toward us and temporarily ended the discussion about food. I followed

Ruth, Miriam, and Eileen onto the bus.

The seating arrangement on the bus, like the lineup before we boarded, was divided by gender. The men sat in the back and the women in the front. In the midsection, two young couples and a few middle-aged men provided a human Mason-Dixie Line. Despite the rigid separation of the sexes, there was plenty of back and forth chatter and movement. We hadn't even left before Miriam walked a few rows back to give her husband his medication. She refused to leave until she saw him swallow the pills, which, for some reason, irritated him.

"What? You think I'm a baby?" he yelled. She patted his head as if he were two, which made him yell again. "Next time, I'm going by myself! I'm going to pick up women. I'll find a young babe who doesn't bother me."

This too didn't seem to disturb Miriam. She made her cautious way back to her seat. "I think he's losing it."

From the back of the bus, he yelled, "I'm not losing it! You're losing it. I'm gonna have to put you in a home. And then I'll have sex with the nurses."

Miriam maintained her good humor. She confided to the bus at large, "If he has sex with anyone, it would be a miracle."

Her husband, who either ignored her comment or didn't hear it, yelled again. "Who's your good-looking friend? Tell her I'll be free in another two months."

Miriam didn't look like a woman on the brink of divorce.

"Is he kidding? You're not going to divorce him, are you?" I framed the last sentence as a question, but if I were she, I would have dumped the guy sometime around the Johnson administration. Having only seen my parents' fiery relationship, and Dad's preternaturally calm marriage to Ann, I had no idea what was going on between them.

Miriam pointed to her gold wedding ring. "We've been married for almost fifty years. In the Jewish religion, you have to get married again. Otherwise, we'll be living in sin. We're planning a big second wedding, even though he wants to elope to"—here she laughed again—"Atlantic City!" She yelled, "Hey, Mike. You got lucky when you met me! I coulda done a lot better."

Ruth joined in, "Never you mind about Mike. Keep your good luck for the slots."

This brought an almost prayerful atmosphere to the bus, as everyone thought about the importance of good luck.

There were some hard-eyed gamblers on the bus, in addition to my self-appointed fairy godmothers. Several men studied the racing form and talked of daily doubles, exactas, and horses that "liked the mud." A few women with elaborately painted and decorated nails studied books with titles like *How to Win at Blackjack*. Ruth, Eileen, and Miriam sipped cardboard cups of coffee and showed off pictures of their grandchildren.

I closed my eyes and began plotting the next few days. I prized my independence, but I had no choice. I would have to depend on other people to help.

And even if my plan didn't work, it would keep me out of prison until Claudia Espina, Dad's hotshot lawyer, returned from the Hamptons.

Chapter Twenty-Five

Dance like nobody's watching.
— Satchel Paige

The bus lumbered in fits and starts through the streets of Chinatown. As we approached the Holland Tunnel, and my escape from New York, the driver hit the brakes right in the middle of the intersection of Sixth Avenue and Canal Street. The honking and yelling from blocked cars and infuriated drivers grew to an operatic crescendo, but I was the only one inside the bus who seemed to mind. The driver calmly fiddled with the radio, and the passengers on the bus viewed the tumult with pleased interest.

Miriam kept a close watch on traffic and Ruth began a silent countdown. After two minutes and three seconds, both women let out a whoop of delight and began high-fiving all the ladies on the bus.

"Ladies, we are winners and we haven't even gotten to New Jersey yet!"

Grumbling, each man forked over five dollars. When we got to the other side of the avenue, the mood was festive on the feminine side of the bus.

Miriam's husband warned, "I wouldn't party too soon, ladies. There's always next time."

Miriam patted his head. "We've got a coupla side bets to help pass the time. If it takes more than two minutes to cross Sixth Avenue, we win. If it takes more than fifteen minutes to get into the tunnel, the men win. But a little birdie told me"—she tapped the side of her nose—"it's clear sailing all the way to Atlantic City. Next time we'll deal you in."

Despite Miriam's rosy report on traffic, the bus came to a halt. And stayed halted.

Flashing lights circled from four police cars that stood guard at the entrance to the tunnel. I slid my baseball cap over my forehead and slumped down, cursing myself for taking a seat by the window. A city bus, going in the opposite direction, stopped to pick up passengers. On the side of the bus, an advertisement for American Ballet Company's upcoming season took all the space from front to back. The ballerina, in a glittering tutu and sparkling crown, soared above a swirl of smoke. It was the Black Swan. The dark and deceitful swan queen, who took the white swan's identity and fooled everyone. Me.

Ruth followed my glance. "You like the ballet?"

I choked a bit, willing her to look away from the picture of me. I nudged closer to her, trying to block the view from the window.

Ruth narrowed her eyes. "Hey, honey, whatsamatter? You don't look so good."

To my horror, she reached over and touched my gray hair. She pressed her lips together and stared straight at me.

Ruth said, too quietly for anyone else to hear, "You're not running from a husband, are you?"

Eileen seemed unaware of anything other than her satisfaction with being proved right. "It's like I said, she don't eat, she don't feel good."

Ruth took out her sandwich again. She pulled off a four-inch section and waved it at me. "Here. Eat. You'll feel better. Trust me."

I shook my head, because I didn't trust myself to articulate a calm answer. I couldn't resist peeking through the window again. The bus with the picture of me was frozen in place, and the police were only a few yards away. We lurched a few feet toward the entrance to the tunnel and hit a pothole. The resulting jolt provoked an earthquake in my stomach that registered at least a seven on the Richter Scale. The smell of Ruth's salami paved the way for a number of secondary seismic shocks so nauseating I feared if I opened my mouth, I would throw up.

Miriam said, "Put that thing away, Ruth. She looks like she's gonna puke.

Honestly, the smell of all that garlic on top of this crappy stop-and-go traffic is making me feel like puking, too."

What made me think I could elude the New York City Police Department? I wasn't street smart. I never even went to college. As every boyfriend I'd ever had has told me, I knew very little about life in the "real world."

The bus inched closer to the cop cars. I put my head between my knees, partly to hide and partly to avoid fainting. The last thing I needed was to be evicted from the bus and sent to a hospital. I stared at the faded blue threads of my jeans and counted backward from one hundred. When I got to eighty-seven, I made up my mind. Unsteadily, I walked to the exit doors at the back of the bus.

I had one hand on the door handle when someone grabbed my shirt. I spun around to find Ruth's eyes looking deeply into mine.

She whispered, "I know who you are. I seen the picture of you on the bus. And on the TV. Don't you go anywhere. Eileen, Miriam, and me—we got your back, honey. No one's gonna mess with the three of us. You gotta get to New Jersey? We'll make sure you get there."

I was terrified. "What—I don't know what you mean. I don't feel well. That's why I want to get off the bus."

Ruth again put a finger next to her nose. "Bad idea. You'll be all by your lonesome. Trust me. Me and my friends. I take one look at your face, and I know you're no criminal. Probably couldn't hurt a fly."

I was a block away from the Holland Tunnel, but miles away from freedom.

Very gently, Ruth said, "Don't be scared of no police cars. They're always here, blocking traffic instead of getting it to move faster. You get off the bus now, you draw attention to yourself. Too risky."

I was paralyzed with indecision. If I stayed, I'd be trapped on the bus. If I exited, I'd be trapped in New York City.

Ruth said, "You come with us to Caesars Palace. We always go there. My husband taught Latin for a million years, and he likes the name. Then we figure out what to do next."

Her face, soft with wrinkles Barbara would never permit, comforted me. I longed to spend the day with her, gambling at the slot machines and eating salami sandwiches. But I couldn't.

"Thank you, Ruth. You've been so kind. But I'm meeting my sister."

Ruth looked worried. "You got a cell phone, right? So call your sister and have her meet you at Caesars Palace."

I hated disappointing her. I felt closer to Ruth than to people I'd known for years. "I'm sorrier than I can say. But I can't. Next time?"

Ruth hugged me back. "Yeah, sure, doll. Next time. We go first Wednesday of the month. Don't forget. We're the lucky Wednesday girls. You don't wanna go on Thursday."

Eileen, who was in the seat in front of us, turned around. "Yeah. Never on Thursday. Those gals are mean. Mean girls. Not like us."

Almost against my will, I let Ruth guide me back from the exit door. She slid into the window seat and kept a careful eye on the police. Fifteen minutes later, we passed the police cars and the flashing lights, and fifteen minutes after that the filthy tiles of the Holland Tunnel welcomed us to New Jersey. At that point in the journey, my sleep deficit caught up with me. We were nearly at Atlantic City when I slowly emerged from my nap.

Half asleep, I heard Ruth say, "No way we can let the kid go it alone. We gotta help her."

Someone, I think it was Eileen, said, "You gotta be kidding me. Bad enough you didn't turn her in when you had the chance. Maybe there's a reward. You think of that? And what if she gets caught? What happens to us?"

Miriam said, "We'll be arrested. We'll be aiding and abetting a criminal. But I still think we should help her." Her tone brightened. "We might get adjoining cells! That wouldn't be so bad."

Eileen's voice was sharp. "I say forget about the whole thing. We've been nice enough, not turning her in. Give her that stinking salami sandwich and say goodbye. That's my humble opinion on the matter."

The others disagreed in vehement whispers. "She said she ain't guilty. You wanna send an innocent kid to prison? What kind of person are you?"

Angry, Eileen said, "The kind that doesn't want to get involved with things that are none of my business. None of your business neither."

I turned around. "Please, ladies. I am so grateful to you. But Eileen is right. I don't want to involve you any further. It isn't fair to you." I took a deep breath. "I'm not your responsibility. I'm meeting my sister, and she is driving me to Philadelphia to meet with a new lawyer. I thank you for your help and your friendship. But you really can forget about me. Pretty soon, I'll have all the help I need."

Ruth was angry. "See what you did, Eileen? You scared her off."

Eileen was unrepentant. "I gotta do what I think is right."

Ruth, who seemed to be the spokesperson for Miriam, as well as herself, declared, "And we gotta do what we think is right."

Eileen fixed me with a cold stare. "Did you do it? Did you kill that girl? I'm telling you right now, I used to be a secretary for a very hotshot lawyer, now dead, God rest his soul. I know a liar when I see one. So, I'm only asking you once."

I appreciated her honestly and her caution. "I did not, and could not, murder Arianna Bonneville. But the police think I did. And the killer has set me up to be the fall guy. I'm not waiting around for someone, besides my parents, to believe me. I'm going to prove it myself. Which I can't do from jail."

Eileen's lips tightened. "Then, like Ruth said, we've got your back. Anybody asks, we never seen you or heard of you. But we'll write down our phone numbers for you. You get into trouble, you call us. From a pay phone, mind. Be smart."

Ruth and Miriam patted Eileen on the back.

Miriam said, "Eileen is the practical one. We're the dreamers."

Eileen rubbed her thumb against her other fingers, as if anticipating a payout. "Hah. Care to place a small wager on that?"

The bus lumbered up to the entrance of the Tropicana. I was shocked to see my new friends swallow tears as they said goodbye. I had barely cleared the steps of the bus when Ruth called me back.

She pressed a small cloth bag into my hand. "For the casino. You get free chips to get you started."

I tried to give it back to her, but she put both hands behind her back. "You paid for your ticket. Gotta take what's yours, doll face." She squeezed my arm and returned to her seat.

The bus roared off. I opened the bag. Instead of casino chips, the women had filled the bag with one hundred dollars in small bills. A gift from my fairy godmothers I vowed I'd repay. With interest.

The noise inside the Tropicana was of the electronic variety. Pinging, ringing, and buzzing filled the air, but there were few customers in the brightly lit halls and dimly lit bars. I hadn't counted on the Tropicana housing more than one bar, and I resigned myself to walking the length and breadth of the hotel in search of Melissa.

My first stop was a cavernous room filled with chairs of an alarming shade of orange. I strolled past three elderly men arguing over a game of pinochle and two very large young women drinking cosmopolitans and giggling. A lone woman with short red hair nursed what looked like a cup of coffee. I couldn't see her face, but I knew the set of her shoulders as well as I knew my own reflection.

The redhead looked past me. When I got closer, she started and nearly strangled me with the force of her hug. "Leah! Oh, I mean, Sarah!"

"What should I call you? Sis?" I tried to act casual, since the whole point of disguising myself was to avoid attention.

Melissa pressed her cheek against me, and her tears mixed with mine. "I'll be your other half, Sarah. Call me Bernhardt—Bernie. Call me Bernie."

I looked over at the bartender. She was reading a copy of *USA Today*. In Atlantic City it must take more than two teary women to provoke attention. Even so, I dropped some money on the counter and steered Melissa out of the bar.

She tried to take my bag, but I didn't let her. "Hey, Bernie. You look pretty good as a redhead. And I can handle the backpack myself. But let's get the hell out of here. Where are you parked?"

"Close by."

I put my red plastic sunglasses on, and Melissa followed suit with her expensive black-rimmed eyewear. I pointed to the golden "C" that sparkled from the side of her glasses. "Nice shades, Bernie."

She smiled back. "I hope yours are part of your disguise. Barbara would faint if she saw you now, even without the gray hair and fanny pack."

"Of course they're part of my disguise. You didn't recognize me, did you?"

Melissa laughed. "You didn't recognize me, either!"

"Yeah, we're quite the masterminds. And speaking of disguises, Melissa, what's with the hair?"

My sister got serious. "There are a million cameras in those casinos. I'll never be as beautiful as you are, but all the same, we do look alike."

That statement made what I had to tell her much easier. A little easier. "Listen, uh, Bernie, that's why I'm here. I need to be you for a little while. Not long. Maybe three days, tops."

She was thoughtful. "You mean, like identity theft?"

I looked at her closely, to see if she was joking, but her expression remained serious. "It's not theft. It's more like identity borrowing."

We took the elevator to the parking lot. Melissa punched at her car's remote control and the lights from a black Mercedes SUV illuminated the way.

I removed a Harvard Crimson blanket from the seat and put it on my lap. The cushioned car seats soothed the insults my back and rear end suffered during the bus ride. I rubbed my hand against the soft leather and admired the space age look of the console. The car felt as spacious as my apartment. "New wheels?"

Melissa looked embarrassed. "David bought it. It has a very high safety rating."

Melissa wasn't comfortable with conspicuous consumption, which amused me.

"Of course it does. It feels like a very padded rocket ship."

Melissa navigated her way through a narrow maze. "Speaking of Barbara."

I knew what was coming. "Were we speaking of her? Because I'd rather not, right now."

Melissa bit her bottom lip, a look I knew well. "She and Dad are frantic. They seem to think you're on your way to New Haven to see Claudia Espina. Dad must have told me a thousand times that you knew Claudia isn't back from the Hamptons. And poor Gabi. She's almost as frantic as our parents, who, by the way, have been calling her every second they're not calling me."

Sometimes you thought you couldn't get any more nervous than you were. But sometimes you were wrong. Apparently, there was always another layer of anxiety to send your pulse racing.

"Please tell me you didn't tell Barbara we were meeting."

My sister was insulted. "Of course not. I figured if you found a way to tell me to meet you, you'd find a way to tell her too. They deserve to know. No one knows where you are."

As if to corroborate her complaints, her cell phone started vibrating. I didn't want to feel guilty. But I also didn't want to give my father a heart attack. Another heart attack. And I could envision Barbara popping pills and smoking cigarettes until five, when she could justify hitting the wine. For the present, my parents were better off not knowing what I'd planned.

I slipped down in my seat as we drove out of the parking lot and put the blanket over my head. As soon as we passed, I sat up. "I feel terrible about putting Barbara and Dad through all of this. And you too, Melissa. But I don't have many choices. I can't go to jail. And I can't wait for Claudia to get back from her vacation so she can work at getting me free. I have to do this my way."

Melissa didn't answer until we got beyond the E-ZPass entrance to the Garden State Parkway. As we drove by the cameras, I again slid off the seat and curled myself into the space below. It wasn't difficult. There was so much legroom, a basketball player could have managed the maneuver.

As we eased onto the Parkway, Melissa said, "What if your way is the wrong way? What if running away makes everything worse?"

There wasn't a way to make things worse. Unless I was convicted, this was as worse as things could be. Although the temperature in the car was comfortable, goose bumps popped out on my arms, and I wrapped the blanket around my shoulders.

I tried to sound calm and reasonable. "I can't investigate this mystery if I'm in jail."

"You wouldn't stay in jail! You'd get bail. This whole scheme is crazy!"

I stared out the window. "What if I didn't get bail? What then? And even if I did get bail, I wouldn't be allowed out of the country."

Melissa clenched the driving wheel so tightly her knuckles were white with strain. "Thanks to this crazy scheme you've all but guaranteed you won't get bail. What if you're caught? How will this look during your trial? Leah, my darling, I am terrified for you!"

"I'm convinced the answer to this mystery is in Paris. I have to go there. Not to jail. I want to go disguised as you. You said yourself we look alike. I'll be back in no time."

The car veered wildly as Melissa tried to get into a lane already occupied by a Mack truck. When the honking subsided, she said, "No one at the conference is going to mistake you for me. That's ridiculous. It won't work."

I had to get her to understand the reason behind my plan. "Please let me finish. I won't be attending the conference. I just need to get to Paris. At first, when the police asked about the attack on Colbert, I ignored the obvious connections. But the detectives didn't. The two episodes became part of their narrative about me—I was in Paris when Colbert was attacked. I was at the studio when Arianna was killed. The fact that I didn't have much of an alibi when we were in Paris didn't matter at the time, because other people had compelling motives. And Colbert, forgive me, was as mean as he was good looking. After a few years directing the Rive Gauche Ballet, the police were probably hard-pressed to find people who didn't have a motive to kill him. The French police interviewed me for about ten seconds before dismissing me."

Melissa, normally a cautious driver, seemed distracted. As the road ahead split in two, she swerved left and then right, which set off another cacophony of honking disapproval from aggravated Garden State drivers. She ignored them. "I wish you could hear yourself. Then you'd know how crazy you sound. So, let me summarize what you've told me. You're now a suspect in an earlier murder attempt. You decided to evade New York City police and run away, in disguise, to Paris, where the French police will be looking for you. Brilliant. Really brilliant."

I was stung by her refusal to understand. "I have to get to Sylvain. And to any other Rive Gauche dancer who can get me information."

CHAPTER TWENTY-FIVE

Melissa burst out, "They'll turn you in! You're—you're an escaped criminal."

"I am many things, but not that. I am an escaped innocent person."

Melissa hiccupped, her sign of real distress. Around the rhythmic bumps in her chest, she said, "I didn't mean that. I meant—well, you know what I meant."

"I do. But you're my only hope, Melissa. My only chance. If you won't help me, I might as well go back and turn myself in. And all this risk would have been for nothing."

She shook her head from side to side. "That will never happen. I will never let you down."

Chapter Twenty-Six

Classical dancing is like being a mother: if you've never done it,
you can't imagine how hard it is.
— Harriet Cavalli

After an exhausting drive, we arrived at a curved street lined with enormous oak and maple trees. Bright patches of flowers bloomed on each green lawn, and it was very quiet. Melissa pulled the car into the attached garage, which was larger than my apartment.

I sat in Melissa's immaculate kitchen while she clattered about, wiping clean countertops and brushing off invisible crumbs. When she'd hunted and killed every last germ, she collapsed into a chair. "You're going to get caught. Innocent or not, you're a fugitive from justice. You've convinced yourself you can solve the murder by going to Paris. But you're running away from your problems. You know what Socrates had to say about that?"

I stroked her hair. "Socrates was unfairly accused of treason and ended up drinking hemlock, taking the rap for a crime he didn't commit. So, not the best example right now. And anyway, I know who the killer is. And I'm going to get proof and then I'm coming back."

Melissa dropped a ball of wet tissues into the empty garbage can. "Who? Who did it?"

In contrast to Melissa's emotion, I was very calm. Because after I figured out who I was looking for, I understood what I was looking for.

"Zarina Devereaux. All the evidence points to her. And no one else."

The tension left Melissa's face. "Then go to the police and tell them!"

208

If only life were that easy. "I know Zarina did it. But no one else does, and it's going to take more than my say-so to satisfy the police. That's why I need to talk to Sylvain. He was the first person the police interrogated. He was close to Colbert and Zarina. He also knew Shevchenko, the Russian dancer who was poisoned the same night. I'll get him to talk to me or die trying."

Melissa leaned forward and put her head in her hands. "How can you be so sure Zarina did it? What if you're wrong? What then?"

Melissa's questions scared me. "Zarina lied about everything. Every single thing out of her mouth was a lie. I need to break her alibi."

My sister didn't look disbelieving, but she didn't look convinced. And if I couldn't win her over, the likelihood I would be able to persuade anyone else was vanishingly small.

I spoke with more confidence than I felt. "Zarina told me, and presumably the police as well, that she didn't arrive in New York until after the murder. But Madame Maksimova said she had lunch with Zarina before the murder. Why would Zarina lie about when she arrived? Obviously, she had something important to hide. Otherwise, she would have been at the rehearsal with the rest of us."

Melissa didn't seem impressed. "Being a liar isn't the same as being a murderer. And how do you know Madame wasn't the one who was lying?"

I couldn't help laughing. "Madame? That's impossible. Madame isn't a suspect. In fact, she offered to go to Paris for me."

She spoke very slowly, and looked at me full in the face. "Why has Madame been so helpful? Why has she been so eager to get involved? Barbara told me Madame has had many problems lately with the company and with Friedrich." Melissa pounded the table. "Don't you see? She started this whole ridiculous investigation in order to keep an eye on you so you don't get too close to the truth. A real friend would have told you to hire a professional detective."

My heart started racing, and, despite the cool temperature in the kitchen, trickles of perspiration crawled down my back. "What possible reason could Madame have for killing Arianna?"

Melissa was eerily calm. "That, we don't yet know. Here is what we do know: The day Arianna was murdered was also the day Madame didn't show up for company class. And you have only Madame's word for why she wasn't there. I don't see any reason why Zarina would murder Arianna. But let's say you're right and Zarina did murder Arianna. Maybe Madame is pretending to help you but is really on Zarina's side."

Here I was on firmer ground. "Skipping over the fact Zarina was in New York when she said she was still in Paris"—I ignored Melissa's headshake and kept going—"Zarina said Friedrich was pursuing her, was jealous of her, and wanted a relationship with her. But when I went to Friedrich's apartment, and she showed up, it was clear she was the jealous one. She was so angry I thought she was going to stab me. Or Friedrich."

Melissa's mouth was set. "I still don't hear a motive, Leah."

"Don't you see? Colbert cheated on Zarina with Sylvain. Colbert gets stabbed. Friedrich cheated on her with Arianna. Arianna gets killed. It all fits. Especially when you add in the fact Arianna was competing with Zarina for the lead role in Bryan's ballet. I'm worried Zarina will attack Friedrich next. Or Bryan. She's obviously out of control."

With annoying logic, Melissa observed, "I seem to remember you telling me that no one would kill for a role in a ballet, no matter how big the role was."

It was no fun arguing with a philosophy major and all-around genius. "I also said the murder was personal. It wasn't just the role. It was also that Arianna was sleeping with Friedrich. And honestly, please forgive me speaking so ill of the dead, Arianna was an incredibly nasty human being. She was cruel when she didn't need to be. She enjoyed it. I think she went too far with Zarina, and Zarina made her pay for it."

Melissa rubbed her forehead, perhaps to get a few more of her Ivy League-educated brain cells working on the problem.

After a few moments she said, "If someone has to go to Paris, it should be me. It'll be less risky for both of us. You can tell me who you need to talk to and what you need to know."

I wasn't sure about many things, but I was absolutely certain about this.

"No, Melissa. I have to go. I can't ask anyone, even you, to rescue me. I have to rescue myself."

Melissa creased her brow, something neither of us did often. Barbara taught us this habit made wrinkles. I smoothed my sister's forehead for her and massaged her scalp. She laughed. She knew exactly what I was thinking.

But she didn't give up her argument. "Be reasonable, Leah. What do you expect to find in Paris? Your suspects are all in New York."

"The suspects are in New York. But the evidence is in Paris. Paris is where Colbert was stabbed, and that's where all this started."

Melissa didn't seem convinced, but at least she was listening. "The dancers at the Rive Gauche Ballet know you. Do you honestly think you can talk to them, disguised as me? If they recognize you, they'll notify the police. And if they don't recognize you, why would they talk to some random person? I fear for your safety. You should be doing the same."

I tried to shrug off her concerns. "If anyone recognizes me, I'll figure out some plausible story. Or I'll get the hell out of there. And stop worrying quite so much. You're making me more nervous than I already am."

Melissa sat back, deflated. "You have all the evidence you need. Why won't you see what's right in front of you? You told me that when you got to the costume room, you smelled Joy perfume. You also told me Madame wears Joy. She's the one who did it. And you're too stubborn to see it."

Two hours and many arguments later, Melissa reluctantly agreed to let me take her identity. But she had yet to give me her passport or her plane tickets. I didn't blame her, but I also couldn't see any other way forward.

I showered, shampooed the gray out of my hair, and rummaged through my sister's closet for some clothes. As a final touch, I cut bangs, in imitation of Melissa's hairstyle. My already awful haircut looked even worse, but it had the benefit of hiding the top half of my face.

Melissa's pants and shirt were laughably baggy, but I wasn't going to Paris to attend a fashion show. I padded my middle once again, cinched a leather belt around my newly expanded waistline, and covered the whole sartorial disaster with a long bulky cardigan. Then I lugged Melissa's neatly packed suitcase into the trunk of the car.

To my surprise, she wheeled out a second suitcase. "Melissa, I'm only going to be in Paris for a short time. All I need is an overnight bag."

She shrugged and didn't answer.

The set expression on her face warned me not to question her further. I placed the extra bag in the car and sat in the passenger seat. Melissa organized everything so well. There was no way she'd listen to a relatively disorderly person like me.

Before going to the airport, we stopped by the bank. She parked on a side street instead of using the drive-thru so I could avoid the cameras, but I hid under the blanket just the same. When she returned, she handed me a thick wad of bills.

"I'll pay you back," I told her, even though I knew money wasn't what was worrying her.

Her grip tightened on the steering wheel. "Don't insult me. You know I don't care about the money. I care about you."

Now came the hard part. "And I care about you. So please, take this." At the next red light, I handed her Madame Maksimova's American Express card and all of the cash she'd just given me. I'd realized, finally, the extra suitcase was for her. Once I left for Paris, she too would have to go undercover. And when she did, she wouldn't be able to use either her credit cards or mine.

She tossed it back in my lap. "The only place for this card is the garbage can. Whichever one of us uses it will probably get arrested."

As we approached the red light of a busy intersection, instead of slowing down, Melissa executed the infamous Jersey slide, screeching across two lanes of traffic and pulling into a gas station. Without bothering to explain her maniacal maneuver, she held out her hand. "I changed my mind. Give me Madame's credit card. And while you're at it, give me yours as well."

I handed them to her, nervous about her suddenly erratic behavior. "Sure. No problem. As a matter of fact, it's good that we stopped. You should give me your passport and ticket now. I don't want to leave without them."

"You're not getting my passport or my tickets. You're not going."

She crossed her arms and stared straight ahead as I pleaded with her. "You said you'd help me! This is the only chance I have! Do you want your only sister in prison? What changed in the last hour?"

Melissa was deathly pale. I tried to force her to face me, but she kept her head averted. Worse, she began to hiccup, an indication of how distressed she was. She pressed her hand against her chest. "Nothing has materially changed. Your plan is good. But I will go and pretend to be you. Same idea. But better."

Weeping, I entreated her, "I can't let you take that risk. What if I'm wrong, and the murderer is in Paris? Or hunts you down, thinking you're me? You're a mother. You can't take that risk."

For a moment, Melissa wavered. But even the thought of Ariel and Benjamin didn't change her mind. She held her breath, trying to stop the hiccups. She finally exhaled. "Let's be practical. First of all, I speak French and you don't." She nodded in anticipation of my outraged objection. "Yes, I know you speak enough French to get by, but you're not going to France to sit in a café. You need colloquial French to talk to Parisians. And you have yet to master the subjunctive."

I got out of the car and started nervously pacing around the parking lot. When I was in the grip of extreme emotion, I had to move.

After five minutes of breathing in gasoline fumes and car exhaust, I returned to the car, opened the trunk, and removed the backpack I'd brought with me to New Jersey.

Melissa ran out of the car. "What are you doing?"

"I'm going back to New York. If you can get me to a bus stop or train station, that would be great."

Melissa beamed. "Exactly! That's my plan."

Wrangling with a genius sister wasn't easy. It was like trying to find size six shoes at a sample sale—frustrating, futile, and fraught with danger. Slowly, in the manner of a kindergarten teacher talking to a recalcitrant five-year-old, I said, "Let's be clear about this. Your plan is to pretend to be me pretending to be you?" I grabbed her shoulders, forcing her to look at me. "Not a good idea, Sis, since by now an all-points bulletin has gone out for my arrest."

She looked smug. "The APB is for you, not me. Don't you see? We follow your plan, but we do it my way." She reached into my bag, extracted the wig with long brown hair, and placed it on her head. "Don't I look like you now?"

I was startled at the likeness. "Uh, yeah, but how is that going to help me?"

Melissa peered into the mirror and brushed the long brown strands so they more closely framed her face. "I'm going to Paris as myself, but in your hair and sunglasses, with your red bag. Of course, I'll use my own passport and credit card, but I'll change hotels and go undercover. Hopefully, the police are smart enough to figure out you've taken my identity but dumb enough not to realize we've executed a double fake."

Thinking of Jonah, I said, "At least one of the detectives is pretty smart. However, his partner may slow him down enough to give us the time we'll need."

Melissa placed her index finger on her lips, in a wordless plea for me to shut up. After a few minutes, she said, "While the police are busy tracking me across every arrondissement in Paris, you'll get to work in New York. Please remember I majored in philosophy, not international espionage, so you won't have much time before I'm arrested. Once they catch up with me, you'll be in extreme danger, from the police And maybe the killer as well."

I threw up one argument after another, but Melissa was immovable. She pressed her lips together, opening them only to say, "I'm not going to argue with you. If you want my help, you have it. But not for a harebrained scheme that's going to get both of us in trouble."

I didn't want to admit it, but Melissa's scheme wasn't completely terrible. If she were detained, what crime could she be charged with? Impersonating herself?

I wondered if Melissa, smart as she was, had figured out the flaw in her plan. I didn't want to further upset her. "While you're in Paris, pretending to be Leah Siderova in disguise, how am I going to impersonate you? I think your husband might notice the difference."

She laughed, but not in a happy way. "Don't be too sure about that. Daniel's been...kind of preoccupied lately."

I was hurt by her lack of trust. "Why didn't you tell me you're having problems with your marriage? You always act as if your life is so perfect. Why didn't you confide in me?"

Melissa was brusque and dismissive, as she always was when we were talking about her life and her problems. "Let's not get distracted. We have work to do." She tapped at her phone and again motioned me to stay quiet. "Hello, this is Ms. Sharon...yes, thank you. All is well...I'd like to confirm my reservation. Yes, that's right...three days, beginning this evening...Excellent. Please use the card I have on file."

She ended the call, and, with a mischievous look, pinched my cheek. "Congratulations, Ms. Sharon. You will be resting and relaxing at the Ultimate Spa Center. I suggest the hot stone massage and a deep cleansing facial. You won't need a card or money. They'll put everything on my account." She brushed her fingers across the back of my hand. "Book a manicure as well. If Barbara could see the state of your nails, she'd forget all about the murder charge."

I pulled my hand away. "You're the one who needs some time in a spa. Every time I talk to you, you're running a school fundraiser or canvassing for clean water. How you manage to work a full-time job, write books, take care of the kids, and volunteer for a million worthy causes, is beyond me. And now you're off to Paris to save my life. It's a lot for one person."

Melissa shrugged. "I look good on paper. But we need to get back to business. Make a list of the people I need to interview and the questions you want me to ask. I don't think I'll have any trouble getting to Sylvain or the rest of the staff at the Rive Gauche Ballet. Several of them are going to be at a luncheon, hosted by the Alliance Franco-Américaine. I'm one of the presenters."

I was impressed. As usual, Melissa seemed to have everything figured out. She was filled with energy and purpose, but now that I wasn't going to Paris, I felt lost. The adrenaline that had fueled my mad dash to New Jersey faded, and a terrible weariness gripped me.

Melissa fingered Madame's Amex card. With biting sarcasm, she said, "How kind of Madame to give you her credit card. Especially one so noticeable."

I was worried about my sister's rapid mood changes. "Uh, yeah. I told you how supportive she's been. She's really gone out of her way to help me."

"How do you know she's not setting you up? How do you know she didn't turn around after you left her and call the police?"

Chills ran down my back as I remembered the way Madame tried to get me to linger with her. She would never let me down. "I refuse to believe she would betray me."

Melissa pinched the corners of her mouth in a stubborn look I knew well. "You can refuse to believe it. That doesn't mean it's not true. Everything you told me about Madame's involvement makes me suspicious. Didn't it make you wonder, just a little, that she thought a real private detective was a bad idea but that she and you and Gabi were capable of handling the investigation? I would have told you how crazy that idea was, if you ever called me back and were willing to talk."

Melissa smacked me on the shoulder with unnecessary force. "How do you know she hasn't already told the police you have her card? How do you know a single swipe won't bring the police directly to you?" Melissa clutched her head. "For heaven's sake, I hope you didn't tell her you were going to see me!"

I removed her hands from her head. "I'm not a complete idiot. I didn't tell her where I was going, not because I didn't trust her, but because I wanted to throw the police off the scent. I told her I was going to see Claudia Espina at Yale. I also told her she should tell the police if they ask her."

Melissa said, with some satisfaction, "Good thinking."

We were starting to attract attention, so we got back in the car and drove to the train station. I reached over to kiss her goodbye, but she pushed me away.

"Give me a minute," she wheezed. "Having trouble breathing."

I knew exactly how she felt. I also knew, thanks to my recent bouts of anxiety, how to coach her through the pain. After ten minutes, some of the color returned to her face, but she was still shaky.

"I'm so sorry, Melissa. So terribly sorry."

She was astonished. "For what? For babysitting me through a panic attack?"

I looked out the window. "For a mental giant, you can be a real moron. I'm sorry for giving you the panic attack. And I'm sorry for never being as supportive of you as I should have been. I'm sorry for being jealous of you—even jealous of your panic attacks. I'm ashamed of myself."

Melissa said, in the same soothing tones she used with her kids, "If you think that, then you really are an idiot. Otherwise, you're completely nuts. You have nothing to be ashamed of. You were always a wonderful sister to me. And I must have been an insufferable little prig, always so proud of being Little Miss Perfect. The kid Mom and Dad wanted. I admired you, always. You had the courage to do what you wanted."

It's a good thing neither of us recorded our childhood. Revisionist historians had nothing on my sister and me.

The train rounded the corner. "Promise me one thing," I said. "Promise you'll keep to crowded places. No solitary walks down deserted alleys. No wandering around the Paris theater, looking for suspects. Don't meet anyone, unless in it's a public place."

Melissa hugged me tight. "Right back at you." Her lips curled in a sarcastic smile. "Maybe I'll call Madame from Paris. Everyone says you and I sound alike on the phone."

I stood up, stretched, and lifted the suitcase out of the trunk. "Good idea. While you do that, I'm going to get the evidence I need against Zarina."

Melissa put on my red plastic sunglasses. "Good thinking. But I don't want you to contact Madame. I think she and Zarina are in it together."

Chapter Twenty-Seven

Classical ballet will never die.
— Ninette de Valois

I got off the train at Newark, New Jersey, one stop short of New York's Penn Station. I took a local bus into the city but skipped the Port Authority stop, figuring I'd be safer if I exited downtown. Exhausted physically and emotionally, I headed to the Ultimate Spa. I checked in as my sister and settled into a room that whispered Zen from every earth-toned, environmentally sustainable surface and fell into a deep sleep.

When I woke up, I was starving. The dining options were uniformly healthy, low-fat, vegan, gluten-free, and non-GMO, but I did manage to scarf down a few carbohydrates in the form of organic brown rice. If—when—this nightmare ended, I promised myself a black and white cookie. Or maybe a pint of salted caramel ice cream.

I ate in my room, partly to avoid meeting anyone, and partly because I needed to concentrate. With Melissa on her way to Paris to interview Sylvain, I had to figure out an appropriate plan of attack in New York.

Melissa had given me her iPad. I blocked the location before logging in and downloading every post and picture I could find from the night Colbert was attacked. I hoped the pictures would provide concrete evidence for what I already knew, that Zarina was a killer.

Arranging the different posts chronologically was about as easy as searching for dark matter. The possibility of a time lag in between when the photos were posted and when they were taken was a further complication.

I ordered and reordered the photos. As far as I could tell, all of the Rive Gauche and American Ballet Company dancers were present when the post-performance dinner began. But halfway through the dinner, things got more complicated. I couldn't find pictures of Zarina during the time Colbert was attacked, but the same was true for Sylvain and Kerry. Grayson had also left early, in order to post his review. Obviously, I too was absent.

Only two photographs of the night were easy to place, for in them Madame and a group of Rive Gauche dancers waved to the camera under an intricately scrolled and decorated gilt clock. Behind them a shadowy figure lurked in the background. In the first picture, the man was to the right of the dancers. In the second one, he was halfway through a doorway that led backstage. The hands of the clock clearly stood at eleven thirty. Twenty minutes later, a stagehand had found Colbert's still-warm body.

Since nearly every corner store offered photo services, I didn't have to wait to print out the picture. And when I enlarged it to the point I could ascertain who the mystery man was, I'd have one very important clue—the identity of Zarina's accomplice.

Theoretically, I was making progress. Nevertheless, for all my confident predictions to Melissa, I was still unsure of Zarina's motives. Worse, I didn't know how she managed her alibis. But, in the complicated and competitive world we inhabited, she was the only person who had the necessary temperament to commit murder. She was passionate enough to have stabbed Charles in a fit of fury and cold enough to have plotted Arianna's death.

She also exerted a magnetic pull on all of the men in her life. Charles Colbert, Valentin Shevchenko, Grayson Averin, Bryan Leister, and Friedrich Holstein all doted on her. And Sylvain? I didn't know much about him, but I trusted my sister to find him and ask the right questions.

There were other men in Zarina's life, and I worried that one of them had the evidence I needed. In my abortive attempt to interrogate her, she'd flashed her emerald and diamond ring and hinted at lovers both foreign and domestic. But was she telling the truth? Thinking back, I realized that everything she told me was misdirection—and that I'd believed her.

Until I saw the picture of Madame and the dancers, I assumed the men who covered for Zarina did so innocently. But after seeing the picture, I knew the guy who gave Zarina her alibi was, at the very least, a willing accomplice.

I didn't bother trying to contact any of my suspects, because, in less than twenty-four hours, I knew exactly where all of them would be.

With plenty of time to kill, I was tempted to avail myself of the Ultimate Spa's ultimate services, but I feared someone would realize I wasn't Melissa. I continued to hole up in my room, making notes, organizing photos, and planning my attack. I did hit the gym, sauna, and pool before eating another obscenely healthy meal. The place didn't even have coffee. I had to make multiple trips to the store to keep myself at a normal level of caffeinated equilibrium.

Two hours before the curtain went up for the opening night performance of American Ballet Company, I was too itchy to stay inside. Needing to work off some nervous energy, I started walking uptown. Clad in Melissa's Chanel sunglasses, her baggy clothes, and a scarf wrapped around my head, I moved unseen and unremarked through the streets of the city.

I had no luck enlarging the photo of the mystery man. His head was averted, and the grainy image that emerged after many enlargements could have been Friedrich. Or it could have been Fred Astaire. Or Ginger Rogers.

I began to tire, and when an empty taxi pulled up to the curb, I jumped in. As the car zoomed through intersections and swerved from lane to lane, I reviewed again the collage of pictures. At Fifty-Ninth Street, as traffic slowed to a crawl, I exited the taxi. With little time left to get to the theater, I sprinted across the street and zigzagged around selfie-taking tourists.

As I charged up the stairs to the Metropolitan Opera House, I became aware of something missing from my usual inventory of aches and pain. That something was pain in my knee.

Such a simple thing, to not be in pain, and yet I'd forgotten how liberating it was to move without that grinding reminder of my frailty. Inside, a glimmer of hope flickered. Perhaps I could still be the dancer I was before. Better than I was before. That fragile hope for the future made it easier for me to see Zarina's face and figure advertised on the same billboards that had so recently featured my image and name.

The performance had long since sold out, but I secured a ticket from a scalper, at twice the price. The throng of people angling to get inside guaranteed my safety; no one was interested in a single woman with a cheap ticket, while nearly everyone was interested in scoring a drink before the show.

The line for the elevator was long, but, with my newfound strength, I headed for the stairs. The sooner I was out of the public eye, the better.

I reached the third flight before I began to feel uneasy amid the press of people behind me. Given the vertiginous height of the climb it wasn't unusual for me to feel anxious, but the fear wasn't a function of my phobia concerning high places. As a performer, I was sensitive to when I was being watched, and I had a strong feeling someone was following me. I sprinted to the top, but two steps short of the landing, I took a hard fall when someone tripped me. My feet slid out from under me, and facedown, I skidded down several steps.

I saved my knees from damage by taking the weight of the fall on my hands. Two elderly gentlemen helped me up and tsk-tsked over the rudeness of modern society. Embarrassed at my clumsiness and fearful they would introduce themselves, which would necessitate a reciprocal introduction, I thanked them and hurried off to climb the next flight. I had more important matters to worry about than the bruises on my palms and the stinging soreness in my wrists and shoulders.

I looked behind me but saw no one I knew. And yet, I still had that itchy feeling on the back of my neck. When I reached the top, I saw several girls from American Ballet Company's school, so I hurried inside the theater. My back row seat had a limited view of the stage but an unobstructed view of the press box. All I had to do was wait out the performance. Grayson never waited for the final curtain to descend before leaving. When he exited, I would be waiting for him. And if I didn't get the information I needed from him, I'd hunt down Friedrich. And then Bryan. One way or another, I'd get the evidence I needed to convict Zarina of Arianna's murder at the same time Melissa was getting enough information to nail her for Colbert's murder.

Five minutes before the overture began, the lights dimmed and a familiar voice instructed the audience about cell phone etiquette. This warning never worked, possibly because the management was unwilling to tar, feather, and otherwise publicly shame and eternally damn people who refused to turn their phones off.

After the usual spiel, Friedrich's well-bred, German-inflected voice replaced the recording. "Ladies and gentlemen, please note the change in this evening's program. Zarina Devereaux will not be dancing tonight. Her role will be danced by Kerry Blair. Thank you, and enjoy the show."

The audience was restive. They had paid hundreds of dollars for this opening night performance, and they expected to see Zarina, the star of the Rive Gauche Ballet, not an unknown dancer. I had too much on my mind to question how a third-rate ballerina from the corps de ballet scored the role, but the people around me were obviously angry about the substitution.

As the orchestra began playing the spectral notes of the overture, I sprang out of my seat. Because I was sitting in the middle of the row, my untimely exit shattered the fragile peace the music demanded. But I didn't care about etiquette. What if Zarina attacked again? I ended up climbing over the railing to avoid further commotion, although the sudden swing of the ushers' flashlights in my direction put me in a temporary, and highly embarrassing, spotlight.

Once in the lobby, I charged down the stairs, outside the building, and around the corner to the stage door. I didn't know who Zarina's next victim would be, but I knew I had to stop her. It was an excellent plan, other than the fact that I couldn't get inside the theater from the backstage entrance without putting myself in extreme danger. The police hadn't publicized my disappearance, but I was sure the security guards were on high alert.

I wasn't brave, and I didn't want to go it alone. I wanted to call the police. More precisely, I wanted to call Jonah. But if I did, I'd be doing my explaining from a jail cell. I simply couldn't take the risk. Zarina would never give up an opening night performance for anything less than murder. I remembered how she bragged that dancers who understudied her never got the chance to perform. I had to find a way to warn Friedrich, who seemed her most likely target. Even if he wasn't on Zarina's hit list, he was best positioned to protect the dancers.

I could think of only one trusted person who could plausibly get past the security guards at the stage door, most of whom had worked there since the invention of the tutu. I texted Gabi to meet me at Lincoln Center and to call me back. I don't know how long I watched for a response, but when the phone stayed silent, I gave up waiting. Part of me was relieved she didn't answer. Gabi was a wife and a mother. It wasn't right to ask her to put herself in danger.

I barreled past a group of die-hard dance fans still hoping to buy a scalped ticket, and I returned to the front door of the theater. One way or another, I was going to get backstage.

A disapproving usher told me, with some disdain, that I couldn't be seated until the first intermission. Nodding, I crossed the lobby and headed for the women's bathroom, but I didn't stop there. Behind a door marked Staff Only was a byzantine maze that provided access to the orchestra pit, the dressing rooms, and the stage.

I hid under the stairs until I heard the closing bars of the first act. All of the dressers would be backstage, helping the dancers navigate their change of costume, which gave me a narrow window of opportunity to grab a disguise.

In the deserted costume room, I picked up a gray smock, which was what all the dressers and costume assistants wore. Each smock came equipped with needles, thread, safety pins, ribbons, and scissors. I expected the room to stay empty for at least five minutes, but as soon as I grabbed the smock, I heard the sound of many footsteps coming down the hall.

With no way out, I hid in a closet and prayed that none of the scratchy costumes would be pressed into service before the women left again. I plopped a sky-blue mass of tulle over my head, scrunched into a corner, and tried to quiet the loud thumping in my chest. For a normal person, being stuck in a tiny place was unpleasant and uncomfortable, but I belonged to that segment of the population that was seriously claustrophobic. This fear of small spaces, of course, was in addition to my fear of high places and rodents. In other words, the next twenty minutes were pure heart-pounding misery.

I had to distract myself or go stark, raving mad. Ignoring the chatter of the dressers, I concentrated on what I would do once I was released from the closet-sized version of Tutu Hell. My original plan had been to corner Grayson and get him to reveal to me the details of Zarina's alibi, in both Paris and New York. When I heard Zarina wouldn't be dancing, my only thought was to warn Friedrich. Sitting in that pile of suffocating fabric gave me time to rethink both decisions.

Despite the stifling air in the closet, goose bumps popped out on my arms. Madame told me she'd had lunch with Zarina on the day Arianna was killed. Which, as my sister pointed out, was the same day Madame, for the first time in twenty years, didn't conduct company class.

Madame had provided Zarina with an alibi for Arianna's murder, and she was among the first on the scene after Arianna was stabbed. Madame was in the theater when Colbert was murdered. At each of our meetings, she was insistent that Zarina wasn't guilty of Arianna's murder. Why? Was Melissa right? Were Madame and Zarina in it together? Or did Zarina have a hold on Madame?

No. Just as I knew Zarina was capable of murder, I knew with equal certainty that Madame was incapable of betrayal. On the other hand, Friedrich would sell his grandmother to the slave trade if it could help his career. Was he the killer? Or the next victim?

The sound of laughter broke my concentration.

One of the dressers said, "I wonder what happened to the Queen of Sheba? The high-and-mighty Zarina never misses a chance to get herself in the spotlight."

A second woman answered, "The whole thing sounded fishy to me. I saw her today, and she looked fine. What do you think, Bobbie? You always know all the dirt."

Bobbie York's gravelly voice filtered through the slats of the closet. "I'm not one to start rumors." In response to the laughing protests from the other women, Bobbie said, "I might know that Bryan wasn't at all pleased with how our guest star danced his choreography. And I also might know that Kerry, accidentally, of course, tripped Zarina as she was leaving the dress rehearsal."

The first voice said, "Maybe the injury is to her pride. Kerry better watch out no one stabs her in the back."

The ladies laughed uproariously at this quip. I, however, found the remark far less humorous. Kerry was the latest person to challenge Zarina's supremacy, and she was quite possibly in danger. Of all the dancers in American Ballet Company, no one had treated me worse than Kerry. If I had to risk my life to save someone, why did it have to be that miserable, contemptuous brat? Life was so unfair.

By the time the dressers left, my muscles had frozen in place. The new list of aches and pains included residual suffering from my inelegant fall on the stairs—or, to be more precise, when I was tripped on the stairs. Two hours earlier, I'd felt strong and good. After sitting in the closet, I was ready to check myself into a physical therapy institute. But before that happened, I had a killer to catch. Or a dancer to rescue.

I didn't waste time stretching my muscles or getting the crick out of my back. Instead, I headed directly to a warren of corridors that circled the theater's new addition. These hallways were still used for transporting large sections of scenery and sets, but performers no longer used them. Unless the stagehands were planning on bringing in a Wagnerian-sized backdrop in the middle of the last ballet, I could safely take this alternate route backstage. If I timed it right, I'd get backstage before anyone was hurt.

I passed abandoned dressing rooms and locked storage closets. It was eerily quiet. In the same way that nighttime transformed well-known streets into unfamiliar territory, the dim lighting made the halls I traversed seem a very different place from the one I used to know. Headless dressmaker dummies threw bizarre-looking shadows on each wall, and racks of costumes narrowed many passageways.

Somewhere in the distance was a loud crash. Two hoarse voices shouted a few curses and one physically impossible suggestion. I paused to listen.

225

From a different location, I heard the sound of a heavy object being dragged across the floor. Then all was quiet. I couldn't even hear the music from the pit.

I quickened my pace. Again, I heard footsteps. This time the sound was directly behind me. Fearful of getting caught, I ran up a half flight of stairs and tiptoed across an open corridor that housed old costumes. Irrationally, once there, I had a change of heart and wanted to get out, but I forced myself to continue.

I tiptoed down the long corridor and turned into yet another dimly lit series of interconnected hallways, none of which I'd seen before. Although Lincoln Center had been built in the sixties, they looked as if they dated from the time of Louis XIV, who was the patron saint of ballet. Once again, I heard footsteps, but I saw no one behind me. The new section of the theater paralleled the old one, and sound traveled in unpredictable ways.

I was completely lost. Also, I had turned myself around at least twice. Conceding defeat, I turned on my phone, hoping to Google my way back to civilization. No service, of course. The stone walls resembled the Bastille more than they did a modern theater, which contributed to my growing disquiet.

With no idea how I got there, I ended up backstage. Too late. The performance had ended, and only safety lights illuminated the stage. It was too dark to see much.

Which was why I stumbled over, rather than saw, Friedrich. On his belly, his head slightly angled, his eyes wide open and glazed.

Dead, of course.

Chapter Twenty-Eight

Great artists are people who find the way to be themselves in their art.
— Margot Fonteyn

I paused to catch my breath, terrified I was going to faint and have to once again explain why I was at the scene of a murder. I had to get away before anyone saw me. Along the sides of the theater, and in the back, exit signs beckoned. Outside the doors, the opening night fundraiser was in progress. The only way to escape notice was to retrace my steps.

I tried to walk softly, but the sole of one of my shoes made a sticky, sucking sound. It was wet with blood. Frozen with horror, I found myself unable to move. A breath of air from what must have been an open door broke the paralysis. I didn't want to leave a Hansel-and-Gretel trail of guilt, so I bent down to remove my shoe. Which was why I didn't see the killer and also the reason why the knife aimed at my back hit only a glancing blow to my shoulder as my attacker tumbled forward.

He fell on top of me, pinning me to the floor. The knife clattered out of his reach and he rolled past me to grab it.

I scrambled to my knees and sprang to my feet. In an instant, he had one arm around my middle and the other across my mouth.

"Too bad, Leah. For a dancer, you've got terrible timing."

I tried to bite him, but his grip was too strong. He pressed harder and harder into my middle, crushing my body in a terrifying embrace. My toes left the floor. I flailed against him, but he had my arms pinned.

Keeping his palm against my mouth, he pinched my nose with his thumb and forefinger. I couldn't breathe.

In a desperate effort, I pulled my legs parallel to the floor. With the force that thousands of grand battements produced, I shot the heels of my feet into Grayson's knees.

He staggered and lost his grip on my face and body. Reaching wildly, he managed to hook the strap on my handbag. With a fierce jerk I broke free and ran.

In my nightmares, whenever I was in danger, I screamed, but no sounds come out. But in real life, I yelled with such volume the sound reverberated through the empty theater.

I bolted behind the backstage curtain, shouting, "Help! Help!"

I ran wildly around stage sets and jumped madly over props. Grayson followed close behind. A metallic crash behind me was followed by the sound of his curses. Instinct propelled me toward the glimmer of a steel ladder. I vaulted over a chunk of scenery and ascended rungs that swayed madly from side to side. Blood from my shoulder wound snaked down my arm and made my hand slippery. Grayson grasped my ankle and tried to pull me down. I kicked madly, but he didn't let go.

I hooked one arm around the railing and quickly withdrew the scissors that were still in my pocket. I plunged them into his hand. Yelling and cursing, he released me, and I started climbing.

The fear of heights that had been with me since childhood didn't go away. It became irrelevant. I clattered higher and higher and didn't look below. Thankful that Grayson's weapon of choice was a knife and not a gun, I figured he'd have to get pretty damned close to hurt me. And there was no way a middle-aged dance critic could outrun me.

The ladder led to a swaying catwalk. I dashed to the middle, where I gripped the handrails so tightly the steel cables cut into my palms.

Grayson stumbled a bit before following me. I wedged my feet into the slats of the bridge and braced my hands against thin steel ropes that functioned as a makeshift railing. Heedless of danger, I swung the structure back and forth in increasingly large and rapid arcs. He'd have to have the nerve and skill of a trapeze artist if he wanted to get close to me.

Grayson got only three steps up the swaying staircase before giving up. He returned to solid ground and took out his cell phone but, of course, had no reception. He looked up at me and, with the most chilling smile I'd ever seen, pulled on a pair of gloves and picked up the scissors I'd used to slash his hand. He opened the blades and stuck them in Friedrich's gaping wound.

I screamed with renewed vigor, but my voice grew ragged and weak. I was exhausted, and my bruised hands and wrists shook with strain. Two floors and a universe away, an elegant dinner was taking place for American Ballet Company's most generous supporters. No one could hear me. Even the loudest orchestral works were inaudible in the lobby once the doors were closed.

Grayson still hadn't returned. I let the steel cables come to a halt and waited in silence for a few agonizing minutes, to make sure he wasn't faking me out. I didn't want to linger too long, in case he came back with a gun. Or an axe, which he could use to sever the cables that held up the catwalk.

Slowly, fearfully, I descended. Although terrified to go anywhere near Friedrich's body, I had to retrieve my shoe and handbag before figuring out a safe way to exit.

The police came well before I had the opportunity to contact them. Detectives Sobol and Farrow, with a dozen other officers, crashed through the side door of the theater as I wiped my feet dry of Friedrich's blood. I remembered Grayson's smile and realized that once again, he had pinned his crime on me.

A battalion of police officers rushed toward me as a second group fanned out across the theater. As if watching a movie, I saw the whole scene as they did. Friedrich, lying in a pool of his own blood. Red footprints that marked a path from the dead body to me. Scissors in Friedrich's back that had my fingerprints on them.

Ugly sobs, the kind that hurt terribly, broke out from deep within me. I knew I couldn't keep running. I had no way out. And no place to go. From behind a blur of tears, I saw Bryan running toward me, his face twisted with fury. Gabi, who was right behind him, tried to push him out of the way. Behind Gabi an excited group of dancers rushed forward.

I was sick with pain and grief and fear. But I didn't give up. I'd always been a fighter. And fighters didn't quit.

I picked up the scissors and waved them wildly at the police officers.

Chapter Twenty-Nine

The path to your success is not as fixed and inflexible as you think.
— Misty Copeland

J onah came from behind and held my arms tightly. "Stop fighting me! You're safe, dammit. Listen, my—it's fine. You're going to be fine."

I didn't believe him, and I didn't trust him, but since I was wildly outnumbered, I stopped fighting. When I whirled around to face Jonah, the floor rose up to meet the ceiling and the exit signs blurred.

I didn't exactly faint. Let's just say I sat down for a rest on a conveniently available stretcher and closed my eyes for a few minutes. When I opened them, the medics went at me as if I were the last survivor of the *Titanic*. They cut my shirt and stanched blood from the still-dripping gash on my shoulder. I stopped pushing them away when I realized the knife wound wasn't going to mend itself. I demanded to see my lawyer, whom I guessed was still Morty.

I called to Gabi, but she was deep in conversation with Detective Farrow, waving her long, expressive arms at him as she spoke. Mid-gesture she stopped to blow me a kiss and a smile.

Officer Helen Diaz kept a close watch on me. *Déjà vu* all over again.

But something felt different. Diaz was kindly, not suspicious. Concerned, not fierce. She hovered over me. "Are you strong enough to talk?"

I still wasn't good at staying silent without my legal counsel. "I wasn't going to hurt you. Please believe me. And I didn't hurt Friedrich. I couldn't—I couldn't hurt anyone."

One of the crime scene technicians bagged the scissors I'd used to stab Grayson, so I amended my statement. "I couldn't hurt anyone unless he was trying to kill me."

The policewoman pursed her lips. "You're one lucky woman."

Lucky wasn't the word that came to my mind, but Diaz was firm. "You got lucky tonight. Ms. Acevedo called about two dozen dancers, and the head of security. They searched the whole building, trying to find you. When Mr. Leister heard you screaming he called the police."

The medics, who apparently outranked the police, pushed Diaz aside and propelled me into an ambulance. Gabi promised to meet me at the hospital.

A short time later, I was back in the emergency room. When I saw my ravaged reflection in the mirror, I insisted upon leaving immediately. What if Zach saw me? I was determined to have that date with him, not in the emergency room but in a chic restaurant with candles and wine and romance.

I didn't get my way. The emergency room doctor, thankfully not Dr. Mitchell, detained me long enough to suture the gash in my shoulder. By the time she finished, Barbara, Jeremy, Gabi, Madame, and Uncle Morty were there to help get me back on my shaky legs.

I had no serious injuries. Aside from the stitches, I had a few bruised ribs and two sprained wrists, which I'd hurt when I fell on the stairs and then strained again during my gymnastics on the catwalk. The ribs hurt each time I breathed, but honestly, compared to losing a few toenails, or having to rehabilitate my knee, the pain was negligible.

The pharmacy at the hospital gave me prescription pain pills, which was nice. When I retired from dancing, I should become a paid promoter of pain relievers. Excedrin was my favorite for headaches. I loved those. Advil for muscle pain—I loved those too. Neither had anything over the stuff I got at the hospital, though. Twenty minutes after I took two tablets, I was ready for a three-act ballet, although I settled for a few repetitions of the breathing exercises the nurse had me practice.

A few minutes later, a wiry woman with dark curly hair and an expression as tough as her jean jacket, joined us. She stuck out her hand. "Hi, Leah. I'm

Claudia Espina, your lawyer."

I grasped her hand with both of mine. "And not a moment too soon."

She nodded. "If I'd known you were going to do a runner, I would have come sooner. But I'm here now. You're going to tell me everything. And I mean everything. And then we'll deal with them." She peered through the windowed section of the door to check on the knot of police officers restlessly milling outside my room.

When we were done talking, Claudia allowed the police officers to enter. Two of the officers spoke to each other in French, and I realized, with a guilty start, I hadn't yet let Melissa know what happened. My second thought was I had created an international incident.

Jonah, after an official preamble, said, "Please tell us exactly what happened this evening." He looked angry and bit off his words as if he had a grudge against them and me.

"Hey, it's not my fault you picked the wrong suspect. Don't be mad at me."

He grew pale. "You damned near got yourself killed. Are you this crazy all the time?"

I looked to Claudia, who gave me permission to answer.

"You gave me no choice. I knew I was innocent. And if you were dumb enough to think I was guilty, I couldn't risk waiting around for you to find the real killer."

The French police officer spoke next. "I am Monsieur Lyon. First of all, Mademoiselle Siderova, I must tell you that Monsieur Averin is in custody. You have nothing to fear. If you can, *s'il vous plaît*, explain to us what happened."

I took a deep breath, ignoring the pain in my ribs. "To tell the truth, I thought Zarina was the killer."

Lyon interrupted, "Zarina? Zarina Devereaux? Why you think that?" He sounded angry.

Mentioning Zarina was definitely a tactical error. She wasn't simply famous. The French considered her something akin to a national treasure. Like the Eiffel Tower. Or brie.

"I apologize, Monsieur Lyon. Obviously, I was wrong." I reached into my bag and extracted the stack of pictures I'd printed. "As you know, I was at the gala the night Colbert was attacked, but I left before he was hurt. When I studied these online posts, I realized Zarina was absent from the party when the attack was supposed to have taken place. I also knew she'd lied about when she arrived in New York. I figured she had the best opportunity, and given her personal relationship with Colbert, the best motive, to harm him."

Monsieur Lyon studied the pictures. "Mademoiselle Devereaux has an alibi for that time."

I nodded. "Yes, of course. I know that now. But I also know she was friends with the Russian dancer, Valentin Shevchenko, who was mysteriously poisoned that same night. She was the only point of connection between all three deaths: Valentin Shevchenko, Charles Colbert, and Arianna Bonneville."

Monsieur Lyon looked only slightly mollified. "Shevchenko—that was an inside job. Nothing to do with the other two murders. If you know Zarina, it is impossible she could be killer. Her dancing? It is glorious."

With hard-earned self-assurance, I pointed out, "You could say the same thing about me. And yet I couldn't continue to investigate in New York unless I wanted to do so behind bars. That left Paris as the only place I could hope to find the information I needed to prove my innocence."

Monsieur Lyon grimaced. "This is why you send your sister? That one, she led us all over Paris. Detective Farrow here, he call us and tell us you have stolen your sister's identity."

I was so proud of Melissa. "But you see now this is not true. My sister was in Paris to attend a conference at the Alliance Franco-Américaine. She agreed to interview Sylvain while she was there, as a favor to me. That is the extent of her involvement."

I don't think anyone in the room believed me, but they also didn't challenge me, so I continued with my story, explaining how I got backstage and what happened after Grayson attacked me.

I pointed to the pictures of Madame and the Rive Gauche dancers. "When I saw this picture, I realized a man was involved. I still thought Zarina was guilty, but I also figured she had an accomplice. When I got to the theater and heard that Zarina wasn't dancing..."

Lyon's eyes narrowed. He asked, in careful English, "I still not know what you doing in theater. I agree with Monsieur Sobol. You almost got yourself killed, Mademoiselle Siderova. Very bad idea it was you had to follow murderer to theater."

Truer words were never spoken. Although, given the way things turned out, it could have been a lot worse.

Claudia smiled slightly as I shamelessly lied to Lyon. "I thought Zarina might be in danger. I was afraid I'd get arrested if I contacted the police, so I went backstage to warn her myself."

A tapping noise interrupted us. Claudia opened the door, and Bryan rushed in. He reached over to hug me, which was extraordinarily painful, given the state of my ribs and my sutured shoulder. But rather heartwarming, given the state of my emotions.

Farrow was impatient. "Mr. Leister. We are in the middle of a serious investigation. Please wait outside until we're done."

Jonah was more forgiving. "Let him stay. We can get his story now, instead of waiting until later."

The two French officers nodded their assent, and Bryan began his account of the night's events. "When I got Gabi's call, I grabbed as many dancers as I could and we searched the whole theater, looking for you. The curtain was down, but as I got closer to the stage, I heard someone screaming. The reception inside the theater is terrible, so I ran back to the lobby and called nine-one-one. Then I got two stagehands to come with me to investigate. Otherwise, that crazy bastard could have murdered me."

Trust Bryan to take care of himself first. When he realized he wasn't winning any points for courage, he said, "I was halfway up the steps when Grayson came rushing out. He said Leah had killed Friedrich. Grayson was shaking and angry. His hand was bleeding, and he said you'd stabbed him. But that didn't make sense. I heard a woman screaming, not a man."

Officer Diaz was right. I had been lucky.

I grasped Bryan's hand. "Thank you. But I must confess, I came to the theater thinking you might be a murderer. Or an accomplice to murder."

He was sober. "I thought the same about you. I'm deeply sorry for that."

Hours passed before we were done. The police had some residual irritation concerning my decision to avoid arrest by crossing a state line. I pointed out that New Jersey was so close to New York, the Holland Tunnel hardly qualified as a barrier.

Claudia interrupted my less-than-legally sound argument. "Leah nearly died in her attempt to find the killer. Her brave and bold actions were a consequence of a profound failure on the part of police departments in two countries to effectively conduct the investigations. Should you have any further questions, feel free to contact me." She spoke quickly at first then slowed her words to emphasize her intent. "My expectation is that Leah Siderova will be hailed as the heroine she is." She crossed her arms. "We don't need the keys to the city. A full exoneration will be sufficient. Having already spoken to the DA, I can assure you Leah's cooperation was, and is, dependent upon that assurance."

The group of men fell silent in the face of Claudia's force of personality. She didn't raise her voice and she stood barely five feet tall, but no one was in doubt who was in charge. Farrow admitted I wouldn't face charges for my flight from the law. The French police officers were interested in arguing about who had jurisdiction over Grayson and didn't care much about anything else.

I refused Barbara's offer to bring me home with her. Dad knew I wouldn't voluntarily spend time with his second wife, but he proposed taking me back to his apartment anyway.

Claudia once again intervened. "I still have a few things to discuss with Leah. Perhaps we could all meet tomorrow."

I shared a cab with Claudia. As she exited, she pressed a small package on me. "I've got a few friends in high places, and I thought you might need this. Use it to call me tomorrow. Not too early."

Inside was my phone. Some kind soul on the way to New Haven must have turned it into the police. It represented a reconnection to myself, as much as to the rest of the world. I felt the beginnings of happiness and hunger. My stomach rumbled so loudly I was sure the driver heard, but I didn't care about him. At the last minute, I instructed him to let me off at the corner, instead of in front of my building. Mr. Kim's bodega was closed, but the diner was open twenty-four hours a day.

"I'll take a black and white cookie," I told the counterman.

He stuck the cookie in a bag. "Anything else?"

I thought for a bit. "Yeah. Make that two cookies."

Apartment 5B was as I'd left it. Knowing the police, and definitely Barbara, would have been there in my absence, I'd cleaned it with unusual passion. My mother would have died of shame had the police found evidence of sloppy housekeeping. My bruised ribs made the uphill climb challenging, but I was so happy to be home.

The sun was coming up, and I hadn't slept. Still, I had those cookies with me, so I made a pot of coffee, put my feet up, and calculated the time difference between New York and Paris. I had promised to provide Melissa with frequent updates. Once again, I'd not been mindful of my sister, and I was filled with remorse.

Before her phone registered a single ring, Melissa picked up. She immediately started crying. "Leah, I tried to warn you—I called over and over again to try and save you. I was terrified Grayson Averin would attack you. Or turn you in."

I know it helped to be a genius, but even so, how did Melissa come to this conclusion before I did? Maybe it was some kind of sisterly intuition.

"I'm fine, my dearest sister. Grayson is in jail."

"Barbara told me what happened, but I think she's still in shock. And I didn't want to give Dad a heart attack by talking about what happened. So spill—and do it quickly."

I took a huge bite of cookie and washed it down with coffee. Melissa was the only person in the world who would forgive me for eating and drinking while talking. "Before I give you all the gory details, how in the world did you figure out Grayson was the killer?"

Melissa hooted. "Did you really think I would sit around, when I knew how much danger you were in? Obviously, I didn't have any time to waste. I checked out of my hotel and used a burner app on my phone to call the

French police and to give them an anonymous tip. I told them you were in Paris, disguised as me. Then I took an ungodly number of taxis, visiting every arrondissement and using my card so the police could track me. But I was afraid the police would keep it quiet, so I had a friend post on Instagram you were in Paris. I didn't want anyone—in France or in the US—to suspect you were still in New York."

I gave a few incoherent squawks. "You lied to me. I didn't think that you, the great philosopher, were even capable of deceit. We didn't know who the killer was. And you could have been thrown into jail."

Because she was my sister, she understood I wasn't chastising her. I was complimenting her.

She sounded proud of herself. "You're not the only one who can go undercover. I was worried about you. I was especially worried about Madame Maksimova. I didn't trust her. Why was she so eager to stick her neck out?"

Non-dancers could be so difficult. "Because she's an old-school ballerina, so she's completely nuts and has no clue about how the real world works."

Melissa snorted. "Leah, Madame wasn't completely honest regarding her whereabouts when Arianna was killed. She was in the costume room right before you showed up. When she heard what went down during Bryan's rehearsal, she went to offer you some Russian tea and sympathy. She didn't see you or anyone else, so she went back to the studio. She tried to convince you that the scent of Joy perfume wasn't a good clue because she's the one who left traces of it."

I nearly choked on my cookie. "That's impossible! Why didn't Madame tell me? Or the police?"

Melissa groaned. "I called her from Paris to ask her. She said she didn't know if Arianna had already been attacked. She was afraid if she spoke up it would further narrow the time frame and that her testimony would hurt you, not help you."

One small mystery solved. But there was more I needed to know. "I still don't get how you figured out Grayson was the killer without getting definitive proof by having him attack you."

Melissa assumed her big-sister-knows-best tone of voice that for the first time ever, didn't annoy me. "You were trying to get Zarina to open up to you. But you're her rival. She was never going to help you. But she was happy to talk to me—a modestly famous writer, who conveniently does not share your last name."

I began to feel rather foolish. "Are you telling me we could have accomplished all this from the privacy and comfort of your suburban paradise?"

My sister ignored the interruption. "I set up a phone interview with Zarina and explained that I had already spoken to a number of people at the Rive Gauche Ballet and that I was, in fact, in Paris. She could hardly wait to tell me her side of the story, though it took nearly an hour for her to stop telling me what a great artist she was. Honestly, Leah, I thought I'd puke."

I still didn't understand. "But Zarina wasn't the killer. How did she help you figure out Grayson was guilty?"

She paused to wait for a loud roaring noise to subside. "I'm at the airport, and I don't have much time."

"I promise not to interrupt. Hurry!"

In a hoarse voice, Melissa said, "Very casually, I told Zarina I knew she was in New York on the day Arianna was murdered. She got very tense and told me she'd spent the afternoon with Grayson. Without asking, she told me she was also with Grayson when Colbert was stabbed. For about five minutes, I thought you were right about her, that she was the killer. When I pressed her about her movements the night Colbert was attacked, she told me, without me asking her, that the rumors that she was with some random Russian ballet dancer were completely false. Leah, I had no idea what she was talking about. So, I googled random dead Russian dancers. Once I saw the date of Shevchenko's death, I realized Zarina was more worried about being tied to his murder than she was about being tied to the attack on Colbert."

I finished Melissa's thought. "So, then you knew Grayson hadn't provided a false alibi for her. She'd provided one for Grayson."

Like I said, it helped to be a genius. "Okay, Sis. You've always been the brains of the family. No surprise there. But if Grayson attacked Colbert because he was in love with Zarina, why was Arianna his next victim?"

Melissa's tone was grim. "I don't know. But I can guess. Arianna had to have seen Grayson stab Colbert. And then she probably blackmailed him—not for money, but for media attention and influence. If you put aside all the complicated bed-hopping, it's a simple case of blackmail on both sides. According to Zarina, Grayson was furious that Colbert seduced her away from him. So, Grayson threatened Colbert—told him he was going to do an exposé on the Rive Gauche Ballet that would ruin Colbert's career."

My head was spinning. "It sounds as if Colbert had more motivation to kill Grayson than the other way around."

Melissa agreed. "Under normal circumstances, yes. But Colbert had an ace in the hole. Three Rive Gauche dancers complained to Colbert that Grayson was sexually harassing them. And Colbert threatened to report him to the newspaper, which would have been the end of his career."

I was stunned. "You got all this from Zarina? How is it she knew so much and never told anyone?"

Melissa sounded out of breath. "Like I say, it took a long time and a ton of flattery. I honestly don't think Zarina ever suspected Grayson was the killer. She assumed he would cover for her because she thinks every man she meets is in love with her. Also, I don't think she realized that France and the US have very different ideas about sexual harassment."

I was wide-awake, still a bit stunned at the whiplash changes in my life. "I'm not sure I believe Zarina is that innocent. She had to have suspected Grayson was the killer."

Melissa's voice was nearly drowned in the noise of the airport. "I don't know anything about that. But I do know that the circumstantial evidence against you, including the threads from your skirt that Grayson placed at the scene of the murder, probably convinced Zarina, and the police, you were the guilty one."

Melissa didn't hang up. I could hear her heavy breathing as she headed for the gate. I felt sick, and it wasn't from eating two large cookies covered in sugary icing.

In the aftermath of Arianna's murder, I worked so hard to figure out where other people were, and what they were doing, that I forgot to follow my own actions. One of the many things I should have figured out much earlier was how the threads from my skirt ended up at the crime scene. I'd tossed them in the garbage right next to Grayson. All he had to do was pretend to throw something out in order to retrieve them. That tiny detail could have set me on the right track. All the same, I couldn't argue with how things turned out.

Melissa said, "You won't get one more detail out of me until you tell me how you figured out it was Grayson—and how you convinced the French police."

"Call me when you get home. I have a lot to tell you."

And I did.

Chapter Thirty

Don't let them tame you.
— Isadora Duncan

Two months later, a shower of bouquets rained down upon me as I curtseyed to a standing-room-only crowd at Lincoln Center. I humbly acknowledged the cheers and then, not because I had to, but because I wanted to, I indulged in one of ballet's tackiest customs. I plucked a flower from one of my bouquets, kissed it, and presented it to my partner. I honestly wanted to acknowledge Daniel. More pragmatically, the crowd would have been disappointed had I not submitted to tradition. Needless to say, the cheers redoubled in force.

Another terrible tradition in the ballet world involved excessive curtain calls and bows. We really did milk the audience, but well-bred New York City balletomanes gamely complied, clapping until I was sure their hands were raw. Personally, I thought it would be better to leave 'em wanting more. But again, there was no arguing with tradition. Of course, if the audience had their way at the closing performance of Bryan's ballet, we would have been there all night, as the newest dance critic of the *New York Times* pointed out the next morning. When Bryan walked onstage and kissed my hand, the applause doubled and redoubled.

After the performance, we had one of our fundraising dinner dances, for those patrons who had an extra few thousand bucks to spend on a single ticket. We also raised quite a bit of money on the auction of dance memorabilia. For the record, my autographed ballet slippers fetched the highest price. The exorbitant amount of money the shoes earned might have been a consequence of my performance, but I knew it was just as likely that my notoriety from the murder case jacked up the value. Well, it all benefited the company. Without the kind of government money that supported the Rive Gauche Ballet, we constantly had to sell ourselves to the highest bidder.

The press had a field day. I garnered the kind of attention publicists would sell their souls for, and Pavel Baron, our acting director, was ecstatic. One reporter, who looked more familiar than the others, made me nervous in his push to get close and his refusal to look me in the eye.

I studied him carefully before answering his questions. "I think I've seen you before."

He poked a finger into his collar, as if his shirt had gotten too tight. "Really? I don't think we've met."

As he looked past me, I stared into his eyes. "The last time I saw you, you were outside my apartment. Stalking me."

He coughed and cleared his throat. "I didn't mean to scare you. I was following a story. Nothing personal."

I swallowed hard and resisted the urge to conk him over the head with a nearby bottle of champagne. "In that case, I'm sure you won't take it personally if I have you thrown out of here. The security at Lincoln Center doesn't like gate-crashers."

He flushed a bright red. "I'm not a gate-crasher. And I apologize most sincerely for scaring you." He took his press pass out of his wallet. "Perhaps you will think differently of me after you read what I've written about your performance. You are an artist. And I am truly sorry." Carefully, he returned the card to his wallet. "Grayson had a lock on the dance beat. I was trying to get a foot in the door. Please forgive me."

Under bright lights and without a hat over his eyes, he was a lot less scary. "I'll get back to you after I read the review."

Although tables at the ball went for tens of thousands of dollars, I wrested from our business manager several tickets for the cocktail hour. Then I threatened to leave if he didn't get me a table. And that was how I ended up at the best post-performance gala dinner of my life. Of course, Barbara,

Dad, Melissa, and Uncle Morty were there. Gabi and her husband, Leo, came as well. Ann, my dowdy stepmother, and David, Melissa's obsessive-compulsive husband, also attended. Rounding out the table were Ruth, Miriam, and Eileen, my Atlantic City bus mates, who were impressed with the champagne and the filet mignon but thought the chic and minimalist decorations weren't fancy enough. Their conversation delighted my mother, and she promised to invite them to her next book launch party.

"A few more ribbons and bows, that's what I like." Ruth eyed the single white orchid in the center of the table.

"Well, it's no Atlantic City, but it's still very nice." Eileen patted my arm and they all headed for the dessert table.

Ann was bemused. "I don't know why you invited those—who are they? Those ladies. You don't even know them."

"They befriended me when I was down. They were kind. I don't think I can ever forget how they cared for me, and believed in me, without knowing one thing about me."

My stepmother seemed unconvinced. She consoled herself with plain water and a handful of vitamins.

Zarina and Pavel swept by the table to offer congratulations. She had danced in the opening ballet, while I had danced the last one. My placement in the program was much more prestigious. Not that Zarina and I were keeping tabs on each other, but she did claim she'd gotten more bouquets than any other dancer. My position was that the bouquets don't count when you buy them for yourself.

Barbara, generous as always, said, "Zarina, your performance was lovely. Simply breathtaking!"

Zarina preened and smiled. She put her gold evening bag on the table and looked for more compliments.

Barbara, who knew all about brand envy, nodded her appreciation of the beauty and expense of the bag before her. "You really are a star. So, why don't you tell us what really went down last spring, the night Colbert was attacked?"

My father looked horrified. Dad was the most restrained and polite of men. I guess that was why he left Barbara and hooked up with Ann. She was as phlegmatic and predictable as Barbara was mercurial and capricious.

Zarina didn't seem at all distressed. As long as she was the center of attention, she was happy.

"Of course, the problem is everyone is in love with me." Zarina waited a moment for the rest of us to acknowledge the truth of her statement.

I withheld any comments to the contrary, and the men, of course, obliged her with vehement assents.

To be fair, Zarina looked exceptionally gorgeous that night. She was decked out in a backless scarlet silk gown, slit from ankle to thigh. She pushed her chair back from the table to cross her legs, and the dress slid back to reveal tanned limbs and fierce-looking gold stiletto heels.

Barbara prodded, "I'm sure there's more to the story than that."

Everyone sat forward.

Zarina said, "It was all very simple at first. Charles and I are lovers. Before Charles, Grayson and I are lovers. But I am not so serious about them, because I love Valentin Shevchenko with all my heart. I feel like dying when he dies." The pathos of that statement was mitigated by her next sentence. "Of course, I have relationships with other men too, depending on what city I am in."

David muttered, "Sounds French."

Melissa kicked her husband under the table. She was discreet about it, but I saw him wince and withdraw his leg.

Zarina, however, didn't seem offended, and she seized on his words. "Yes! It begins very French, very civilized. But then, Charles find out about my Russian lover, and he has much jealousy." Zarina's expression hardened. "Charles say he not going to release me from Rive Gauche Ballet so I can perform with other companies. And then Grayson, he has much jealousy too. I say nothing, of course, because he is writing book that is all about me."

None of us pointed out that Grayson's book was nearly five hundred pages long and that Zarina was featured in one chapter only.

"So what provoked Grayson to violence? His love for you?" Dad couldn't help himself. I could picture him writing this up for his philosophy students.

Zarina smiled upon my father as if he were the new love of her life. *"Non.* It was more, how you say? More complications than that. Perhaps I forget to keep secret, and I tell Grayson that Charles's new ballet really choreographed by Sylvain. Which is of no importance. Everyone know that."

I doubted the veracity of Zarina's last statement, but I let it pass. Listening to her talk was like watching a master puppeteer. She played Grayson, Charles, and Sylvain against each other, as unmoved by their emotions as only a pathologically self-centered person could be. She was lucky Grayson didn't kill her instead of Charles.

Melissa was impatient. "Thanks for all this, Zarina. Fascinating. Really, really interesting. But why did you give Grayson an alibi for Colbert's murder?"

Zarina was defiant. "I leave theater to see Valentin. He tell me he is sick. That he thinks he die. I run to him." Her eyes filled with genuine tears. "The whole street, it is blocked off with police. I run away. I am not afraid, no. But our affair—we kept it always a secret. He was married to a terrible woman. The father of his wife, he was very high in police department, and Valentin, he afraid of him. And her."

My sister observed, "This is riveting, of course. But you haven't answered my question."

Zarina resumed her narrative. "I decide to go back to the party, but through the back door, so no one know I have been gone. Grayson see me. I am very upset. What if Russian police find out about me? I tell him everything what happened with Valentin. He say he will tell everyone we were together in my private dressing room. Now I have alibi for both murders."

I was curious if Zarina had ever considered the situation from anyone else's point of view. "Did you ever question Grayson? Or wonder if he had a motive beyond his love for you?"

She was uncomprehending. "Of course not. I am, as you see, me."

My father frowned. "Who is this Valentin Shevchenko?"

Zarina dabbed her eyes. "Valentin is brilliant Russian dancer and choreographer. He die—he was poisoned. Many people in the West think

246

Russian government kill him. My Russian friends say Valentin was spy. But that not true! Valentin was artist, not spy."

Zarina finished her champagne and Uncle Morty leapt up to refill her glass. She smiled a thank you. "I think everyone know rest of story. Grayson stab Charles. Poor little Arianna, who is following Charles around all night, she sees Grayson's attack. And then she blackmail Grayson. And then he kill her."

My father still seemed unsatisfied. "I understand everything you've told us. So far. But what prompted Grayson to kill Friedrich?"

For the first time, Zarina looked regretful. "Friedrich? I am not guilty. But I...the fault, it is mine. I tell Grayson I will marry Friedrich and we will be international power couple. And Grayson, he see Friedrich as standing in his way. So, Grayson go a little crazy. He want to kill Friedrich, but happy to kill Leah too." A flash of her usual snarky attitude briefly resurfaced. "He probably think Leah too nosy."

My belief that Zarina was at the nexus of the tangled relationships was right after all. My conclusion, that she was the killer, was wrong. But everything else connected directly back to her. I asked her, "Weren't you afraid he would kill you as well?"

She raised her delicate shoulders. "It was possible, yes. But I not know he was killer. How terrible if world were deprived of me."

The whole table was silent. The story was absurd and it was ugly. And four people were dead and one was awaiting trial. We already knew Arianna's sudden celebrity—her gig on television with Bryan, her photo on the cover of *Vogue*, her picture in the newspaper—was thanks to Grayson, and not to the Bonneville family or Tess Morgan, Bryan's wealthy and well-connected girlfriend. Grayson had called upon every contact he had to make Arianna happy and to keep her quiet.

I was wrong about so much. I was certain Arianna and Friedrich were lovers. But they weren't. Like so many partners, they simply took advantage of what the other had to give.

Barbara was never one to mince words. "What were you doing in the studio the day Arianna was killed? And why did you lie about being there?

If it weren't for you, Grayson might have been apprehended before he killed Friedrich."

Zarina showed no trace of remorse. "Grayson call and say he must see me. He is dying of love for me. I go, so I can make Friedrich get jealous. When I get there, there is ambulance and police. Grayson see me and he say he will tell police I was with him when the attack happened. Same as in Paris."

Dad, who taught moral philosophy, actually started making notes on a napkin. I had a feeling he'd be using some version of Zarina's story in his classroom for a long time to come. "Do you always use sex to further your career?"

Zarina at first seemed unsure of what he meant. I clarified it for her, and she nodded. "*Oui*, but only if man is good-looking. Otherwise, no. I have my standards, of course." She must have sensed the disapproval emanating from most of us. "One must have sex, yes? Why not have sex that is helpful?"

Zarina, seeing she'd lost the admiration of her audience, left the table and floated over to one of our biggest patrons, Jonathan Llewellyn Franklin IV. He took both her hands and kissed her on both cheeks, lingering more than as usual for friends. I still loathed Zarina, but a tiny part of me admired her grit.

Barbara put her arm around me and hugged me close to her. I took strength in her strength and finished the story. "Grayson pretended he saw me kill Friedrich. If it weren't for Bryan, I could be in prison right now, charged with two murders. Or dead."

No one spoke for several moments. And then my father stood up and lifted his glass. He tapped on it. "To Leah. The bravest and best of ballerinas!" It was the sweetest of curtain calls.

The music began, and my date held out his hand to me.

I hadn't wanted to attend the party alone, and Dr. Zachary Mitchell happened to have been available. He'd left almost as many messages on my cell phone as Detective Jonah Sobol. Not that I would ever be like Zarina and play one man against another. I would never do that.

Nonetheless, things were, as they said, definitely looking up.

A Note From The Author

If you know anything at all about dancers, it will be clear that this is a work of fiction.

Acknowledgements

First, I want to thank my editor, Shawn Simmons, who so generously gave of her time and her talent. I also want to thank those other intrepid Dames of Detection, Verena Rose and Harriette Sackler. I owe a debt of gratitude to my agent, Dawn Dowdle, who provided invaluable advice from her wealth of experience.

I am indebted to my kids: Becky, Jesse, Gregory, Geoffrey, Jacob, and Luke, for their inspiration, advice, and hilariously ironic sense of humor.

I can't imagine life without my sisters—Karyn Boyar, my actual sister, Lisa Robbins, the one I got through marriage, and of course, all those wonderful New York City Sisters in Crime.

Much gratitude is due my critique partner, Corey LaBranche, and my many dancer friends. Their kindness and generosity is boundless.

This book is dedicated to Glenn, who still thinks—after all these years—that he's the one who got lucky.

About the Author

Brooklyn-born Lori Robbins began dancing at age 16 and launched her professional career three years later. She studied modern dance at the Martha Graham School and ballet at the New York Conservatory of Dance. Robbins performed with a number of regional modern and ballet companies, including Ballet Hispanico, the Des Moines Ballet, and the St. Louis Concert Ballet. After ten very lean years as a dancer she attended Hunter College, graduating summa cum laude with a major in British Literature and a minor in Classics. Her debut mystery, *Lesson Plan for Murder*, won the Silver Falchion Award for Best Cozy Mystery and was a finalist in the Indie Book Awards. *Murder in First Position* is the first book of her new mystery series, set in the world of professional ballet. She is currently working on the second book in both series. Robbins is a vice president of the NYC chapter of Sisters in Crime and an expert in the homicidal impulses everyday life inspires.

CPSIA information can be obtained
at www.ICGtesting.com
Printed in the USA
LVHW101453030123
736271LV00028B/234